THIS GIANT LEAP

THIS GIANT LEAP

A Collection of Short Stories

EDMUND R SCHUBERT

Falstaff Books
Charlotte, NC

Copyright 2016 Edmund R. Schubert

Cover Artwork copyright M. Wayne Miller
www.mwaynemiller.com

Cover Design: John G. Hartness

Interior Design: Susan H. Roddey
www.shroddey.com

All rights reserved. No part of this book may be reproduced in any form by any electronic or mechanical means including photocopying, recording, or information storage and retrieval without permission in writing from the author.

All Rights Reserved.

ISBN-13:978-1533450241
ISBN-10:1533450242

Published by Falstaff Books
June 2, 2016
Charlotte, North Carolina

Printed in U.S.A

CONTENTS

Introduction _____ 3

Foreword _____ 5

Mean Spirited _____ 7

This Giant Leap _____ 19

Tangible Progress _____ 45

A Hint of Fresh Peaches _____ 77

Breakout _____ 103

The Last HammerSong _____ 119

A Little Trouble Dying _____ 135

For the Bible Tells Me So _____ 149

Lair of the Ice Rat _____ 191

Batting Out of Order _____ 219

Feels Like Justice to Me _____ 239

ACKNOWLEDGEMENTS

No book is created or completed in a vacuum, and the greatest risk in thanking people is forgetting someone who played an important role. But I'll take the risk and hope for the best.

Speaking of the best, by contributing specifically to this book, or to my career as a writer in general, these folks definitely make the short list:

Terry Schubert, and Katrina and Alexa Schubert
Alethea Kontis and James Maxey
David B. Coe, Faith Hunter, and Misty Massey
Kathleen Bellamy and Orson Scott Card
John Hartness and Emily Leverett
Joshua Palmatier and Patricia Bray
Dena Harris
Dan Hogan
Stuart Jaffe

INTRODUCTION
John G. Hartness

It's not about the most brilliant words or most purple prose. It's not about some magic bullet to become an award-winning author that tops the *Times* list with every release. It's not about getting an MFA from the University of Whateverstan and being ironic and too deep for mere mortals to comprehend. It's not about being David Foster Wallace and having as may footnotes as dialogue tags, or José Saramago and not using punctuation or capitalization, or Cormac McCarthy and being so bleak that you make *Game of Thrones* look like *Friends*.

It's about telling a story. It's about that primal feeling of sitting around a fire and painting pictures with words to beat the darkness back, just a little bit. It's about taking people out of their ordinary, and showing them a world of such wonder, or such terror, that they never walk past a closet door without closing it, never pass a bed without keeping a close watch on your ankles, never pass a mirror without glancing in it to make sure nothing is reflected behind you that shouldn't be.

It's about touching lives with words. It's not about ripping someone's heart out with a story, it's about reaching deep down into their very soul, and leaving your initials there. It's not about what you take from someone who reads your work, it's about what you give them. It's about telling a story. It's about creating honest characters that we can relate to, no matter if they're lost in space or wandering through the middle of the zombie apocalypse.

It's about being so painfully honest with yourself that

your own truth spills out onto the pages. It's about creating characters so real that everyone can relate to them. It's about touching that primal piece of humanity that lives deep within all of us, touching the lizard brain that doesn't think, it just reacts. It's about reaching into a reader's chest and grabbing hold of their still-beating heart and making them *feel* something. It's about telling a story.

Storytelling is the most primal way in which human beings communicate. Whether it's parables, anecdotes, fish tales, or fairy tales, stories are how we say the things we cannot say. Stories are how we get the big ideas across, and nobody has bigger ideas than Ed Schubert, and nobody is better at communicating those ideas.

As a publisher, I was excited when Ed mentioned he'd be willing to talk to me about publishing this collection. As a friend, I was honored when he asked me to write the introduction. As a writer, I'm just blown away by the stories contained in this volume. While I read these stories for the first time I laughed out loud, scaring the cat. I stayed up too late, making for a drag-ass morning, and I wept big salty tears as my heartbreak mirrored the characters in these pages.

This is a remarkable volume of stories, from horror to science fiction, from fantasy to adventure, but every single one of them touches a chord of truth within the reader. I mentioned to Ed that we should call it *This Giant Leap*, after one of the stories contained herein, to mirror not just the huge leap he's taking hanging up his editorial hat to focus on writing, but also the leap of faith he's taken entrusting his stories to an unknown startup publisher. And now, you're taking the leap with us. Thanks for coming along, I promise it'll be a hell of a ride.

FOREWORD

Well that's good; that's the direction giant leaps ought to go in, isn't it? Forward is good. I'd feel pretty stupid writing This Giant Leap: Backward. This bit of scribbling here is only intended to serve as a warning that there are Afterwords ahead (to go along with the forwards and backwards).

I suppose I should also mention that the afterwords are full of personal, rather unapologetic opinions about life, the universe, and everything. Blunt begins to describe it, as I discuss everything from Right Wing Evangelicals to rocky moments in my marriage to paleontology. Sometimes I even talk about writing and the craft of storytelling. All I'm saying is: be prepared. Prepared to absorb, prepared to skip over. The choice is entirely yours.

But there is a brief essay after each story, mostly because I don't like collections that slap a bunch of tales between the covers and send them off alone into the world. To me the essays between the stories are the glue that binds the book together, the thing that gives the whole thing a sense of cohesion. Without them, it's like wandering around blindfolded in the author's mind. But with them, it's like the author has a flashlight and is giving you a guided tour of the dark corners. And isn't that so much more interesting?

I think so. And damn it, it's my book.

I'll meet you on the other side of the first story…

MEAN SPIRITED

As I picked up my pistol one last time, I found my attention wandering away from the weapon itself and to the withered hand that held it. It looked like a mummy's hand, collapsing from the inside after too many millennia of desiccation. What a grotesque hand. My entire body was so close to death; why not finish the job?

Yes, at seventy-eight years old, I could easily come up with plenty of reasons to kill myself, some of them even logical, valid reasons. Blowing my brains all over Trish's favorite Monet for pure spite probably wasn't one of the better ones, but it was good enough.

I had considered blowing my brains out on the Jackson Pollock in the main hall, but given the nature of Pollock's work, I wasn't sure Trish would even notice. She neither knew nor cared anything about art; she collected it simply because that's what obscenely rich people do. However, a spray of blood-red blood over the renowned Frenchman's white water lilies — that would not only get her attention, it would really piss her off. Oh, how it would piss her off.

Dear God, how that made me smile...

And it wasn't the loss of the money that would make Trish mad. Even if the painting hadn't been insured, the ancient hag had enough cash to buy fifty more. She'd probably let some museum clean the painting, then donate it to them and use the insurance money to spend a month sunbathing, topless, on the French Riviera. That wrinkled, sagging, melanoma-ridden bitch.

No, what would piss her off to no end was the knowledge that I had ruined a century-old masterpiece *just to piss her off*. Trish and I had raised the art of spite and malice to that high a level. We were grand masters; we had been at each other's throats for thirty-seven years now.

Turning my attention back to the black-barreled pistol in my hand, I imagined Trisha coming into the library. Her hazel eyes would go wide as she beheld the horror of the scene. I prayed that the power of the moment, the memory of it, would haunt her for years. Hell, for all eternity.

I could envision the scene with transcendent clarity. Standing in the doorway, one of her hands would drift unconsciously to her open mouth, the tip of her forefinger coming to rest on the tip of her nose. Her hand would then move slowly away from her face as her dumb-struck expression transformed into one of unexpurgated rage. She'd rush forward, hurdling my still-bleeding corpse in her haste to get to the painting. "Nooooo!!" she'd howl as her fingers hovered inches away from Monet's bloodstained masterpiece, afraid to touch it for fear the blood might still be damp, that it would smudge the delicate petals of the water lilies beneath.

Then she'd turn back to my body, looming over me like I was an old dog who had just relieved himself on the carpet for the thousandth time.

"You..." She'd kick me in the head. "Arrogant..." She'd kick me again, even harder. "Pompous..." Another kick. "Prick..." Kick.

Her tempo would increase, and she'd punctuate each word with a blow, as if her legs were gigantic, living exclamation points. "You think you've won, don't you," she'd rant, legs pistoning merrily into my corpse. "You think you've stuck the last needle under my fingernails and gotten away with it, don't you? Well you haven't. This isn't over; do you hear me?" Aiming a final kick at my ass, her rage would crescendo. She'd be shouting at the top of her lungs, her eyes bulging, her hair disheveled from the fury of her efforts. "It isn't over *until I say it's over!!!*"

Of course, she'd be wrong.

That was the beauty of it; it *would* be over. And I would have won. After nearly four decades of tormenting each other, I would have finally, ultimately, unequivocally won. There was no way for her to retaliate because I'd be gone, gone, gone, and there was nothing she could do about it.

I felt like doing a little song and dance.

Nothing you can do about it, nothing you can do about it, nothing you can...

Not a good reason to kill myself? I was giddy with excitement. I couldn't imagine a better one.

I brought my .45 to my head, made sure I was properly aligned with the Monet so I would splatter it without putting a bullet through it, and stuck the bitter tasting barrel into my mouth. I embraced the trigger.

• • • • • • • ● • • • • • • • •

I had expected a loud noise when the gun went off, followed by nothing. Darkness. Sweet oblivion.

What I got was pain.

Dear God, what pain. Agonizing, excruciating, unimaginable pain. Vicious, angry icicles of pain clawing their way out from the center of my brain, tearing through flesh and bone in a frenzied effort to be free. But every time they broke through to the surface, they'd vanish—poof, just like that—only to start over again from the center, digging and clawing their way through my brain, over and over, again and again.

Had I screwed up? Had I managed to put a pistol in my mouth, pull the trigger, and not kill myself?

I dearly hoped not. That would give Trisha too much satisfaction.

But those cruel icicle claws wouldn't stop. They went on and on, ripping and tearing. And all I could do was clench my eyes and endure the unendurable. I heard nothing, saw nothing, and felt nothing. Nothing but pain.

I *was* pain.

Finally, after what seemed like days, I managed to open one eye. It wasn't that the pain had lessened. It had not. I'd simply become more accustomed to its presence. Not much; just enough that I could tolerate the movement of one eyelid by about half an inch.

What I saw jolted both of my eyes open.

Lying beneath me... was my body.

My body!

It didn't move. If it had, I would have been stunned, because the hollow-point bullet had blown away a massive chunk of skull and brains. There was no chance I had survived that.

Which meant I was dead—and still experiencing the gunshot. I was frozen in that split second where the hollow-point tore through the roof of my mouth, mushroomed out, and then shredded my brain before blowing open the back of my skull.

And suddenly I knew I would feel this way forever. I had no idea how or why, but I knew it with perfect certainty.

Whether it was punishment from God or simply an unknown fact of the afterlife made no difference.

I was trapped. Trapped in this moment of Promethean pain for all time.

• • • • • • • • ● • • • • • • • • •

They say people can get used to anything. Apparently this applies in the afterlife, too, because a week later I was in no less pain than before, but I had grown accustomed enough to it that I was able to think and move with a touch more ease.

All those schmucks who had heart attacks while getting laid, they had no idea how lucky they were. I pondered that fact angrily. Of course, I did everything angrily. The pain kept me in an eternally sour mood.

And as if the pain weren't enough to maintain my foul demeanor, when I first began to move around, I learned quickly that I was not only trapped in the moment of my death, I was also trapped in the room where I had shot myself. I could open and close the library door, pull books off the shelves, even stumble over my own rank-smelling corpse. But leave the room? Never.

I grew angrier with each passing moment.

And speaking of rank smelling, where the hell was Trish? An entire week and she hadn't come home yet.

For that matter, where was the staff? The maid? Butler? Cook? All were gone.

I had been glad enough they were out of the house the day I shot myself; I didn't want to be interrupted. But someone should have come home by now. Especially that wretched wife of mine. The thought of her seeing what I had done to her Monet—and I had made a royal mess of it, more than I ever could have hoped for—was all that kept me going.

So where was that witch of a...

"Honey?"

Trish! I hadn't heard her come in, but that was her voice. No doubt about it.

I made sure the door to the library was open and sat down in an over-stuffed chair to watch the show. Briefly I wondered if she would be able to see me sitting there. That would certainly present some interesting possibilities. I hadn't considered it before, but being trapped here like this... well, as long as *she* stuck around, I could haunt her to my heart's content. I was a poltergeist. An angry, noisy ghost with a foul disposition—one I would be more than happy to inflict on her for as long as possible. That had the potential to generate some real fun.

"Honey?" I heard her call again. "Margot and I jetted down to the Bahamas for the week. Since you'd be all by yourself, I didn't think you'd need any help, so I took the staff with me. That didn't cause you any problems, did it? I *surely* hope not."

After all these years, that was the best she could come up with? Take the staff away to inconvenience me? She was losing her touch.

"By the way," she began...

Ah. Here it comes. The Big One. I should have known better; taking the staff had just been foreplay.

"I got tested about three months ago and I have AIDS. You should have contracted it by now, too."

Wow.

She was so smooth, so matter-of-fact. So calculated. Based on her delivery, I couldn't help but think that she had intentionally sought out a way to get AIDS solely for the purpose of infecting me.

It also explained a lot: why she had suddenly grown amorous again; as well as those new medications she had recently started taking. She'd hidden them well enough that I couldn't find them, but I'd known she had been taking a new drug cocktail.

If I hadn't been dead, that would have really gotten to me. It would have infuriated me.

But I was dead. Beyond her. If my head hadn't hurt so much, I would have laughed. To tell you the truth, though, I hurt too much to ever laugh again.

I heard Trish call out again; obviously she was expecting some sort of reaction. "Sweetie pie," she called, "did you hear what I said?"

I grabbed a paperweight off my desk and threw it against the wall, hoping to attract her attention. It *whumped* twice, once against the wall and once more when it hit the floor.

"Sweetheart?"

Her voice was getting closer. Finally, an advantage to being a poltergeist. I threw a book.

"Are you in here, pudding?"

She came through the door...

And froze.

Oh, it was beautiful. She spotted my body with her eyes at the exact moment the smell hit her nose. She wears so much perfume that there was no way she could have picked up the stench until she was right on top of me, and it was perfect; I couldn't have planned it any better.

Stunned, she brought her hand to her mouth, exactly as I'd anticipated.

But she just stared at my body. She couldn't take her eyes off of it.

I wanted to shout, but I knew she wouldn't hear me even if I tried. But I wanted to. Oh how I wanted to.

The painting, damn you! Look at the painting!

I contemplated throwing a pen or something at her precious Monet.

She took two steps toward the spot where my body rested.

"Nooooo!!" she wailed.

I was stunned. After all these years, was she actually distraught over losing me?

Snatching up my pistol, she fired three quick shots into my fetid corpse.

Okay… now things were getting interesting.

"How did you find out?" she screamed. "*How did you find out I gave you AIDS?*"

She kicked my body in the small of the back.

"How did you find out?!" She screamed again, bending closer to my body as if I could hear her better that way. "*How?*"

Straightening up, she looked around the room. But she never saw the stupid painting. The look in her eyes was one of someone gazing off into infinity.

Then she started shaking her head.

"Oh no," she said. Very softly. "You're not leaving me here to deal with this infernal disease by myself. You don't get to do that. I decide when this is over, not you."

She brought the gun to her head, lowered it for just a second, then brought it back to her head again. I saw her fingers stiffen with resolve as she repeated, "I decide, not you."

And just like that, the ramifications of what she was about to do hit me like a Learjet.

Nooooo, I wanted to scream. *Noooo!*

Damn it, no! *No!* Kill yourself if you want, I don't care. But not in here. Please, God, *not in here!* I'm not spending eternity trapped in this room with—

Ka-blam.

This time I heard the gun shot.

It was *much* louder than I expected...

Afterword

Afterword of an after-life. This story has been one of my most popular, reprinted in several anthologies. But it's also the one associated with one of my most painful memories, and what fun is happiness, so let me share my pain with you…

It was Spring of 2010. Or maybe it was 2011. I'd been invited to teach a class about writing science fiction (and fantasy) at the North Carolina Writer's Network Spring Conference on the campus of UNC-Greensboro. I was tickled to have been invited, feeling like it was a step up the ladder of recognition and respectability because the NCWN is a big deal in North Carolina. My class was one of the morning sessions, and in the afternoon (if I wanted to) I was allowed to sit in on my choice of one of the other classes. It cost several hundred dollars to attend this conference, so getting paid a couple hundred to teach at it was a sweet deal, too.

The only part I wasn't excited about was the faculty reading scheduled for the lunch hour. Initially I declined to participate, concerned that reading speculative fiction to a literary crowd was inviting everything from disdain to disaster.

But at the last minute, two of the other faculty members cancelled and the organizers asked me to fill in, and in a moment of reckless abandon, I said, "What the hell" and took the plunge.

It went *spectacularly* well. These literary people and poetry lovers (and about fifteen of my students from that morning) all laughed their heads off. Every line that might have been considered slightly amusing got guffaws. Every play on words got howls. Every character foible drew 'amens' and 'halleluiahs.' In a ballroom filled with 125 people, every one of them conspired to make me feel like a writing god.

It was, to this day, the single best reading I've ever done.

But this story also has an epilogue, one that still makes me cringe.

You see, after the reading I went to the classroom for the afternoon session. It was a poetry class. Not my usual fare, but I wanted to stretch and try something new.

And while my fellow students and I waited for the poetry instructor to arrive, the other students turned their attention to me, telling me how much they loved my story and asking me questions, including that old standard, "Where did you get the idea?"

I explained that I had read another story about someone killing themselves and then finding themselves trapped in the moment of their death, but with a very different ending, one that I found less than satisfying. I told them I wanted to write my own version of the idea, which would include two characters instead of just one, and have a different outcome.

Seemed straight-forward enough at the time.

That's when a middle-aged woman piped up, saying, "Oh, so you plagiarized it."

Naturally, I calmly explained to her that I had done nothing of the sort. I explained that my story was no more plagiarized than *West Side Story* was plagiarized from *Romeo and Juliet*. I explained how you could plagiarize lines and sentences and paragraphs, but there was no such thing as plagiarizing a concept. There are simply too many different ways to explore any one idea.

Unfortunately, that's not how it played out in real life. Not even close. What I just described now is the perfect version that plays in my head, *looooong* after the fact.

What actually happened was that I got so angry at being accused of plagiarism that I momentarily froze, afraid that if I said anything at all, it would come out so badly that it would make the situation worse.

I tried counting to ten. I counted to a hundred.

I tried breathing deeply to trick my body into thinking it was actually calm when it was nothing of the kind.

I tried a bunch of things, but somewhere in the middle of all my *trying*, the poetry instructor arrived, started talking (completely unaware of what had just transpired), and the moment transformed into something else. Gone was my chance to explain why this woman was wrong. Gone my chance have these people think I had not just admitted (through my silence) that I had committed plagiarism. Gone every ounce of joy after the best reading of my life.

Years later, the reading is still the best I've ever had. But the memory of it is irrevocably attached to the wincing, cringing, painful memory of those twenty-odd people hearing a woman accuse me of the worst thing you can accuse a writer of, and me sitting there in silence.

Part of me is — in a beautifully symmetrical irony — trapped in that horrible moment for all time. Just like a certain character in a certain story. Or two stories, really.

So much for not making the situation worse by responding angrily, eh?

Such is life, my friends, as it perfectly imitates art.

sigh

THIS GIANT LEAP

My co-pilot Vlhasa and I comprised the third crew to attempt a landing on our planet's lone, gray, rocky moon—a feat Ssirratis-kind had thus far failed to achieve. But our mission would have never launched if the previous crew hadn't sent back that astonishing final message before they died in a blaze of glory. Indeed, the entire space program would've died along with those two astronauts if their final words hadn't been: "There's a craft of some kind, sitting on the moon. Aliens have been here before us, and they left artifacts. Get a fix on our…"

"Get a fix on our position." That's what they would have said if they'd had two more seconds before their spacecraft plowed into the moon's surface. But they didn't have those extra seconds and they knew it—pilots are excellent judges of that sort of thing—so they said the important words first.

Aliens. Artifacts. On the moon. They had seen it with their own eight eyes.

Vlhasa and I were the follow-up to that message.

Those damn fool astronauts had realized they were about to die, so they aimed the Jin-ree 7 near the alien's landing site. Not *at* it, of course—they would never risk destroying such an incredible find. But close enough that it would be easy to locate. Close enough that the next Ssirratis expedition would know where to look.

That went a long way toward them dying as heroes

instead of failures. The public had already proved to be fickle about the space program. The Jin-ree 3 had had too many close calls when it orbited the moon, and the explosion of the Jin-ree 6 had set *everyone* on edge.

The politicians at Colony Prime were already planning hearings by time the Jin-ree 7 launched. The findings of those hearings would have been irrelevant; the simple fact that they were held would have marked the beginning of the end.

But the effect of the Jin-ree 7's message had been enough to delay the hearings; the astronauts' dying words had bought the space program one more shot at the moon. One more shot at history.

Still, if Vlhasa and I didn't get this right, she and I might be the last Ssirratis to leave our planet for many generations.

So everyone in the program knew where the last mission's astronauts had crashed, and what their final words had been. And now the next craft was on its way — Vlhasa and me — flying in the same type of ship, the same kind that had crashed last time. And exploded the time before that.

But we had to go.

More to the point, *I* had to go. I had to know. You see, one of those damn fool astronauts had been my breedmate, Merla, and we hadn't been on the best of terms when she took the ship's controls in her claws and rocketed into a history-making fireball.

I stood a better chance of finding creatures from another planet than I did of finding peace with my deceased breedmate, but I saw no alternative.

I had to go.

I had to find out for myself what had gone wrong.

• • • • • • • • ● • • • • • • • • •

As we descended to the moon's surface, I braced myself with all four arms and all four legs, praying to every goddess I'd ever heard of, preparing all the while for the worst.

Yet even as I prayed, I couldn't keep my eyes off the viewport. Framed in that tiny window, I could see the landing site of the alien craft right next to the crash site of the Jin-ree 7. The alien ship looked like a mechanical version of our prehistoric ancestors, a bulbous body centered within a collection of spindly metal legs. The main difference was that the gold and black alien craft had only four legs, whereas ancient Ssirratis had had eight — at least until our bodies evolved over millions of years to differentiate into four arms and four legs.

Vlhasa did her usual marvelous job, bringing the Jin-ree 8 in for a smooth landing. She could fly any kind of craft, anywhere, anytime, and she put us down on the surface so smoothly that it wouldn't have broken a newborn babe's first web.

In fact, the landing went *so* smoothly, *so* easily, that my immediate thought was to wonder what had gone wrong with Merla and Qitx. The Jin-ree 6, which preceded them, had had engine troubles — the boosters accidentally fired when the main sections separated, causing both to explode — but the Jin-ree 7 had simply plowed headlong into the moon.

"Too easy," Vlhasa said, shaking her head as we touched down. "No way something that easy kills Merla and Qitx. It also rules out the theory that something from the alien ship killed them. I didn't see anything down there that moved, much less looked like a weapon. Whatever that thing is, it doesn't look dangerous. In fact, it looks ancient."

Vlhasa's tarsal claws were a blur of motion as she secured our ship. Seeing her move so deftly made me realize my own arms and legs were still locked with anxiety. I shook them out, trying to look casual.

"Agreed," I said, pleased we were thinking the same thing. We made a good team, Vlhasa and I, always on the same page. That's one of the reasons why Merla fretted about us, always worrying that my relationship with my co-pilot smelled like more than just being friends. And my words to the contrary never seemed to soothe her.

I opened a channel to mission command and informed them we'd landed. At mission command Kneskt had final authority; he was the official voice of the space program. But he'd made it clear that he'd give us a degree of latitude once we landed on the moon.

"Can you confirm the Jin-ree 7's final message?" Kneskt asked. "Are there really alien artifacts on the moon?"

"Absolutely," I said into the microphone. "No question about it."

"What are you going to check out first, the artifacts or the Jin-ree 7?"

"Aliens," Vlhasa said enthusiastically.

I blurted out, "Merla—"

So much for being on the same page.

"Of course," I said. Merla was dead, one look at the wreck-site made that painfully obvious. "Aliens first."

Suiting up took no time: an insulated suit, air tanks, a bubble helmet, and we were ready to go. The suits made it impossible to hear or smell anything through the hairs on our legs, but the scientists assured us the moon had no atmosphere, so even if we hadn't needed the suits for protection, no air existed to carry sounds or smells to us.

As I moved through the airlock, toward the ladder, I heard Vlhasa say over our private channel, "You're two minutes away from the most important moment in Ssirratis history, and I'd be willing to bet my last egg sac that you have no idea what you're going to say when you touch the ground."

I grunted, glad the folks back at mission-command couldn't hear us. Because as usual, Vlhasa was 100% correct. Back home some had argued for words that would commemorate the historic nature of the event, while others argued for something to honor the sacrifice of the four fallen astronauts. Though discussed extensively, the final decision was left to me. Everyone knew that making it prematurely would have invited bad luck.

"Don't worry, Tkit," she added. "I have faith in you. The words will come. When it's time, they'll come."

Vlhasa always had faith in me. Always. That's why I had feelings for her—even if I'd never said so. Not to her; not to Merla. Not to anyone.

I tried to hold those thoughts at bay, but how could I not feel something when someone that amazing expressed that level of confidence?

Was this the moment to tell Vlhasa how I felt?

Of course not. But it was definitely on my mind.

Merla had been dead for two months—that's how long it'd been since she and Qitx crashed. But to say something this close to the wreck site? This close to a historic moment that would be remembered for thousands of years, standing beneath a canopy of stars that was as breathtaking as she was?

Goddesses, was I trying to talk myself out of it, or into it?

Focus, Tkit, *focus*.

I said into the private channel, "I guess it's time to find out."

I simultaneously opened the hatch and a communication channel to mission command, determined that no matter what happened, I would not blurt out something historically inappropriate.

"Kneskt, I'm climbing down the ladder now," I said, feeling oddly light. "I have to say, after experiencing the zero-gravity effects of space, moving around in partial gravity is disconcerting."

When I'd descended to the bottom of the ladder, I extended one foot barely above the lunar surface and said, "Ssirratis-kind has been leaping for centuries. Today, in honor of those who fell while attempting this leap before us, we complete this most giant leap of all."

I looked up at Vlhasa, who held a video camera, getting live footage of the event. Despite the device between us, I could see the immense grin on her face.

It made me feel even lighter. And guiltier.

I took that final step, planting my foot firmly on the moon's surface. Inside my helmet the sounds of cheers from mission command rang long and loud. They whooped and hollered — I could identify at least four different languages from the international team — and it was impossible not to feel immense pride. Not for myself — I hadn't done anything more difficult than climb down a ladder — but for our entire race. We had finally done it. Set foot on the moon. For the first time in history, living beings from our planet had taken the next step into space.

Silently, I added a prayer for Merla and Qitx. We would never have gotten here but for them, and I swore I'd never forget that.

Seconds later, Vlhasa skittered down the ladder and stood at my side, her grin wide, glowing, and vibrant.

Together we took the short, anticipation-filled walk to the alien ship.

"Keep the camera steady," Kneskt said as Vlhasa panned across the lunar plain, filming the terrain, the alien ship, and our own craft.

The first landing attempt had been broadcast live, but when both Jin-ree 6 and 7 had ended in disaster, it was decided that the Jin-ree 8 would be filmed, but broadcast to the public at a later date. Still, I knew the world would be seeing this soon enough.

As we drew closer to the alien craft, the details became ever more clear, as did the various items scattered around it. The camera took everything in, and I reflexively started narrating.

"The alien ship isn't that large," I began. "Maybe 25% the size of the Jin-ree 8. The hull is entirely made of metal, with large parts of it—the sides and the legs—wrapped in gold foil. The top is black and it looks like there may have been another section attached up above. It's possible they left the moon in that other section, leaving this one behind."

I approached the ship and placed a claw on it. The gold foil crinkled soundlessly in the vacuum. I don't know why—maybe the way the ship reminded me of our prehistoric ancestors, maybe something else—but this ship felt beyond ancient, like it had been here for… I don't know. Forever. For hundreds of thousands of years. Maybe longer.

"Any sign of the aliens?" Kneskt asked. "Or any kind of weapons?"

That was an unusual question for Kneskt; he wasn't the sort to think militarily.

"Negative, command," Vlhasa replied. "Nothing remotely weapon-like. But there is a second, smaller vehicle parked near the alien's lander. It might provide a clue."

"How so?" asked Kneskt.

She scanned it with the camera, saying, "It looks like a rudimentary transportation unit, with four wheels and something that looks like an upside down umbrella attached to it. Might be some kind of an antenna. The vehicle is open-air, which makes me wonder if the aliens even needed spacesuits. I wouldn't want to meet the species that can survive the extremes of space without protection. That would be one nasty alien."

I switched my helmet-mic to our private channel and said, "They might have worn suits like ours when they drove. Maybe that's why the vehicle has an open design, so their suits didn't snag on something while climbing in and out."

Vlhasa kept the camera pointed at the smaller vehicle. "Damn, I didn't think of that. I feel like a real idiot."

"More like someone who's open to possibilities. But it wouldn't hurt to make that clear to mission command."

Vlhasa reconnected to Kneskt. "Of course, it could be that they didn't bother closing the vehicle in because they wore suits. There's nothing definitive either way. Except that the seats are much too small for us, so we won't be taking a joy ride."

That got a laugh from everyone at command.

Good.

I noticed something else and pointed to the edge of a nearby crater. "The transport's wheels match up with tracks that go off in that direction. The tracks are so faint you can barely make them out, but at some point we might try following them, see where they lead."

Kneskt said, "Eventually we'll get around to exploring. In the meantime, let's stick with what's right in front of us."

"Makes sense. Regardless, the alien expedition seems to have been focused on exploration. Both the ship and the vehicle are too small and simple to be military-issue."

Vlhasa and I worked our way around the other side. "There are several symbols on the body here, right in the middle of the hull. They're faded but you can make them out: a pale, blue rectangle filled with white stars, and to the right and beneath it there are pink bars running horizontally. Seven pink bars, with six equidistant white spaces separating them. Immediately below that are a very different group of symbols. Two lines of... something, maybe letters or numbers. I don't know. Vlhasa can show you better with the camera."

I stepped back and let Vlhasa zoom in on the symbols until they filled the screen.

"Never seen anything like it," I said. "Any ideas, command?"

"Sure," said Kneskt. "Let me grab my pocket translator."

Laughter came through the radio from the scientists back home.

Truth be told, now that we stood in front of it, the alien craft seemed almost anticlimactic. As much as it represented something amazing and perception-altering, the ship itself, or at least what remained of it, looked small and fragile.

Vlhasa and her video camera backed away from the craft and focused on the gizmos and gadgets dotting the area, filming each in turn.

Communication devices? Science experiments?

I had no idea. The more I looked at the artifacts, the more I wondered how they could have come from another planet, much less another solar system or galaxy. In such a tiny craft, with such simple-looking devices? It didn't add up.

Neither did Merla and Qitx crashing.

It was time to check out the crash site of the Jin-ree 7.

"Vlhasa," I said over our private channel. "I want to see if

I can find the 7's black box. Maybe there's something about the audio or telemetry data that will give us a clue what went wrong."

"Wait up," Vlhasa called. "I'll come with."

"No," I said. Possibly too abruptly. "Study the artifacts. Figure out how much is practical to bring home with us. You know the science nerds are going to want to study everything they can get their hands on."

I didn't care about alien artifacts or the science nerds. Truth was, I knew I couldn't predict how I'd react when I got to the crash site. Merla and I had fought right before she blasted off.

We fought a lot. That made it easy to be attracted to the tough but supportive Vlhasa.

By contrast, Merla was outright combative. And stubborn. And never met a hill she wasn't willing to die on, as long as she won the argument.

On the other hand, she was also smart and beautiful, and when her stubbornness wasn't being used against you, it looked an awful lot like fierce determination. It was impossible not to respect that. And as contradictory as all that sounded, it was precisely why I loved her.

I needed to do this alone.

I opened our private channel and said to Vlhasa, "I need a minute. With Merla." I paused, not sure what else to say.

"I'll go follow that smaller vehicle's tracks and see if there's anything worth examining at the other end," Vlhasa said in a way that made me think splitting up was what she'd been planning all along.

In hindsight it should have struck me as peculiar, but I had other things on my mind.

The wreckage of the Jin-ree 7 rested at the bottom of an impact crater caused by the crash. I climbed down into it, careful not to snag my suit on any of the fragments.

Whereas the alien's landing site had been relatively neat, the 7's crash site was a complete mess. Merla and Qitx had flown head-first into the moon's surface. In fact, it didn't look like they'd slowed before impact at all.

The crash had caused a massive explosion, but the fire could only burn as long as oxygen was present in the ship, so while some of the debris had charred, a lot more had shattered and been flung but not burned.

On the other hand, because of the low gravity, the debris flew a long way.

I started my investigation at the point of impact, figuring I could work my way out as needed.

Turns out I didn't need to go very far at all. In the dead center of the wreck site laid the bodies of Merla and Qitx, charred, but still strapped into their seats in what remained of the main cabin.

Merla was a great pilot. Not as good as Vlhasa, but you didn't get into the space program unless you were tops on the planet. And there she lay, blackened. But there was no question about her identity. Not to me.

Words came into my mind unbidden, unavoidable.

I'm sorry, Merla. Sorry for everything.

I wasn't sure why I was apologizing; the words just ran through my brain.

So sorry. So, so sorry.

I turned away. I couldn't look at their bodies anymore.

I turned my attention to the reinforced seats Merla and Qitx were still strapped into. More precisely, I turned my attention to the metal housing that attached both seats to the floor. The housing served a dual purpose: in the event of a rough landing, it would be sturdy enough to hold things together and keep the pilot and commander from being hurled about; and in the event of a catastrophic landing, its reinforced housing would protect the black box data-recorder nested in its core.

A crash like this back home, involving this much rocket fuel, would have resulted in an explosion comparable to a volcanic eruption. There would have been no bodies. No debris, no black box. Nothing but ash.

But here on the moon, the fire had as much chance as Merla and Qitx did.

Zero air meant zero chance.

I pulled a power-claw out of the pouch strapped to my side and pried into the housing surrounding the box. The metal had fatigued enough to pull apart without much effort, and the black box itself looked pristine. The so-called 'black' boxes were actually widowbelly red under the theory it would make them easier to locate.

I pulled this one from its housing, then plugged an audio cord from my suit into the box. I'd need to take it back to our ship, possibly to a computer lab back home, to study the telemetry data. But I could listen to the audio.

I'd just need to keep my legs from trembling too much. If I rustled inside my suit, my leg hairs wouldn't hear a thing. And the thought of what I was about to hear... terrified me.

Nervously I tapped the coded pattern onto the top of the featureless box, cuing up the final transmission.

Instantly I heard Merla's voice.

"There's some kind of craft, sitting on the moon. Aliens have been here before us, and they left artifacts. Get a fix on our..."

Then silence. No sound, no explosion, no static.

The recording simply ended.

I'd already heard the replay of this message hundreds of times: on the news, during training sessions, in my sleep. I knew her every inflection and intonation.

I glanced over at Merla's blackened corpse.

I couldn't believe the powers that be had let me come. I had been sure mission command would pass me by and go with the next crew in line.

Now I wished they had. Goddesses, what had I been thinking? Coming here? With Vlhasa? This was so wrong, in so many ways.

I tapped another pattern into the box, rewinding it further.

"...*to that, mission command. We're going around the far side of the moon now; we'll be out of radio contact for approximately thirty-five minutes. See you on the other side.*"

About to tap yet another pattern into the box's surface, I stopped, remembering that going around the moon took you out of touch with the planet but had no effect on the box, which recorded everything that was said inside the ship, not just what was said between the ship and mission command.

I let it play on.

At first I heard only silence. I thought perhaps the box had failed.

Then I heard Qitx speak.

"*We need to talk, Merla. I need your help.*"

"*Of course, Qitx. You know —*"

Qitx cut her off, his voice so serious it made my leg-hairs rise against the skin of my space suit.

"*Don't say that. Not until you hear what I'm asking.*"

"*What could possibly be so serious?*"

"*How about if I told you they intentionally blew up the Jin-ree*

6's second-stage rockets?"

"What!?"

What?!

That had to be an error. I rewound and replayed it again. It said exactly the same thing the second time. And the third.

I considered getting Vlhasa to hear this too, but I didn't want to waste time tracking her down. She'd hear it soon enough.

Qitx continued.

"There are aliens on the moon. Well, alien ships anyway. Several. We've observed them through the new superscope at Mt. Tchicksum. You and I are going to investigate."

Merla's excitement was palpable. Nothing thrilled her as much as discovery; it's the reason she joined the space program in the first place.

"Are you kidding? Of course. This is fantastic."

"But you can't tell anyone. Not even Tkit. Nothing we do can be part of the official record."

"What are you talking about? We've got to tell Tkit. We've got to tell everyone. This is going to change the world."

She was right. I knew it. Qitx knew it. Irrefutable evidence of intelligent alien life would change everything.

"Changing the world is exactly the problem. Ssirratis-kind isn't ready for this. They'll panic. We have to protect them from themselves. We have to ease them into it."

"You've got a poor opinion of the average Ssirrati."

Qitx's voice grew stern. He wasn't interested in debating; in his mind the decision had already been made. Always the good soldier, that was Qitx. Everything by-the-book.

"Merla, you know I'm right. Mission command told me how it is. I asked out of courtesy, now I'm telling you. We have an obligation to protect – "

"We have an obligation to the truth! Scientifically, spiritually, socially — this is going to change everything."

"I know, I know. That's why it's so important we do this right, ease the public into it. The government has studied this, figured out the best way to handle it. Trust them."

Merla laughed. "Are you kidding me? Trust mission command? They're the ones who sent me into outer space without telling me there's an alien ship parked on the moon. And why would they tell you and not me? I'm the pilot for flack's sake!?"

"Look, we're here now, and there's nothing you can do about it. Find a way to live with it. Work with me. Because you can't change it."

That had been Qitx's fatal mistake.

I knew Merla too well. Without listening to another word, I knew that was the moment she had decided to plow the Jin-ree 7 into the face of the moon.

Oh, she'd have said all the right things to Qitx beforehand, exhibiting professional behavior every step of the way. And then at the last possible moment, when it was too late to do anything to stop her —

Wham. She'd have struck.

And in case you're wondering, yes, she really could be that obstinate.

Or determined, depending on which side of the argument you stood on. She always had a crystal clear idea about what constituted 'the right thing.' And she'd see it through, no matter the cost.

"I think you're right, Merla," I said aloud, surprising myself. "I think Ssirratis do deserve to know about it. About all of it."

I shut the box down, knowing full well what had happened even without listening to the rest of the recording.

But how was I supposed to get the black box home and into the right hands without anyone knowing? At least until it was too late to stop me? The information recorded in that box was the only way to prove what the government knew. Hopefully something on it also specified the government's responsibility for the destruction of the Jin-ree 6. Qitx had said mission command knew about that, too. They must have had a hand in it.

Of course they did. And Kneskt must have known, too. So innocent-sounding when he asked me to confirm Merla's final words.

Were there really find alien artifacts on the moon? As if he didn't know.

So many moving parts.

From behind me, Vlhasa tapped my helmet. I almost screamed.

"Find anything?" she asked.

What kind of question was that? I was standing next to two charred bodies, plugged into the black box.

Was she fishing? Testing me?

I inhaled deeply, enjoying the sweet taste of paranoia.

"There's nothing out of the ordinary on the audio," I said, hoping my voice didn't betray me. "We'll have to take it planet-side to get the telemetry data properly analyzed."

Maybe I could copy the voice-data somehow, get it to the media. I'd have to publicly confirm its accuracy, which would be the end of my career as an astronaut.

But Merla had died for the truth. Was I such a coward that I wouldn't risk far less?

"Okay," said Vlhasa. "Pack up the box and bring it along. We'll drop it off on our way to the alien ship. In the meantime, we need to talk. I need your help with something."

I froze.

We need to talk. I need your help.

Those were the exact words Qitx said to Merla.

"What is it?"

"Come with me. I think Nlnuh and Sdekk will be able to explain it better than I can."

All four of my legs went numb. Nlnuh and Sdekk… were the crew of the Jin-ree 6.

"That's not possible," I said. "Nlnuh and Sdekk are dead."

Vlhasa put a claw on my arm. "Do you need a minute to compose yourself?"

"I need answers," I said.

"Because you look like you're going to pass out."

I roared. I was angry and confused and hurt and grieving. I grabbed all four of Vlhasa's arms. "What the flack is going on!!"

"Follow me," she replied, nonplussed. "You'll understand when you see Nlnuh and Sdekk."

That's all she said. Then she broke free of my grasp and strode away.

• • • • • • • ● • • • • • • • •

We walked in silence, pausing long enough at the Jin-ree 8 to drop the black box at the foot of the entry ladder. In the lower gravity I could have easily leaped to the entryway to put the box inside, but that was far too buoyant an act for someone in my state of mind. And I didn't want to be conspicuously protective of it. If I carried it with me, it would have been all I could think about.

Vlhasa and I walked past the alien landing craft and

began following the transport's tracks. The silence weighed more than a mountain.

At the crater I'd spotted earlier, two astronauts emerged from inside of it, dragging gear up over the rim. The gear perplexed me. Vlhasa had prepared me—told me that we'd see Nlnuh and Sdekk. Good thing, otherwise I'd have had a heart-attack when they appeared. But what they were hauling made no sense. It was a large light on an even larger tripod.

Vlhasa called out, "Nlnuh, Sdekk. I found Tkit."

"Great," Sdekk said. "Give us a hand with these, will you? Now that you've finally landed, we need to set up the photo shoot."

I instinctively grabbed hold of one side of Nlnuh's tripod. In the low gravity of the moon it wasn't heavy, just awkward.

In my state of shock, I didn't know what else to say, what else to do. The words 'You're alive' may have crawled out of my mouth, but I can't be sure. I just grabbed a tripod and started helping move them.

"Good to see you, too, Tkit," Nlnuh said. "Sorry about the way things ended for Merla and Qitx, but we're damn glad you made it. Don't know how much longer we'd've lasted if you hadn't shown up."

I bobbed my head once or twice because words still eluded me.

"All right," Sdekk said. "Let's get one of these things aimed this way…"

Vlhasa twisted the light to aim it in the direction Sdekk indicated, saying, "What's the plan?"

"We're going to add some extra light coming from angles besides where the sun is. That will create a few shadows that shouldn't be there. The conspiracy theorists will spot it and denounce the alien lander as a fraud."

"Proof of alien life is no small thing. What if no one takes the bait?"

Nlnuh chimed in. "We've been studying this stuff for a couple of months, and I don't think this is an alien ship. Sdekk disagrees, but I'm convinced these artifacts are from the species that ruled the planet millions of years ago, before they suddenly disappeared and Ssirratis-kind evolved into the dominant life form."

Vlhasa got a disdainful look on her face. "The Googlerth? On the moon? Ninety-eight percent of everything we've found from their time period is plastic. Or really, *really* tiny." She gestured to the gold and black lander we were preparing to photograph. "That ship is metal, not plastic. And though no one would call it huge, it's certainly not miniscule like all the things Googlerth culture seemed obsessed with."

"That's what I say," Sdekk chimed in. "But ultimately it's beside the point."

I found my voice. At least a little.

"What in the world is going on here?" I whispered.

With all of the movement, no one heard me. I cleared my throat as my wits came back to me, saying again, loudly, "What's going on!?"

Nlnuh and Sdekk chimed together, "Ah, look who's back."

Vlhasa added, "I wondered how long it would take you to work through the shock."

"Will someone please tell me what's going on?" I said a third time.

"For starters, the Jin-ree 6 didn't really blow up," Sdekk said matter-of-factly. "We staged an explosion in the booster rocket so we could go dark and do research on the alien ship. This little thing," he waved a claw dismissively at the lander and the surrounding artifacts, "this crap is a few million years old. Tests indicate that all of the raw material came from the home-world. Whether it's Googlerth or not is inconsequential. The really interesting artifacts are in that crater…"

Sdekk marched toward the crater they had dragged the lights out of. The one the small transporter's tire tracks led to.

I followed.

And I saw it.

With my own eight eyes, I saw it.

What I had thought a pretty standard crater was actually the end of a long gash in the moon's surface.

And wedged into the middle of that gash lay an enormous spaceship.

It looked nothing like the pathetic little thing behind me. It was enormous, at least one hundred and fifty meters from tip to tip and pointed on both ends. And most curiously, the hull was covered with etchings, curious markings carved down the length of the ship.

I saw no sign of a porthole, door, or anything else. Just etchings. Over every square centimeter. And this ship wasn't small or insignificant. It wasn't half a ship like the smaller craft behind us.

It was truly, fundamentally, *alien.*

"This is what we came to study," Sdekk said. "This is what we need to keep from the rest of Ssirratis-kind until they're ready. The Googlerth ship will be a perfect smokescreen though, to keep them off-balance and guessing."

"I… I don't…"

I had no words. My brain was full and my mouth wouldn't work.

"I need to know one thing, Tkit," Sdekk said, one claw on my arm. "Can we count on you? Are you with us?"

I thought hard.

I stopped trying to talk, and I thought.

About Vlhasa.

About Qitx.

About eternally principled Merla and her doomed last stand. About her charred body, not 500 meters in the other direction, and how this discovery would fundamentally change the world as we knew it.

· · · · · · · · ● · · · · · · · · ·

"And?" asked the reporter.

"And what?" I replied.

"What did you decide? What did you do?"

"I'm here talking with you, aren't I?"

The reporter absentmindedly tapped a tarsal claw against her small recording cube, processing what I'd told her.

"I don't know," she said. "I mean, you're clearly who you say you are. I checked you out before I agreed to this meeting."

"You checked me out?"

"What kind of reporter would I be if I didn't? I'm a journalist, not a tabloid hack."

"I meant no disrespect," I said. "I would have just thought that an astronaut—the first astronaut to ever set foot on the moon, no less—would be given the benefit of the doubt."

"Well, see, that's one problem, right there in a nice neat web. According to your story, you weren't actually the first Ssirrati on the moon. You were the third."

"I misspoke," I said. "The first Ssirrati to *officially* set foot on the moon."

"It's not just that, though. There are other things. Little details I can't wrap my spinner around. Like why wouldn't they tell Merla about the mission before it launched? For that matter, why didn't they tell you? And even if you could come up with a reasonable explanation for that, how in the world do you expect me to believe that Nlnuh and Sdekk survived alone on the moon for four months? Or that they came home from the moon again and no one ever recognized them? I could go on and on with these kinds of questions. It's just not..." She slipped her recording cube into her pocket. "Your story. It's got too many holes."

"I could plug every one of them," I said. "Answer every question you've got."

The reporter looked straight into all eight of my eyes, and I detected something I'd seen before. Something that I'd seen from a lot of people since I started telling my story. Something I hated.

Pity.

She said, "Everyone at the space program, every one of your fellow astronauts, they all say you came unhinged at the death of your breedmate. That losing Merla broke you. I agreed to this meeting out of respect for what you've been through. You'll always be a hero. But I think they're right. I don't think you're dangerous, but I do think you've lost touch with reality. I'm sorry, Tkit, but there's no story here."

She stood, locking onto my eyes with hers, the pity unmistakable.

Then she walked away.

I sighed.

I had done it. Again.

But the pity grew tiresome.

I decided then and there that this would be the last real journalist I talked to. Time to move to the final phase of the plan: the tabloids. The tabloids would giddily print my story, ensuring its utter lack of credibility.

And that would be that.

Between the ancient-alien theorists feuding over whether or not the pictures we took of the smaller alien craft were faked, and the deep conspiracy theorists who postulated the whole thing was merely a smokescreen for something bigger, I think we had successfully wrapped the whole affair in so many layers of mystery that no one outside of the space program's innermost circle would ever know the truth. If the astronaut who'd seen it with his own eight eyes had no credibility, *no one* did.

Despite what Merla may have thought, Ssirratis-kind isn't ready for this. Not yet.

Someday they will be. Someday we'll be able to tell them. When the moment is right. When the answers have all been unearthed.

In the meantime, we'll keep studying the real alien ship, looking for a way inside.

Looking for answers.

And we'll find them. Of that I have no doubt.

It's just a question of time.

Afterword

When the publisher of Falstaff Books, John Hartness, decided to use the title of this story as the title for the whole collection, he said he liked the symbolism it represented in me taking a giant leap of my own, from being primarily an editor to primarily a writer. I don't think I would have ever thought of that on my own, but I like very much.

Having worked as the head editor of the online magazine *InterGalactic Medicine Show* for the past decade, I've learned a lot, made a lot of friends (and probably an enemy or three—for any number of fanged, clawed, virulent examples, Google the insanity of the 2015 Hugo Awards when it was hijacked by certain Sad/Angry Puppies and then reclaimed by even angrier so-called SJWs). I believe I've also progressed professionally in ways I never could have imagined when I first accepted the position as editor.

But as much as I've gained from being an editor over the past ten years, I lost something, too, something that was always higher on my list. Truth be told, being an editor was never really on any 'list' in the first place. Becoming editor of *IGMS* effectively fell in my lap through a series of interconnected coincidences, the result of saying 'yes' to a number of other, unrelated, less glamorous projects and positions.

I have no regrets about becoming an editor. I think I did good work and helped more than a few writers in the process. But what I found over time was that the more I let other writers' stories and characters run around in my head, the less time there was for my own stories and characters to develop. I effectively lost both the time and the ability to write my own stuff. And writing my own stuff was always the thing that *was* on the original 'list.'

About two years ago, I had grown restless enough to recognize it as a desire to return to writing. I asked the publisher of *IGMS*, Orson Scott Card, for a brief hiatus so I could see what happened if I tried my hand at writing again. It had been so long since I'd written anything (and finished it — I had *many* half-completed pieces, proof to me that writing and editing simultaneously was beyond my grasp), and I needed to convince myself that I could still produce publishable fiction. Orson was not only gracious enough to let me take the hiatus, he was generous enough to continue paying me, even though two of our assistant editors produced the next couple of issues entirely on their own.

I made the most of my hiatus, writing several of the stories in this book, including "This Giant Leap," as well as "Batting Out of Order" and "Feels Like Justice to Me." I even sold most of them pretty quickly.

My confidence bolstered by success, I seriously contemplated resigning as editor of *IGMS* and going back to being 'just' a writer. It looked good. It felt right. I wanted it.

Then my wife lost her job.

I never made a lot of money editing I*nterGalactic Medicine Show* (it was, from day one, a part-time job that I supplemented with other writing and editing projects), but when it suddenly became the vast majority of the income flowing into my household, it also became impossible to justify giving it up simply because I felt like being writer again.

Eventually I found a full-time job with a more stable paycheck and resigning from IGMS became an option again. Except that almost immediately upon securing said full-time job, my managing editor and dear friend, Kathleen Bellamy, called me to say the cancer she'd been battling for four years had spread into her lungs.

insert numb silence here

I was angry after receiving that phone call—angry at the world, at the universe, at God, at everybody and everything—for allowing such a shitty thing to happen to such an amazing person. I actually scared my wife when she first ran into me after that phone call. I explained what was going on and her response was, "Edmund, you need to chill. You can't punch cancer," to which I venomously replied, "*You don't know that.*"

Probably the best thing that came out of that exchange was that when I retold it to Kathleen, it made her laugh. So maybe that was my punch in the throat to cancer, making her laugh and forget for just a few moments about the crappy hand life had dealt her. I dearly hope so.

Naturally there was no way I was walking away from *IGMS*—and Kathleen—in the middle of that kind of crisis, so I worked my day job from 9-5 and edited *IGMS* at night and on the weekends and waited and watched and hoped and prayed—and in the end, cried when the prayers seemed to go unanswered and she died. I edited one more issue after she passed because I thought she would have wanted me to, but it just wasn't the same without her. And I knew that it never would be.

Then and only then did I resign. It was bittersweet, to say the least.

Time will tell what kind of writer I'll become as a result of my years as an editor, but having Kathleen as my managing editor and friend definitely made me a better editor. With her gone, it was finally time to make The Giant Leap.

TANGIBLE PROGRESS

July 29, 1935 – The Shenandoah Valley, Northern Virginia

Despite the absence of the moon, the star-filled summer sky glowed brightly—bright enough for the Blue Ridge Mountains to throw stark shadows across the grassy field. Eleven-year old Gabrielle Ortello walked halfway across the meadow with her mother, then took off running to catch up with her lean, intangible, naked friends. There was just no way to be intangible and clothed at the same time.

The four other girls had almost reached the dense stand of pine trees on the other side of the meadow, and as Gabrielle ran, her mother, also intangible, also naked, called out those familiar words: "Watch out for *people*!"

Gabrielle waved without looking back. "I know, Mama," she said. "I know."

She had heard it a thousand times. Make sure no one sees you walk through tree trunks. Make sure no one sees you pass through boulders.

What was Mama worried about?

Besides, walking through stuff was fun. And the Rem'n were intangible for only a handful of days each month. Did they really have to be *that* careful?

Yet every time the moon was about to disappear, the whole Rem'n tribe—nearly twenty families—hid from the outsiders, the *estraneos*. They took off faster than a flock of crows at the sound of a farmer's shotgun. They took their horses, wagons, and their rickety, spoke-wheeled pickup truck, and they camped out in the middle of nowhere, hiding; waiting for that first pie-slice of moon to peek out and turn their people solid again so that the men, women, and children could all get dressed and walk amongst the *estraneos*.

Sprinting across the meadow, Gabrielle caught up to the other girls, joining them as they strolled through the last few yards of the swaying grasses. When they reached the woods, the group chattered on, going deeper in.

Except Gabrielle, who paused.

Gabrielle listened to the breeze as it rustled through the pine trees. She gazed up at the silhouettes of the swaying branches, which looked like airborne brooms trying to sweep the stardust out of the sky.

It was a perfect night to be intangible, to explore the world.

The wind rustled, whispering to her, just as the other girls called loudly, breaking her reverie. They waved, beckoning from the woods, gesturing for her to join them.

Gabrielle sighed. She didn't agree with so many things some of them did, but they were the only friends she was permitted to have. Though they were intangible only during the new moon, even during the rest of the month the Rem'n didn't interact with *estraneos* unless absolutely necessary.

And how was she supposed to make friends like that? Real friends. Not self-centered, self-important nitwits like...

"Come *on*, Gabrielle," said Celia.

Twelve years old, Celia was the oldest of the group—nearly a teenager—and she never let anyone forget it. "You're supposed to be the werewolf. We can't start without you."

"I played the werewolf last time. We agreed I could be a Hunter this time."

Celia crossed her arms over her thin, translucent chest. Her eyes and lips narrowed like a set of blacksmith's vices. "That's right. I forgot; it's Diana's turn."

Gabrielle immediately saw her mistake. Poor Diana may have been named for the goddess of the moon and the hunt, but she was only eight; playing the werewolf gave her nightmares.

And Celia knew it.

"You know," Gabrielle said, "if you're going to be manipulative, you could at least try to be subtle…"

"Why? This works just fine." Celia gave the other two girls—Julia and Leabe—a satisfied waggle of her black eyebrows.

Gabrielle strode up to her—close enough to touch, if that were possible. "If I were solid right now, I wouldn't pull your hair, and I wouldn't smack you." She raised her fist. She had to reach up to do it because Celia was taller, but Celia stepped backed regardless. The other girls gasped.

"You wouldn't dare!"

In Rem'n culture, passing yourself through someone else's space—*invasione*—was a serious violation.

Gabrielle pushed her fist through Celia's nose and out the back of her head. "Torment my friend again and you'll find out what else I'll do."

"We'll see," Celia retorted. But she retreated several steps.

Gabrielle pointed to a large pine tree. "Are we going to play werewolves and Hunters or not? Stick your heads in that tree and count to fifty. No cheating."

The other girls walked to the scaly-barked pine. As they

inserted their heads into the tree, Gabrielle said a quick prayer to Diana—the goddess, not her friend—that Celia would stick her face into a rotten section filled with beetles and ants and grubs. Or better yet, a hollow spot with a snake in it.

Once certain that no one was peeking, Gabrielle ran back to the edge of the woods. She had learned long ago that backtracking would allow her to circle around and pick them off one at a time. If they were going to hunt her, she would hunt them too. Isn't that what real werewolves did?

But when she got to the forest's edge, she forgot about their game. Her tribe's campsite on the other side of the meadow had been abandoned. Abandoned by the Rem'n, anyway.

'People' walked around the site, poking through things like so many ants exploring a giant picnic basket.

Gabrielle stood at the edge of the woods, watching. Fascinated. She had to get closer. There had to be some way to sneak closer. To hear what they said, see what they did.

Were they like the Rem'n? Were they stealing things? Rem'n would have…

That's when she noticed a large group of men moving across the meadow. She didn't think they'd spotted her, but they were headed straight toward the pines where she and her friends were, yelling. Calling a name.

They were searching for someone.

Gabrielle didn't wait to find out who; she ran at once to her friends. They all had to hide—quickly.

The *estraneos* couldn't hurt them, but if they discovered them and the adults found out, the girls would be in trouble. Big trouble.

Gabrielle ran straight through every bush, tree, and rock in her path, the world flashing black each time she passed through one. Finally, she arrived at the spot where she'd last seen her friends.

"Diana! Julia!"

Gabrielle went to the pine tree where the girls had counted, trying to guess the most likely direction they'd have gone. Almost at once she spotted an area where the pines stopped and a rocky outcropping jutted up out of the sloping ground. The Rem'n had been traveling south through the Shenandoah Valley for several days and everyone—kids and adults alike—had been fascinated by the large mounds of rock nestled among the trees.

This was the logical place the girls would have been drawn to.

"Celia," she called. "Julia. Diana. Leabe. Listen, there are people coming. You've got to hide."

No reply.

"Come on!" Her desperation grew. "This isn't a trick. There are people are coming. *Estraneos.*"

Gabrielle stopped at the edge of the rocks, listening. The wall of rock loomed long and tall, like a two-story train station made of gray stone.

Gabrielle began to repeat, "This isn't a tri—" when she heard the crunching and crashing made by the estraneos entering the forest.

"*Girls!*" she whispered furiously. "*Hide!*"

Still no reply.

But the herd-of-buffalo crashing grew louder and louder, and Gabrielle could only hope her friends heard it, too. Or at least understood what the crashing noises meant.

Gabrielle took three steps backwards and slipped directly into the wall of rock, intending to hide there until the *estraneos* passed—

—and found herself standing inside a cavern.

The cavern itself wasn't a surprise; her mother had told her this valley was littered with massive caverns. Luray, Shenandoah, Endless, Grand. Mama had said some of them even had electric lights inside and promised they would try to visit one.

No, the surprise came in the form of a light, inside the cavern, in the middle of the night.

Gabrielle... was not alone.

A yellow light came bouncing around the corner, twitching like a drunken firefly, shadows lurching as the source moved closer, and Gabrielle's mother's words came to her for the thousandth time. *You can't let anyone see you like this, Gabby.*

Gabrielle backed halfway into the rock until only her eyes, nose, and chin stuck out from the rock like the work of a mad sculptor's chisel.

A young man strolled into view. Gabrielle guessed he was about thirteen, with the finest, blondest hair she had ever seen. Even his eyebrows looked like golden layers of spider webs. All of the Rem'n had dark hair and dark eyes, and this blond-haired boy was so different. His hair was too bright, his skin too light. But as odd-looking as he was, Gabrielle found herself with a growing urge to speak with him. To get to know him.

Wearing a pair of coveralls but neither shoes nor shirt, the boy carried a railroad-style oil lantern and seemed to be casually wandering around the network of caverns, enjoying the pointed, reddish-orange stalactites that hung from the ceiling like so many rusty icicles.

Gabrielle could scarcely believe how different the inside of this cavern looked from the plain stone outside. And how insignificant it all seemed compared to the chance of meeting someone new.

Her mother's words came to her again. But she didn't want to watch out for people. She wanted to *meet* people.

Gabrielle knew she would startle the boy no matter what she did, so stepped directly out of the rock and cleared her throat. When the boy turned, Gabrielle said, "Hey. What you looking for?"

He stumbled backwards, almost losing his lantern, and it looked like the flailing lantern threw lightning bolts around the edges of the stalactites. When the boy regained control, he slowly lifted his free hand and pointed at Gabrielle.

"A ghost!" He paused, then added, "A n… n… *naked* girl ghost!"

Gabrielle glanced down at her translucent body, then at the boy. Then she raised an eyebrow. "How are you supposed to wear clothing when you're intangible?"

All Rem'n went naked for the three or four days known as the Phase of Grace. Nudity was commonplace, a monthly part of their lives. But no one in her tribe had ever looked at her like this. This boy made her *feel* naked.

"I never heard of no naked ghosts before," the boy said.

Gabrielle tried to cover herself with her intangible hands, but they proved as effective as a picture window on an outhouse. "I'm not a ghost. I'm a Rem'n. We're cursed. Have been for thousands of years."

The boy climbed to his feet and reached a hand toward Gabrielle. She took a step back, thinking about running.

Then she remembered the only other person who had ever gotten this close to her during the Phase of Grace. He had run away. This new boy might have been surprised, but he wasn't afraid. And Gabrielle wasn't going to let a little discomfort make her miss something interesting.

"How did you die?" he asked, trying to pass his hand through her head.

"I'm not a ghost!" Gabrielle said vehemently, dodging his attempted *invasione*. She closed her hands into fists. "I told you I'm a Rem'n. My name is Gabrielle."

"Wow. Dead, and she don't even know it."

Gabrielle rolled her eyes. How many times did she have to tell him…?

"Watch. I'll show you."

She turned to the rock wall. She was about to re-enter it when it occurred to her that it would prove only her intangibility; it would do nothing to prove she was alive.

She stepped toward the wall anyway, unsure what else to do.

The boy must have thought she was about to leave because he called out frantically, "Wait! Don't go."

Gabrielle stopped, but enough was enough. "Say I'm dead one more time and I'll kick right through you for sure."

Unaware that he had just been threatened with *invasione*, the boy moved a small rock across the floor with his foot.

"You, ah, you haven't got anything to eat, have you?" he asked.

"Oh sure," said Gabrielle, passing her hands through her thighs. "Right here in my pockets." She made sure she had a big smile on her face so he'd know she was only kidding around.

The boy sighed. "Yeah…"

That's when the truth struck Gabrielle. Suddenly she felt sorry for him. "You're lost, aren't you?"

The boy squinted, studying her. "Not lost, exactly. I've just been exploring down here for a *looong* time. I sure am cold though. I thought it would be warmer underground, not colder. That's why I took my shirt off. I had no idea it'd be so cold down here." He rubbed his hands against his arms and shoulders, and Gabrielle noticed for the first time that he was covered with goosebumps.

Gabrielle put two and two together. "That explains all those people poking around in our camp. They're looking for you."

The boy perked up. "They're looking for me?"

Gabrielle nodded. "How long have you been… 'exploring'?"

He shrugged; the gesture made his lantern rise and fall. The shadows danced, but the boy's expression was sad.

Gabrielle wished she were tangible so she could give him a hug, maybe warm him up. "When's the last time you ate?"

"Breakfast," he replied, kicking the stone across the floor.

"Breakfast? Sweet goddess, that's all day ago. It's the middle of the night! It's a miracle your lamp hasn't run out of oil."

"Is it that late?" The boy raised the lamp and the shadows shortened. "I only use the lantern while I'm moving. When I get tired, I rest in the dark, which saves oil. I hug it for warmth and make sure I don't move."

"Wouldn't you keep warmer if you kept moving?"

"Maybe. But I also almost fell off a ledge the last time I tried walking in the dark. There are some crazy deep chasms down here." After a moment he added, "Wait a minute, if you're, umm… what's the word… intangible, how can you walk? Shouldn't you sink into the ground or float in the air or something? And how can you talk? How can you do *anything*?"

Gabrielle knew the answer to this from listening to her father and the other men around the campfire. "We're cursed by Mars, the God of War," she said. "Gods' curses don't obey rules or science."

That didn't seem to mean anything to the boy, and the moment turned into uncomfortable silence.

"Hey," Gabrielle finally said, not wanting to the conversation to die, "you never told me your name."

"Isn't it bad luck to tell a ghost your name?" He set his lantern on the ground.

"I warned you," Gabrielle snapped. She stepped toward him and swung her foot in a perfect arc to kick through his shins. Of course, her foot passed through him with less effect than a cloud through the sky, which only set the boy to laughing.

"It's not funny," hollered Gabrielle. It had never occurred to her that someone could think an *invasione* was a laughing matter. She stepped back and took another swipe at him, which only made him laugh harder.

His laughter was pure and infectious, and before she knew it, Gabrielle was laughing, too. He began kicking at her, too, and the whole thing turned into a bizarre square dance, two lithe young bodies swinging feet and pivoting and twirling, doe-se-doe-ing until the boy fell to the ground, landing on the rocky floor and holding his sides from laughing so hard.

Gabrielle laughed so hard she started crying. It had been a long time since she had done anything so freely, so uninhibitedly. She wished she could give the boy a hug or lean on his shoulder or *anything*.

But she couldn't, and for the first time ever, she regretted being intangible.

"My name is Willie," the boy said though glittering tears. But his laughter faded and the tears grew increasingly less funny. "Willie Kitterman… and… and I want to go *home*."

That's when Gabrielle remembered that Willie was still a kid, even if he was a few years older than she was—a kid who had been lost all day, hungry and tired and cold and scared.

"I haven't been exploring," Willie confessed, the tears subsiding. "I've been lost down here all day. I have no idea how to get out."

"I could tell," she said softly.

The young teen snuffled loudly. "You can?"

"It wasn't hard to figure." With all the confidence she could muster, she added, "But I'm going to find a way to get you out."

Willie grasped the lantern's wire handle and raised it, looking around the cavern hopelessly. "How?"

How. That was the question.

"Have you ever been in here before?"

Willie shook his head. "My parents told me a million times to stay out of here." He looked around again. "I guess they knew what they were talking about."

Gabrielle followed his eyes, but her mind wandered out into the woods where the herd of *estraneos* crashed through the forest. The local people probably knew the caverns well enough to navigate in and out in no time. All she had to do was march up to one of them and say *Hi, Willie Kitterman is in there and he's lost. Would you please come save him?*

Piece of cake. One that would get her into a mountain of trouble.

"Look, Willie," she said, trying to find a gracious way to explain her dilemma. "If I go out there and talk to people and my parents find out—"

But the wounded look on Willie's face stopped her.

"I thought you were my friend."

"You also thought I was a ghost, and clearly that's not—" Gabrielle cut herself off. Whatever else happened, she wasn't going to abandon Willie like a sack of kittens down a well. There had to be some other way.

"Do you remember what the opening of the cave looked like? Could you describe it to me, the place where you went in?"

"What good will that do?"

"Because I can walk through walls, remember? I'll go outside, find that opening, then pass back and forth through the rock until I find the fastest way back out. Easy as falling through a log!"

Willie chuckled. "I think you mean easy as falling *off* a log."

Gabrielle shrugged. "You have your sayings, we have ours."

Willie described the cave opening to Gabrielle vividly, but the more he detailed every leaf and rock, the less likely she thought she was to find it. She didn't know the difference between a cedar and a pine, or shale and quartz. And if she couldn't find the way in, she'd never get Willie out.

There was just no way—until she remembered the shirt Willie left behind.

"Willie," she interrupted. "These rocks and trees look the same to me. Tell me what your *shirt* looks like. Spots, checks, stripes? Did you drop it on the ground or drape it over a stump? That's what I need to look for."

He described a plain white t-shirt hanging from an equally white sycamore branch.

"I have no idea what a sycamore tree looks like, but I'll be right back," she said excitedly. She walked through the cavern wall and the world went momentarily black.

Emerging on the other side, Gabrielle hoped Willie

wouldn't be too scared when he realized he was alone again.

Outside the cavern, it took a minute for her eyes to adjust to the silvery-blue starlight. Before she had adjusted, though, a voice whispered severely, *"Hey! Gabrielle!"* She looked around but didn't see anyone.

"Up here, stupid."

Celia squatted atop the rocky outcrop. She looked like a frog on a bloated lily pad. Leabe, Julia, and Diana stood behind her.

"We know about your boyfriend," Celia taunted. "We've been watching the whole time. You were talking with that *human*." She said the word 'human' with utter contempt.

"We're human, too," Gabrielle said. "Don't you listen to anything our parents tell us?"

"Look who's talking, Miss Don't-worry-I'll-save-you." She brought her hands together over her heart and said mockingly, "I'm not a ghost, I'm a Rem'n." Her voice took on an extra-syrupy quality when she added, "We're cursed. Have been for thoooooouusands of years."

Celia pointed down at Gabrielle. "You are going to be in so much trouble when I tell your parents. How many times have they told you to watch out for *people!*"

Gabrielle knew Celia was just using their parent's words because it suited her purposes. But she also recalled the whipping she'd received the last time she had let *estraneos* see her during the Phase of Grace; it had been hours until she could walk straight and days until she could sit.

"I don't need to let anyone else see me. And if Willie says anything, he'll probably say a ghost saved him."

She set off toward higher ground where Willie had said he thought his t-shirt would be. But the moment she started moving, Celia said, "Have fun. We'll keep your boyfriend company while you're gone."

"No, you won't," Gabrielle replied sternly, but she knew what Celia was capable of. A hole opened up at the bottom of her stomach and her heart dropped straight down through it.

Celia was already gone.

"You'd better not leave him alone with them," said Diana, the only one who had stayed behind.

Gabrielle shrugged. "They're as intangible as we are. What could she do?"

Diana shrugged back. "It's Celia. She'll think of something. Something mean."

Gabrielle fumed. She didn't have time for this. But Diana was right. Celia would do it—whatever *it* turned out to be—just to be spiteful. She walked back through the rock, into the cavern, just in time to hear Celia's voice.

It took a moment to realize Celia was above her, sticking her face out from the ceiling.

"Ruuuuun," Celia droned in the softest, sweetest voice she could muster, her voice echoing eerily around the chamber. "Run awaaaay!"

"Who is that?" Willie said, twitching. He twisted his head from side to side, raising his lantern. It never occurred to him to look up.

"I am the spirit of the cave," Celia replied in that singsongy voice Gabrielle so despised. "And I'm here to warn you about the ghost who calls herself Gabrielle. Do not trust her. She's an angry ghost who pretends to be your friend. Follow her and she'll lead you to your death."

"*That's a lie!*" Gabrielle shouted, emerging from the wall.

Willie jumped back.

Gabrielle looked up at the ceiling, where Celia's face beamed with silent laughter.

"Knock it off, Celia. It's not funny."

"Ruuun," Celia repeated. "Ruuuuuuun."

Willie began to back away.

"Come on, Willie," Gabrielle said, reaching out. "You know me. You know I'm trying to help."

Celia wasn't done taunting. "If she wants to help, why isn't she out looking for the entrance to cavern like she said she would?"

Willie's retreat increased in urgency. "That's a good question. Why are you still here? What do you want?"

"Turn off your lantern, Willie," Celia instructed. "If she can't see you, she can't find you to hurt you."

Instant blackness. Not a single star or anything. It was unnerving.

"Use your brains, Willie," Gabrielle said in the darkness. She was struggling to keep her cool. "The only one who's trying to hurt you is stupid Celia. And blundering around in the dark is the quickest way to do it."

Silence.

"Come on, Willie. I came back into the cavern because I knew Celia would do something mean. I came back to protect you. From her."

More silence. Clearly Willie was unconvinced.

Gabrielle changed tactics and turned her attention to Celia. "We both know you can't actually hurt him when you're intangible. You're wasting your time. And mine. Why don't you admit it and get out of here?"

Suddenly the darkness filled with the sound of high-pitched wailing. At first it was just Celia's voice, but the wailing grew, adding Leabe's voice, then Julia's. Gabrielle prayed that Diana wasn't doing it too, but at this point she couldn't tell anymore. She couldn't distinguish between all the voices. She was also stunned at how much of a racket they were capable of making. A hundred condemned souls being dragged into the underworld couldn't have caused a more horrifying din.

It must have sounded to poor Willie like death itself.

Gabrielle heard the sound of his feet shuffling, then running in the darkness.

But that sound was almost instantly replaced by three others, nearly simultaneously — a *whoof* of expelled air and the shattering of glass, followed almost immediately by a short, terrified scream.

"Willie!" Gabrielle cried. In the pitch black, she couldn't see a thing. But it sounded like Willie had tripped and fallen over a ledge.

"Willie, where are you?"

"Ruuuun," came Celia's sing-songy ghost-voice again. "Run for your liiiiife!"

"It's not funny, Celia. If you just killed him…"

"Not… dead…" Willie's voice sounded incredibly strained.

"Where are you?" Gabrielle asked, trying to locate the source of his voice.

"Help me, Gabrielle," pleaded the voice in the darkness.

"Willie!" she cried again, clutching at nothing, with nothing, into nothing.

But there was nothing. Blackness and more blackness. Not a single sound besides the far off drip drop plop of water.

"Willie!" Gabrielle shouted for what felt like the millionth time. But she was already running, sprinting though the darkness, through the cave wall. She kept right on running until she emerged from the cavern and into the silvery-blue of the night. She took a moment to get her bearings, then continued running toward the meadow.

You like being a snitch, Celia? she thought to herself. *You're going to* love *this.*

Near the edge of the woods she caught sight of a small group of estraneos and sprinted toward them, yelling, "Hey!"

The people took one look at her and ran away, screaming.

Gabrielle watched them flee. She had miscalculated.

Behind her she heard hysterical laughter. There stood Julia and Leabe. Celia must have sent them to spy on her, which meant Celia was probably still in the cave.

"That was great, Gabby," Leabe said. "Do it again."

Fool, Gabrielle chastised herself. The only reason Willie didn't run away is because you were careful not to scare him. You have to be gentle with *people*.

Gabrielle walked back through the woods, searching for other *estraneos*. There had to be someone still here. Leabe and Julia followed her, chattering noisily the whole time.

"Quiet," Gabrielle snapped.

"Why? I thought you wanted people to find you."

A voice in the distance called out, and Gabrielle recognized it was calling for Willie.

Gabrielle followed the cry. Except this time, when she got close enough to see the men calling for Willie, she called back from a safe distance.

"Hellooooo," she cried. "Helloooo? Is anybody out there?"

"Willie?" a man's voice replied.

"Willie!" came the second man's voice, stronger. "Over here, boy."

As the men came closer, Julia and Leabe vanished inside a nearby tree.

"Hello?" Gabrielle called again, seemingly wandering aimlessly, gazing vacantly and doing her best to act like a ghost.

Both men caught sight of her at the same time and froze in place like they had looked into a Gorgon's eyes. But at least they didn't run.

Gabrielle wandered in their general direction, careful not to get too close. Not knowing how badly Willie had been hurt made it agonizing to be moving so slowly, but she knew it was the only way her plan had any chance.

"Hellooooo? Won't someone please help me?"

She started walking slowly back toward the cavern where Willie lay, walking straight through a tree to reinforce her ghost-like nature. She also made sure she moved at a pace the men could easily follow and still keep a safe distance. They weren't going to reveal themselves to her, but they didn't need to.

"Hellooooo?" she said as she fought the urge to run. "Hellooo?"

As she neared the rocky area where she had left Willie, she checked the men one last time, saying, "*Please,* someone help me..."

Then she walked right through the stone.

Immediately Gabrielle climbed up through the top of the cavern to the same place where Celia had been perched earlier. Celia was nowhere to be seen. From up high Gabrielle had a perfect view of the men who'd followed her.

"Did you ever see the like?" one man gasped.

The other man shook his head tightly, speechless.

"I bet some little girl died in those caverns years ago and that was her ghost, still wandering, still looking for help."

"I think I heard a story about that when I was a kid," the second man said, finding his voice. "My grandfather used to tell us about her. I thought it was just a tall-tale to keep us out of the caverns."

Come on, Gabrielle thought with impatience. Put the pieces together.

She debated calling out to them again.

"Hey," said the first man. "You don't suppose…"

The second man seemed to catch the idea simultaneously, two men hooking the same fish. "Yes, I do suppose," he said excitedly. They looked back and forth between themselves and the rock. "Willie went in the cavern! We got to go get Fred. He knows these caves better'n anybody. If Willie's in there, Fred'll find him in no time."

Yes, Gabrielle said to herself. *Go get Fred.* She breathed a sigh of relief. Go find Willie.

She watched the men run off, crow-cawing for Fred all the way. Then she slipped through the blackness of the rock and into the equally black cavern.

"Willie?" she asked tentatively, not really expecting an answer yet hoping she would receive one.

Drip.

"Willie?" she called, louder.

Drip, drop.

"Wiiiiillie!" She bellowed at the top of her lungs.

Drip drop.

She sat down, her head hung low. "I'm sorry, Willie."

She sat. And waited. She didn't know how long she waited, or even exactly what she was waiting for.

Eventually she heard voices in the distance. Lots of them.

This time the voices were inside the cavern. And when she saw the lights bouncing around the corner, she called back to them.

"Here! I'm over here!" Gabrielle called, trying to deepen her voice. It sounded silly and not much like Willie, but she hoped that in the echoing cavern no one would notice.

"Willie?" came the reply.

"Yes. I'm right here."

"Where, Willie? Call out again."

"Down here. Look for the ledge."

As the approaching torches and lanterns caused a flash-flood of light throughout the cavern, Gabrielle backed once again into the rock, leaving just enough of her face that she could see what was happening.

The approaching group continued calling. "Willie?"

This time Gabrielle remained silent. The men were close enough to find Willie on their own now.

One of them, a hefty man with a ruddy nose and bushy beard, threw an arm out to stop the others. "Whoa," he said. "There's a big drop-off here." He leaned out over the edge with his torch.

"Whoa!" he repeated. "He's down there."

Someone tied one end of a thick rope to one of the snow-white columns, and then a thin young man tossed the other end over the ledge and shimmied down.

Gabrielle wished she could see what was going on down on that ledge. She wished she knew if Willie was alive or dead.

"He's breathing," shouted the voice from the end of the rope. "Looks like he's unconscious, though. And I think his arm's broke."

"Unconscious?" the ruddy-nosed man barked back. "He was just talking a minute ago, calling out to us."

"Don't know what to tell you. But he's unconscious now, that's for sure."

"It's a miracle we found him at all. Tie a rope on him and let's pull him up."

Gabrielle watched with anticipation as the men hauled on the thick rope, dragging Willie and the other man up from the depths. The instant Willie came up over the edge, the entire search party closed in around him, checking him, talking softly among themselves.

Gabrielle's frustration increased at her inability see anything. She took a single step out of the rock, trying to get a closer look.

One of the men stood in the center of the group, holding Willie in his arms. Gabrielle froze.

Willie's eyes fluttered open, looking directly at her.

She waved at him. A tiny wave, with only her fingers.

He smiled at her.

Then he closed his eyes again.

Gabrielle breathed a sigh of relief and slipped away.

· · · · · · ●● ● ●●● · · · · · ·

Back at camp, the *estraneos* had left and the Rem'n had congregated once again. They sat together, telling each other stories while they waited. It's what they did when they were intangible: they told each other their best stories. It would be at least three more days before they were solid enough to clean up the mess that had been made by the people looking for Willie.

Gabrielle snuck into her family's canvas tent, hoping no one would notice her. It came as no surprise though, when five minutes later Mama and Papa appeared along with one of the tribe's Elders, Elder Dukas. Thank the goddess they were intangible; Elder Dukas smelled like rotten garlic when he was solid.

"She told you, didn't she," Gabrielle said.

"Celia told us everything," Papa said.

"And Diana told us another version," Mama added. She

glanced at the Elder before adding, "We're not happy about either version, but we are more inclined to believe Diana's."

Gabrielle breathed a small sigh of relief. It hadn't occurred to her that Celia would embellish the tale to get her into even *more* trouble. Thank the goddess for Diana.

A small chortle escaped Gabrielle's lips. Thank the *goddess*, Diana, for her *friend*, Diana. She didn't mean to laugh; it just sort of happened.

Her father failed to see any humor. "You think this is funny? You break one of our most important rules and laugh about it?"

Papa proceeded to lecture her about rules, seemingly forever, but before she could utter a word, the Elder interrupted Papa's lecture.

"In a few days you will take her into town and find this boy, Willie," the Elder said. "Introduce her to him."

That got Gabrielle's attention. She searched the faces of the Elder and her parents suspiciously. What kind of punishment was this?

"Yes, Elder Dukas," Mama said as if she understood. "There's a farmer's market every Saturday. The whole town turns out. I'm sure the boy will be there, too."

The Elder nodded, but before he could speak, Papa added, "Luray is a particularly close-knit town. They watch out for each other."

"All the better," Elder Dukas replied.

• • • • • • • ● • • • • • • • •

Six days later, with a waxing crescent moon hanging in the sky and the mess the had made of their caravan cleaned up, Gabrielle and her mother put on matching green and white dresses and went into the town of Luray, Virginia, with Papa. They strolled together down the main street, Mama looking casual and Papa trying to, but not quite pulling it off.

Gabrielle was conflicted. She was thrilled to be in town, to see the farmer's market and all the people. And, of course, she would get to see Willie. She had no idea how they were going to find him, but she was thrilled about seeing him again.

On the other hand, she was still suspicious about Elder Dukas. He had something up his sleeve when he told Mama and Papa to bring her here.

As they walked down Main Street, Gabrielle spotted a head of hair so blindingly blond that it could only belong to one person. His right arm was in a sling.

"Willie?"

She released her mother's hand and ran toward him.

Willie turned at the sound of his name.

"Over here, Willie," she called. "It's me, Gabrielle. How's your arm?"

No sooner had she called him than the light of recognition spread across his face.

"Holy begonias. You're real."

Except instead of coming toward her, he ran off in the opposite direction.

Gabrielle stopped.

"Willie?"

She turned to her mother, who glanced over her shoulder at Papa.

Gabrielle wished they would both go away. How was she supposed to talk to Willie with them hovering like that? They were probably the reason he ran off.

However, before Gabrielle and her mother had walked another block, Willie reappeared with four other boys, all about his age.

"Look at this," he said to his friends. "I told you she was real. Hi, Gabrielle." He smiled.

A dark-haired boy walked up to Gabrielle and poked her hard enough that it hurt.

"She's not a ghost," the dark-haired boy said. He poked her again.

"Ow," Gabrielle said, shoving his hand away. "Quit it."

"And she's sure not naked," said a third boy, sounding disappointed. "You told us she was naked."

"She said she wasn't a ghost," Willie said. "Intangible is the word she used. She called herself something else, too." He turned to Gabrielle and said, "What was that word, Gabrielle? Roman?"

Gabrielle's mother spit on the ground. "We are no Romans," she said with contempt.

Willie put his left hand on Gabrielle's face, clearly favoring his injured right arm and thrown a little off balance by the weight of the cast. His hand was rough but warm on her cheek, and she closed her eyes and leaned into it.

"I swear, it's true," he said. "Before, you couldn't touch her. It was the weirdest thing."

Gabrielle's eyes snapped open. Willie wasn't touching her because he was glad to see her; he was testing to see if she was solid. Suddenly his hand had all the welcome warmth of a branding iron.

She grabbed his hand and flung it away. "What's wrong with you?" she demanded. She spun to her mother and repeated, "What is wrong with him?"

"I'm sorry," Willie said to Gabrielle. "I wasn't sure if you were real. Some of the other adults kept talking about ghosts, and, well, I thought maybe I was seeing things, you know… because I hadn't eaten all day." After a moment, he added, somewhat sheepishly, "Thanks for saving my life."

Gabrielle beamed. He *had* seen her after the men pulled him up from the ledge.

"So you couldn't touch her, huh?" one of the other boys said. He leaned in and grabbed Gabrielle's shoulder.

"I said quit it," she snapped.

Willie looked at the other boy but didn't say anything, and before Gabrielle knew what was happening, suddenly all of the other boys were closing in, touching. Testing. Probing. To see for themselves if she were real.

One boy grabbed her wrist; another grabbed her by the elbow. A third boy grabbed her from behind by both shoulders and suddenly there seemed to be hands everywhere, touching, prodding, poking—

Where is Mama, Gabrielle wondered frantically. Why isn't Mama—

A hand brushed across her chest.

Gabrielle screamed.

Papa jumped in an instant, even before Mama could react. Yet despite Gabrielle's screams and Papa's presence, the hands kept touching. Papa slung one boy to the side, grabbed another by the shirt and hauled him back, which left Willie facing off against the boy who had touched Gabrielle's chest.

"Apologize," Willie spat.

"Make me," replied the other.

That's when Gabrielle stepped in. She was embarrassed at having screamed. She had just been overwhelmed by all those boys, all those hands.

She punched the boy squarely in the jaw.

He reeled, just for a moment, then rushed at her, bellowing.

Willie, broken arm and all, met him head on. Gabrielle jumped in too and the three of them exploded into action, a blur of arms and legs and angry words.

Almost instantly Willie's other friends rushed in as well, followed by Papa. Suddenly everywhere around Gabrielle flew a hum and a whir of movement. The boys fought with the kind of abandon that only young boys can, Willie using the cast on his arm as both a defensive shield and a weapon.

Papa tried to separate them, though he showed no more care than he would have in separating a pack of fighting dogs. Fists flew and bodies were hurled. Noses and lips bled. Gabrielle landed several blows, hitting as many people with her elbow when she drew her arm back as she did with her fist when she punched forward.

Then suddenly Gabrielle saw there were even more people, the townspeople, looking up, looking toward them, then moving toward them.

Papa noticed too and let the boys go. The entire group of five boys sprinted off together, disappearing into the red brick general store up the street.

"Are you all right?" Papa asked, checking Gabrielle.

"I'm fine," she said, distancing herself from her father. She didn't want to be touched by him either. She didn't want to be touched by *anyone*.

Mama raised a hand, stepping forward as if to greet the *estraneos*.

"We don't mean any harm. We were only protecting our daughter."

"From what?" came a voice from somewhere in the crowd. "I didn't see them kids hurting none of y'all."

"And we didn't hurt those boys, either," Papa said.

"Then why was they bleedin'?" retorted the same

anonymous voice.

"They did that to each other," Papa said aggressively. "It was their own doing."

The crowd didn't like his tone. Their angry buzzing grew louder and they flowed closer, like a swarm of bees prepared to sting.

Just as the swarm seemed ready to make a surge, a roofless black Model T Ford came chugging around the corner. It pulled to a stop directly between Gabrielle's parents and the crowd of *estraneos*.

"So many people congregated in the middle of the street always makes me nervous," said the man, standing up inside the Model T. He put his left hand on the front windshield and his right hand on the gun at his hip, looking back and forth between the two sides. Sunlight glinted off the silver star pinned to his chest.

"These strangers assaulted some of our young'uns," said a wrinkled old lady standing on the porch of the general store. She looked down at Gabrielle with her one good eye. Her other eye was the color of milk and cherry blossoms.

"Yeah!" shouted the mob.

"But not before those boys acted in a most ungentlemanly fashion toward the young lady here," the milk-cherry-eyed old lady continued. She pointed at Gabrielle. "Called this one here a ghost, too. It was most peculiar."

The sheriff looked at Gabrielle, then her parents, seeming to size up the Rem'n. "They look like regular enough folk to me," he said.

He added a little more loudly, gesturing to Gabrielle's parents, "I think it would be best if you all went back wherever you come from." He turned to the mob and waved his hands as if shooing a herd of cows. "All of you. Go on. Go back to your homes or shops. There's no trouble here, so let's not make."

The ebbing crowd slowly but compliantly receded.

The sheriff sat back down in the driver's seat, looking at Papa. "Y'all are heading home, right? Not going to see you here again, am I?" It wasn't a question. It was barely polite.

Papa shook his head, and apparently that sufficed. The sheriff chugged off again, his Model T making coughing noises.

When the car vanished, Willie and his friends appeared one by one from inside the general store. They stayed on the white-painted porch next to the old lady, Willie fidgeting with his cast, trying to get it properly settled into the white cotton sling. Gabrielle marveled at how, despite the blood that was still drying on their noses and lips, the boys stood together quite comfortably, as if the fight had never happened.

Mama pulled Gabrielle close, caressing her hair and inspecting her green and white dress for damage. "Those boys weren't trying to be mean. They just don't know any better."

Gabrielle pulled free from her mother. "He brings his friends to *touch* me. Like I'm some kind of freak! And all you have to say is 'They don't know any better'? Whose side are you on?" She felt like hitting somebody. "It's stupid. You're all stupid!"

Tears formed in the corners of her eyes and Gabrielle felt her jaw tremble. She looked up the street at the general store where Willie and his friends openly stared.

Then Gabrielle looked at Mama and Papa, and a flare of anger burst up inside of her, burning away her desire to cry. Her parents and the Elder had *known* this would happen. Known that Willie and his friends would treat her this way.

Her parents had done this to her *on purpose*.

It was unforgivable.

Unpardonable. And she wouldn't stand for it.

She wished the moon would vanish so she could be intangible, so she could run away. Run away from them all.

I'll go... I'll go...

Where would she go?

Gabrielle shook her head.

That was the problem. And it was inescapable. The Rem'n were her people.

Trying to run away from them would be like trying to run away from her arms and legs. Like trying to run away from her heart and lungs.

Only the other Rem'n understood what it meant to be *this* different.

We call these people *estraneos,* she thought. But we're the real *estraneos*. We're the outsiders. And no one else can truly understand what that's like.

Knowing that, however, did nothing to make the moment any less painful, or the stares from Willie and his friends any less galling.

But looking at them, she realized that staying with her people she was right. As quickly as Willie and his friends had fought with each other, they had immediately come back together again when things got dangerous.

So did the Rem'n. They had to depend on each other, there was no one else.

Still, she wished again that the moon would disappear so she could become intangible and disappear, too. Even if she couldn't run away, she wanted to crawl inside the nearest rock or tree and vanish.

Disappearing sounds good, Gabrielle thought as she eyed her surroundings.

But not right now. Not in front of all these people. You've got to watch out for *people*...

She looked up at Willie and his poking, prodding friends. Then at her parents. She thought about the sheriff and the townspeople and the cherry-milk-eyed old lady. About the other Rem'n in her tribe. About Celia and Diana and smelly old Elder Dukas. About all of them.

Yes, Mama, she concluded. You do have to watch out for people.

The trick is in figuring out which ones to watch out for.

Afterword

You can talk a book to death. More specifically, you can talk the life out of it. Allow me to elaborate.

Over a decade ago I had an idea to link the origins of werewolves—as well as a race of werewolf hunters—to the legend of Romulus and Remus. It was a neat, tidy, tight, tremendous idea, full of possibilities. Everybody said so. The reason everybody said so was because I told anyone who would listen. Possibly a few who didn't listen, too, because I talked about it *endlessly*. I wrote a little here and there, made several false starts on a novel featuring the idea. And finished nothing.

And then one day I was done. *Finito*.

I was done because I had talked about it so much that I no longer needed to write it. I had explored the concept. I had navigated its nooks and crannies. Delved its deepest recesses. And grown tired of it. A person only has so much energy to expend on any one thing, and me being as ADHD as they come, my stock of reserve focus is shallower than that of your average four-year-old. And I had exceeded it.

So I set it aside. Reluctantly, of course, because I still thought it was a great idea. But it was also an idea for which I had *absolutely nothing to show* (besides the hearty affirmations of the dozens of people I'd regaled, or bored, with my telling of it).

So abandoning it was the only thing left, the only real option. I clearly wasn't going to write the damn thing, and talking about it was keeping me from writing anything else.

So I set aside my numerous stalled efforts and looked for

new ideas, new projects, new momentum. And found some. A little here, a little there.

And life went on. As it always does.

But all the while, a small part of my brain was waiting, lurking, hoping for that day when enough time would pass and I could try again. It took many years because I had been *that* stupid with the idea. I had been that callous with my treatment of it, that thickheaded about my ungentle mishandling of it.

But I eventually found my way back to it. Or it found its way back to me, I'm not really sure which. Just this one story, very intentionally about werewolf hunters when they're *not* hunting werewolves. And then I set it aside again, hoping that flirting with the idea but not fully committing to it would make my brain hungry to write more.

Will it? Will I write about these characters or in this setting or with these concepts again?

Only time will tell. I'm optimistic though because I already have the third book in what will be an amazing trilogy planned in my head. It was the book that came most naturally, but it soon became apparent that it was the last one in the series, not the first.

Still, it's an amazing idea. Let me tell you all about…

Yeah, right.

Like I'm ever going to make *that* mistake again.

A HINT OF FRESH PEACHES

She had died again, just three days ago. It was the eighteenth time this year; the ninety-second time since she'd started using the Machine. Yet each time, the dying only got harder. Not because of the throbbing in her head and her joints. No, that would pass.

It was the ache in her heart, an ache that grew more wrenching with every passing year.

No parent should ever lose a child. But for Helena Moore, it should have been *beyond* impossible. By hooking herself up to the Machine, she had the power to bring a human being back from the dead by taking their death onto herself. Yet three years ago her daughter had died and she'd been powerless to do anything about it.

Logically she knew it wasn't her fault. But logic be damned. Who else could have saved Katie? Who else had failed to?

Today, sitting on the front porch of the Caribbean beach house still half-owned by her ex-husband Frank, Helena wondered how long it would be until she recovered from her most recent Machine-induced death. How long until the inexplicable odor of fresh peaches faded from her nostrils and the heavy taste of blood left her mouth. How long until her vision cleared and the Caribbean Sea was anything but an angry turquoise blur.

But no matter what happened, no matter how quickly

she bounced back from each session with the Machine, her thoughts remained the same.

I could have done better.

I could have done more... *if only I'd tried harder.*

So four times a day she tied her frizzy red hair up into a ponytail and sprinted on the beach. She lifted weights in her private gym; sat in a soundproof room, meditated, and did yoga. She would have swum laps around the entire Caribbean if she thought it would've helped. Anything to strengthen her mind and body so as to speed up the recovery time.

But it wasn't enough. It hadn't been then, and it wouldn't be now.

It would never be.

Stupid alien machine, she thought. Stupid scientists.

Stupid me, for ever getting involved with any of them.

Stupid, stupid, stupid...

A familiar voice inside of her head interrupted her. Her ex-husband Frank may have been gone from the island, but when she got introspective, his voice had a way of showing up, chirping in her ear when it was least appreciated.

Stupid, or just bad timing? Why does it have to be anyone's fault...?

She wasn't in the mood for his Jiminy Cricket bullshit, not today. And there was only one good way to flush him out of her head: exercise. Rising from her wooden chair, Helena stepped off the porch and padded down to the ocean's edge. Strong winds blasted sand into her arms and legs, and she turned her freckled face aside to protect her eyes, sending her ponytail flying sideways. Despite the approaching storm, it was time to swim—

Well, it would have been. Except for that boat.

Even with blurred vision, she had no trouble spotting the

boat on the horizon: a chugging, puffing, sputtering brown blob carrying what would surely be another client.

Once upon a time her clients had all come in private helicopters. In those days, if you couldn't afford your own helicopter, you couldn't afford Helena's services.

That seemed like so many lifetimes ago.

Watching the approaching ship draw nearer, she realized her eyesight was clearing a little. Not much, but enough for her to make out the brown shape on the horizon: a fishing trawler—a battered vessel crossing a choppy River Styx, delivering the dead.

About a hundred yards off-shore the trawler dropped anchor and launched a rowboat. It had to; Helena had long since torn out the dock. Just because she wasn't charging exorbitant fees anymore didn't mean she wanted everyone to have easy access to her. She could never have handled them all.

Government trainees handled one or two clients per year, and federal guidelines restricted newly-certified professionals from doing more than four. Taking someone else's death onto yourself was too taxing. Even seasoned pros knew better than to do more than eight or nine a year; their bodies wouldn't stand up to it.

Unless, of course, they spent every minute of every day conditioning their body and mind, tweaking the tiny alien machine.

So here came corpse number nineteen for the year, floating on a decrepit, puke-green rowboat that had been dropped off the side of a tattered fishing trawler. Clearly this one would have to be kept secret from the government; there was no way these people could afford the official fee. Uncle Sam called it a 'fee,' but really it was nothing more than a creative way to tax the world's richest people. Judging from the state of their boat, though, these people couldn't afford a fee of any kind, much less the seventy-million-dollar price tag this procedure officially carried.

She would do it anyway. She didn't give a damn what the Feds thought. The Feds weren't likely to take the Machine away from her—she was one of only thirty-seven people in the world capable of using one. But it did occur to her that if they discovered she was handing out freebies, they might post someone on the island to monitor her. That would be intolerable.

It was also a problem for another day. Today her only concern was the as-yet unidentified corpse on the rowboat.

As the boat drew closer, Helena could make out a pair of Hispanic-looking people pulling at the oars.

South American, she wondered? Central?

Both regions were near enough to reach her by trawler, but far enough away that at trawler speed, the client/corpse had to have been dead for at least twelve hours. Not good. After twenty-eight hours, there was no way to bring a corpse back to life. And the longer it had been since the person died, the harder the revival was on her: it was like trying to jump-start a car that had been abandoned by the side of the road for too many years.

As the rowboat pulled closer still, Helena saw that it was being rowed by a middle-aged man and woman. Probably husband and wife. They had to have been pretty desperate to risk jumping into such a small craft considering the size of the storm that was brewing.

Seeing them, her throat tightened, the lump inside feeling like she'd swallowed a pineapple. An approaching couple inevitably meant one thing: a dead child.

Please, she prayed, *let it be a girl.*

She couldn't help it.

Katie was the only person Helena ever worked on who didn't rise again...

• • • • • • • • ● • • • • • • • • •

Three years earlier...

Helena winked at Frank, who was always nearby during the procedure. There was nothing he could do to help — not until it was over — but he was there just the same.

And right behind Frank was his red-headed shadow, Katie. Thirteen-years old and deep in the throes of that reverse-Oedipal-thing teenage girls do: believing her father could do no wrong and that her mother was the most awful creature ever to walk the Earth.

Lately Helena and Katie fought more often than not. Helena knew it was just a phase, but it was a phase that couldn't end soon enough. Every time Katie glowered, Helena could feel her own jaw clench, her stomach tighten.

She didn't need that. She didn't deserve it.

She glanced at the sixty-eight-year-old man laid out on the table before her. Sixty-eight years wasn't terribly old, but this playboy had a reputation for partying. If he kept pumping drugs and alcohol into his system, he could die again within a matter of months. It had been his heart that gave out this time; who knew when his kidneys or lungs would fail.

On the other hand, what did it matter? Let him have a stroke for all she cared; see if he could get on anyone else's schedule. Although it had been nine years since the alien ship carrying the Machine had crash-landed in the Rocky Mountains, there were still few people in the world capable of using one. From a mechanical standpoint, the Machine was surprisingly simple and the government had reverse-engineered it in a matter of months.

It was the individuals capable of running them that were in short supply. Successfully operating one took a rare combination of physical and mental strength combined with an extraordinary level of empathy, all channeled through the Machine. For a client to get on Helena's schedule was as much a matter of luck of timing as it was money.

Helena waved Frank out of the treatment room as the client's personal assistant came in. Many clients had the procedure videotaped, as if they were tourists or, worse yet, expectant parents in the delivery room.

Helena tried to catch Katie's attention. But her daughter had a knack for keeping her long red hair hanging directly in front of her eyes.

"Talk to Katie," she called after her husband. "Make sure she secures the sailboat like I told her. There's a chance that storm might veer this way and it's a pretty nasty one."

Frank laughed, trying to redirect the conversation, to overcome the awkwardness that pervaded every conversation that involved Katie and Helena. "You sure are some kind of Boy Scout, Hel. Always *prepared* for everything." He said the word 'prepared' like it was an evil thing, but his grin made his joshing obvious.

"You know any Boy Scouts who made fifty-six million dollars last year?"

Frank shrugged at her as he ushered Katie through the kitchenette, slipping out the door at the back.

That was Frank. If he wasn't Jiminy-Cricketing his conscience in her ear, he was making lame jokes. She would rather have heard from Jiminy though, because Frank only made jokes when he was worried about something and him worrying made *her* worry. She trained more than most Olympic athletes; what was there to worry about?

Only now she *was* worried. She had caught it from Frank like the flu, even though all that was left to do was to plug herself into the Machine, push a button, and enter a meditative trance.

She glanced at the old man's corpse. The next time she saw him he'd be strolling around this coconut-tree-covered island. The clients always recovered from the procedure before she did.

Helena inserted three fingers into the side of the Machine and began chanting her self-hypnotic mantra. "So that life may endure… So that life may endure…"

"Why do you say that?" asked the client's assistant.

He was leaning against the white stucco wall, talking to her but keeping both eyes glued to the screen of his video camera.

Irritated at being interrupted yet keenly aware of the fact that the client would see this video before he left the island, Helena put on a faux smile. "It's what the aliens said the only time they were observed using the Machine. At least, it's as close as we can come in English. The other translation was 'Life goes on' and everybody agreed that sounded lame. The government's scientists did a series of tests and decided the exact wording wasn't the important thing; what mattered was focusing the mind in the right place."

The assistant swung the camera toward her. "How could they understand what the aliens were saying?"

Helena wanted to tell this clown he was wasting precious time, but she held her tongue. Entire books had been written on this subject. Did he not know how to read?

"The aliens communicated telepathically. Even so, they were difficult to understand. Their thought-process was... well, alien. And within a week of landing they all were dead — too badly wounded during the crash — so it's not like anyone had much time to ask. Now either shut up or get out. I need to concentrate."

The assistant left, and Helena pushed the button.

And then she died.

• • • • • • • • ● • • • • • • • • •

Helena stood at the waterline, waves crashing against the beach and stealing the sand beneath her feet. The Hispanic couple was halfway to shore and rowing frantically. Too frantically for such choppy conditions.

Seconds later the boat flipped, dumping all three bodies into the sea. It was instantly clear that neither of the living ones were decent swimmers.

Helena rushed to the water's edge, aimed herself at the upside-down rowboat, and dove into a crashing wave. Repeatedly she rose up with a cresting wave to get her bearings as she swam, spitting saltwater and calling at the top of her lungs. Swimming, rising, swimming. Calling. Spitting. Swimming.

Finally, a wave heaved both her and the upside-down rowboat high enough for her to spot it. She swam toward it, grabbing onto its side with breathless relief when she arrived.

"Hello!" she called, trying to catch her breath. "*Hola!*"

"*Hola,*" came the pitiful reply from the other side.

Saltwater smacked Helena's face as the waves pounded the side of the boat. She worked her way hand over hand around the edge until she met up with the man. Seeing him, her first thought was that his receding chin reminded her of a turtle pulling its head into its shell, and his being next to an overturned rowboat only highlighted the effect. It would've been almost comedic if his dark-brown face weren't drenched with concern.

"They're gone," he said frantically, eyes staring at the frothing sea. "They went—" He gestured sharply with one hand. "Down."

Helena grasped the side of the flat-bottomed boat and heaved herself up on top of it. Then she pulled the man up next to her. "Stay here," she shouted over the growing storm, pointing emphatically at the overturned bottom of the boat. "*Aqui.*"

She dove off and immediately began pulling herself downward. It would take a miracle to find either of the other two, but after eight years of working with the Machine, Helena Moore had seen her share of miracles.

Normally the Caribbean would have been spring-water clear, but the storm had whipped the sea into an underwater blizzard of sand. Helena knew better than to open her eyes, so when she hit bottom, she turned in circles, arms outstretched, feet kicking awkwardly, seeking, searching.

But not for long. She was running out of air.

Pushing herself off the bottom, she headed to the surface. Breaking through, she gasped, gulping air greedily but briefly, knowing that time was of the essence. Then she kicked and turned herself over, diving again, swimming again until she found bottom, spinning again in gangly circles. She didn't know how much more of this she could take; the sea was so turbulent it was rapidly depleting her.

Out of air once again, she swam for the surface.

Halfway up, she bumped into something, something

large and puzzling. As she felt with her hands she realized it was *both* bodies, linked somehow.

Lungs afire, she grabbed a leg and headed to the surface. She didn't bother trying to inspect what she had found; she simply swam for shore, dragging the pair up onto the beach and collapsing next to them in a fish-gasping heap.

When she finally caught her breath, she turned to the tangle of bodies.

Mother and son were locked together by the mother's death-grip. The boy was about fifteen years old, the mother maybe forty. Apparently she'd grabbed her dead son's wrist and simply refused to let go. She chose death over letting go.

And the woman was as dead as her rigid son, who clearly had been deceased *far* longer than twenty-eight hours. That meant she'd died for nothing.

Helena looked back out to sea where the father clung atop the capsized rowboat. She was in no hurry to bring him in; doing so would only require telling him what had happened.

I've got to, though, she finally concluded. *Unless I want to lose him, too.*

She ran her hands across her tangled hair, pulling it away from her face. She dove back into the sea.

Towing the boat to shore made more sense than trying to get the man to swim with her. When they were a dozen feet from the beach, he jumped off, landing awkwardly.

He pulled himself up in the middle of the surf only to be beaten down, pummeled by wave upon wave of white-capped fists even as he dragged himself out of the water and onto the beach.

Eventually he staggered up to his wife and son, who lay side-by-side. Falling to his knees between them, clutching at them, he wailed unintelligibly in Spanish. Helena looked away. She tried to focus on the howling of the wind, to ignore the cries of the man. There was only one thing left to do, really; only one course of action that made any sense. But she would give him a moment to grieve.

• • • • • • • • ● • • • • • • • • • •

When Helena had regained consciousness, the old man was gone and a powerful moaning filled her ears. From all appearances the tropical depression had not only turned in their direction, it had strengthened into a hurricane.

With a thin, rasping voice, she called out: "Frank?"

Nothing.

"Frank?"

Frank was always there when she regained consciousness. He had to be; she had the strength of a newborn jellyfish when she first came to.

Helena could smell the peaches; the scent lingered in her nostrils like it always did. She tasted the blood in her mouth. The procedure had worked; the old man would live to party another day.

But where was Frank?

She willed her hand toward the call button next to her bed, reaching, slowly. Two inches. Three. It took a full minute for each inch and by the fourth she was depleted.

She needed to rest. To sleep…

• • • • • • • • ● • • • • • • • • • •

"No!" the Hispanic man shouted, shaking his turtle chin side-to-side. "That is not how she would have wished it."

Helena and the man—Diego—carried mother and son through the main house and into the treatment room. Together they laid the woman on the table next to the Machine.

Diego pleaded with Helena every step of the way.

"I don't think you're hearing me," Helena said for the fourth time, shouting louder as if the increased volume would make him understand. "Your son has been dead for three days! Even if your wife were standing right next to you, there's nothing I could do for him. You need to stop thinking you have a choice, because you don't."

Diego took a step closer and for a moment Helena feared he might get violent. She didn't fear for her own safety; she was far too strong for him to hurt her. But the last thing she wanted to do was hurt him.

Violence, however, was not on Diego's mind.

"*Por favor,*" he said. "How could I explain to her that I let you save her and not our *Jesús*? How am I supposed to live with her—with myself—if I allow that to happen?"

She gripped him by his shoulders. "Look, I understand your dilemma. But if you don't let your son go, you'll lose them both."

No sooner had those words escaped her lips than she heard Frank's voice in her head, echoing her words.

Your choice is to let go, or lose them both.

"I know!" she shouted. "You think I don't get it! You think I don't see the parallel?"

Diego shrank in fear, but Helena didn't care. She continued shouting at Frank. He could be *so* infuriating. "It's not the same," she screamed.

She snatched a coffee mug off the table and threw it against the white stucco wall where it shattered. The ceramic shards rained down on the floor, but coffee clung to the wall like a caffeinated Rorschach test.

Diego fled the room, hands raised to protect his head. Helena watched him run, Frank's words fading away with him.

"It's not the same," she repeated.

It seemed like the perfect time to cry, but for Helena the crying days were far behind. Instead, she attached wires to the woman's body, then adjusted the Machine, hooking herself and her patient up.

Truthfully, this was going to be the easiest revival she'd ever done. After all, this woman had only drowned within the last hour and seemed to be in perfectly good health.

This was going to be a piece of cake...

• • • • • • • • ● • • • • • • • • •

When Helena had woken again, it was pitch black outside and the wind wailed with even greater intensity.

The call button was still a tantalizing six inches away from her outstretched arm—and Frank was still nowhere to be seen. Something bigger than a hurricane must have kept him away.

She willed her arm forward again. It went no faster than before, but this time she forced herself to wait a full minute between each inch, counting in her head, *one-one-thousand, two-one-thousand, three-one-thousand...*

The delay was agonizing, but if she lost consciousness again, she might lose several hours instead of several minutes.

When her hand was an inch from the call-button, the door between the main house and the treatment room opened. It was the client, the old man. He looked awful.

"If..." he began. "If there was any way we could have

known… any way to let the girl…"

"Girl?" Helena asked. Except it was more of a gurgle.

The old man—Oliver something. Oliver Rinehart?

Whatever his name, he refused to look her in the eye.

Then it hit her. He was talking about Katie.

Helena's mind jolted awake. She couldn't move, but she wanted to fly.

"Where—" She struggled. "What—"

The old man would come no closer.

"She's dead," he said.

Helena's vision curled. Her world swam and blackness sought to claim her.

No, she willed. *No! I'm. Not. Passing out.*

The old man's assistant entered the room, still clutching that damn video camera.

"Take it easy, Mr. Rinehart," the assistant said. "It's been a rough day for everyone."

Helena stared at the assistant, begging with her eyes. *Please, tell me what's going on. Tell me where my daughter is.*

The assistant sat in the leather chair next to her, the one Frank used.

"There's no good way to say this, Mrs. Moore," he said. "So I may as well say it straight. Your daughter is dead, and your husband is in a coma."

Helena's eyes strained, trying to process what she'd heard.

"Right after you finished with Mr. Rinehart," he said, "your husband came in carrying your daughter. Apparently she slipped between the boat and dock. She was wearing a lifejacket, but she hit her head and went in face first.

"Your husband tried to wake you. Tried for a long time. Eventually he gave up and hooked himself to the Machine.

But… well…"

The assistant shrugged, clearly not wanting to say the words again.

Your daughter is dead.

Helena didn't need to hear the words again. Her mind had converted the whole thing into a movie, a movie she couldn't stop.

It started with Frank walking down to the dock.

Growing increasingly irritated and anxious with each step. Irritated because he doesn't see Katie doing what she's been told; anxious because he dreads the fight that will surely result. These fights, they're wearing him down. He's tired of them.

Then he spots Katie, face first in the water.

At least he thinks he does: the waves are pitching and the sailboat is going up and down, so it's only a glimpse, only a moment.

He breaks into a run. Because deep inside, he knows.

Ten feet away there's no question. Katie, face down in the water. Her orange-red hair fanned out around her head like a pumpkin-colored halo. Her life jacket is keeping her afloat.

Frank grabs the back of the vest and deadlifts her out of the water with a strength born of panic. She's not breathing. He immediately pushes down on her chest to force the water out, performing CPR and breathing for her. He keeps pushing her chest and breathing, pushing and breathing. Because he knows Helena just hit that goddamn button back in the house and can't possibly help. He knows that if he doesn't save their daughter, no one will.

Except Katie won't breathe. No matter how much Frank pushes and breathes for her, all she does is lay there. Lay there with her bangs plastered over her eyes. Like she's hiding behind them. Like she's always hiding...

Helena blinked.

She looked around. The room was empty except for the old man and his assistant.

"Where...?"

It was a struggle to get more than one word out.

"Your husband?"

Helena shook her head 'no'.

"Your daughter is in the house. Mr. Rinehart's nurse is looking after them. Not that there's much she can do."

"Bring... girl," Helena said.

The assistant shook his head. "Mrs. Moore," he said. "I sympathize. Really, I do. But there's—"

"*Bring her!*"

The assistant recoiled but his resistance was brief. "All right."

One minute later he reappeared with Katie in his arms. Her red hair and blue bikini were still soaked and dark, but it was the whiteness of her skin that captured Helena's attention. Skin wasn't supposed to be that white.

Helena wanted to rise up and take Katie into her arms. To stroke her hair. To rub warmth and color back into her skin.

But she couldn't. She was trapped in her Machine-addled body.

She didn't have the strength to weep, nor did she have the luxury. There was work to be done.

Rinehart's assistant lay Katie on the table where the client had been just hours earlier. And for Helena that was the crux of the matter: time was of the essence. The body couldn't have been overly damaged, and it couldn't have been more than twenty-eight hours since they died.

Katie was neither of those. She was young and, until her lungs had filled with water, in perfect health. Under any other circumstance, this would have been the easiest revival Helena had ever done.

Under any other circumstances...

But right now Helena barely had the strength to utter a few words. Trying to revive Katie was more likely to kill Helena than anything else.

"Hook... her up," she said.

The assistant did as he was told. It wasn't complicated. The difficult part took place within Helena's body and mind.

But Helena struggled to even get her fingers into the Machine. She couldn't line them up.

When it became clear she couldn't do it, the assistant came over, and he took her hand. As he inserted her fingers into the Machine, she heard him whisper, "So that life may endure..."

• • • • • • • ● • • • • • • • •

Of course, it didn't.

It hadn't been Katie rising on a Phoenix's wings; it'd been Helena flopping about with Icarus's wings, crashing just as hard. There would be no scent of peaches this time. No fruit-filled happy ending.

Logically, Helena knew she should have been grateful to survive another session with the Machine so soon after the first, and doubly grateful that four days later Frank emerged from his Machine-induced coma. But logic had nothing to do with it. She couldn't get past the fact that Katie *should* have been the easiest revival she'd ever done.

She couldn't let go.

She did, however, learn why most marriages don't survive the death of a child. Two years later, Frank was gone. In the letter he left when he moved out, he said he couldn't stand being around someone who wouldn't, who couldn't, who didn't ever talk about anything besides Katie's death. It hurt too much. Katie was his daughter, too, but he needed to live again, to move on; and he had come to question whether Helena would ever be able to do that. He said she talked about 'doing more,' but it was always more for the dead, when she ought to focus on the living.

He was right, and she couldn't blame him.

Nor could she let Katie go.

Because she knew she could have done better. Could have done *more*. If only she had tried harder…

· · · · · · • • • ● • • • • · · · · ·

Several hours later, Helena awoke to the feeling of a cool washcloth on her forehead. Her eyes remained closed, but she heard a soothing male voice muttering in Spanish.

Diego.

Helena instinctively checked for peaches. Sure enough, the scent was there.

Good, the procedure had worked.

Helena allowed herself to drift off.

She slept for several more hours.

· · · · · · • • • ● • • • • · · · · ·

The next time Helena awoke, Diego was still sitting next to her in Frank's old leather chair. Instead of putting up with the blurred vision that always came after a session with the Machine, she closed her eyes.

"*Hola,*" Diego said. "You are feeling better now?"

Helena wasn't going to get up any time soon, but she felt well enough to speak.

"A little," she replied.

She was much stronger than she'd been three years ago, and this session had been the cake-walk she'd expected, with minimal blood in her mouth and only the faintest hint of fruit in her nose. She was actually surprised at how good she felt, considering she'd just revived someone last week.

"How long until you can help my Amaranta? You say time is *importante, si?*"

Though Helena's eyes were closed, she could envision Diego pointing at his son's decomposing body. Pointing and growing impatient.

Helena would have laughed if it weren't so tragic.

"We're not going to be helping Amaranta. We can't."

"Of course we can," Diego replied. "She is right here in this room."

"Look, Diego, you said it yourself; your son has been dead for three days."

"*Si,*" he answered. "Just so. But I am not talking about *Jesús.* I'm talking about—"

Helena interrupted him. She didn't need excuses; she needed him to accept reality.

"Look, I don't know what you've heard, but after twenty-eight hours the procedure doesn't work. It just doesn't."

Diego paused, confused. "Amaranta is only dead for three hours. You saw her, helping me to row our little boat before flipped."

She? What the devil was he...? "Isn't Amaranta your

son?"

Diego shook his head vigorously. "No, no. My Amaranta. My wife. You said you could save her. Hook her to your machine. She is still dead. Waiting for you."

But that was impossible. The clients always recovered before she did.

"She's not alive?"

Helena turned her head and looked to the table. The body lay there, unmoving. Helena watched for any sign of breathing. There was none.

This was unheard of. *No one* had ever failed to respond to the Machine. Especially not under such ideal conditions.

"Did you check for a pulse?"

"Pulse?"

"Yes. Did you put your hand on her heart, can you feel it beating?"

"*Si*, I did that," Diego replied. "There is nothing."

Helena's eyes narrowed.

How could that be? She'd tasted the blood in her mouth; she'd smelled the peaches. She felt the same way she *always* did after using the Machine. When she'd failed to revive Katie, she felt nothing, nothing at all.

"But I did everything…"

She looked at Diego. Watching him; his face, his melancholy—Helena knew.

"Your wife doesn't want to come back, does she? She wants to stay where she is." Even as the words tripped out of her mouth, they made no sense. Why would anyone *choose* to stay dead? *How* could they choose that?

Diego stood, shrugged his shoulders, and showed his empty hands. "Maybe I think she wants to be with her *niño*. Her *Jesús*." He paused before adding, "Maybe I do, too."

Helena stared at the ceiling. *She wanted to be with her baby?* Of course she did. Helena did, too. But that wasn't an option. That—

A clattering drew Helena's attention. In the kitchen Diego was fumbling with a large knife, the one that Frank had used to cut up fresh pineapple. Diego had dropped the knife on the floor, but he was picking it up again.

There was madness in his eyes.

Three hours ago, Helena had had no concerns about her ability to defend herself. But this was different. Right now she was no match for a five-year old with a pointy crayon, much less an angry man with a carving knife.

Yet even as she studied him, she saw that what she had at first mistaken for anger was actually Diego staring off into infinity, looking for his family. They were out there somewhere, his wife and son, together. But they had left him behind. How could they do that to him? How could they go off like that and expect him to carry on alone?

"No," Helena called.

Diego turned toward her, his turtle-chin bobbing up and down.

"*Si.*"

With the knife in one hand, Diego held his other arm over the stainless-steel sink. The blade rested across his wrist.

"No!" Helena cried again.

She tried reaching out but her arm barely moved.

No.

Helena refused to lay there and let this man kill himself. She rocked her body from side to side, rocked until she built up enough momentum to roll herself off the bed.

Unable to brace for impact, Helena smacked into the floor with a sickening *whump*, landing on her face. Blood ran from her nose and a salty, coppery, dark odor flushed away the fresh peaches.

To her relief, Diego dropped the knife and rushed to her, scooping her from the floor.

"You are *loco*," he said, lifting her back to the recovery bed.

Weakly she said, "I could say the same about you."

"My mother and father were killed by feuding drug gangs when I was nine," he said vacantly. "I lived on the streets, by myself, for twelve years. Until I met my Amaranta. I won't be alone again."

Helena heard Frank's voice. *Are you running away from something,* he asked, *Or toward something?*

"Shut up, Frank," she said. "He doesn't need your crap right now and neither do I."

Diego didn't seem to notice. He was looking right through her. Not far away, the knife waited on the edge of the sink, gleaming under the kitchenette's bright white lights.

Diego's pain was so palpable anyone could have felt it, but with the level of empathy Helena possessed, it was eating her alive. The problem was that she'd spent too many years rerouting her empathy into the Machine. That was how the Machine worked: you poured your empathy into it and used it like a grappling hook to grab hold of death and drag it through yourself and back out.

Problem was, Helena had no idea how to do that with a living person. *Without* the Machine. 'Doing more' had been her mantra for years, but this was a situation she'd never conceived of.

Well...? she heard Frank's voice say in her ear.

It was all he had to say, because as much as she hated the idea, Helena knew Frank was right. She knew precisely what she needed to do in order to reach Diego.

She needed to talk about Katie. About her death, and about how it had made her feel. She needed to open up, because Diego needed to know he wasn't alone. And the only way to do that was to prove to him that someone else...

...that *she*... had also endured the pain he was feeling right now.

But how? She'd clung to her pain for so long it was a part of her. She couldn't just give it away. You didn't just rip something like that off and... throw it away. How much more pain did Frank expect her to endure?

Yet for the first time, Helena saw clearly: it wasn't *her* pain that mattered. This wasn't about her at all.

So she mustered every ounce of physical and mental strength she possessed. She focused every bit of yoga and meditation she'd ever done; brought to bear every bit of training, every hour of weight-lifting, and every stroke of swimming.

And she turned, internally, and aimed her empathy at something besides a machine. She used her empathy as if she herself were something besides a machine.

She reached out and took Diego's hand.

"Listen," Helena said. "I have a story to tell you."

Afterword

This story is the anti-*Tangible Progress*. Unlike that story, whose basic concept I talked to death without ever really writing anything, I have been trying to get "A Hint of Fresh Peaches" right for over a decade. It's *that* story, the one I could never get right but could never let go of either.

The opening is essentially the same as when I first started... but oh, the endings! There was one where the main character ended up in an office in New York City. There was even one where she ended up giving birth to a bunch of alien babies. I tried *so* many different things.

The problem for me is that if I start a story with some kind if ending in mind—*any* kind of ending, really—I'm usually in good shape. I don't always hit the same ending I started out for, but if it's a good enough target, it will get me where I need to go.

When I first started writing my only novel, I read about some famous writer who wrote the last chapter of his or her book first and then wrote *to* that point. That struck me as an intriguing idea, and I decided to give it a try. So I wrote the final chapter as I envisioned it at the time.

Two years later... the ending I ended up with bore nothing in common with that first ending. Nothing whatsoever. The main character wasn't even the same gender. But the exercise had been enough to point me in a direction. To get me started.

I like to make the analogy that if I get in a car, even if all I know is that I'm traveling from New York to California, there are a lot of interesting routes I might take to get there, a lot of interesting detours I might pursue, and several worthwhile final destinations I might arrive at. Los Angeles is very different from San Francisco. But they're both interesting destinations at the end of a potentially fun journey. And for me that's enough.

But if I get into a car in New York and just start driving, I'll meander all over the place, looking at Wisconsin, then Georgia, then Maine, passing through Nebraska twice. How the hell do you know when you've arrived if you have no idea where you're going?

That, for me, was "Peaches." I had sat in a workshop as a fledgling writing and put down the words, "And then she died. Again." No idea where I was heading, just those five words. Typically, that's a recipe for disaster. Or at least an abandoned story. (I've started *many* short stories that way and most die on the vine.)

But "Peaches" was different, and the funny thing is that to this day I can't tell you why.

I can't claim to be in love with the characters, and I can't claim to have had any kind of theme or point I wanted to make. I just had an opening that compelled me, and I had to have an ending to go with it. I had to see this one through.

Whether I did it justice or not I leave to you, the reader, to decide.

BREAKOUT

Brian Byrd was headed, with much relief, to prison again, when he spotted a small patch of nothingness overhead. It was located near the North Star, a void of light where HD172167 should have been. Given that HD172167 — also known as Vega — was the fifth brightest star in the sky, Brian was eager to get to prison so he could get a better look at what was going on.

With the yellow headlights of his dented old jeep reaching into the night, Brian pressed harder on the gas pedal, speeding faster down the deserted stretch of Route 10 between Phoenix and Tucson.

Glancing upward through the windshield again, Brian found his gaze drifting from the splotch of nothingness where Vega should have been to the bright orange orb that was Mars. He couldn't help it; as compelling a mystery as the sudden disappearance of Vega was, Brian was hopelessly in love. There was something about Mars that had always captivated him, and this summer a happy coincidence of orbital mechanics had brought the Earth and Mars closer together than they had been in almost 60,000 years.

Sweet Mars…

Brian pinched his lips and exhaled through his nose. If only the proximity of Mars and Earth could do something to improve the relationship between Mars and Venus. But it didn't — not in the Byrd household, anyway.

Where did I go wrong, Brian wondered for the thousandth time. *How did my wife become my boss? My overseer? My warden?*

It hadn't always been that way. It had been wonderful. Once.

But now…? Now Brian was happy to be going to prison once a week, just so he could get away from her.

Back when things were good, his wife, Zelda, had suggested he quit his job as manager of the local bookstore and go back to school to get the degree in astronomy he had always dreamed of. She worked extra hours to keep them afloat while he studied, and he appreciated her efforts to support him. But somehow, somewhere along the line, her responsibility for the family's finances subtly morphed into her *controlling* the finances, which eventually turned into outright domination of the relationship.

By the time Brian got his degree and discovered how precious little money astronomers made, Zelda had completed the transformation from a supportive friend to a power-mad demon. And although Brian could theoretically have walked out at any time, divorce was not an option. As miserable as he was, in the end he had to admit he was more afraid of being alone.

Brian eased his jeep off the highway, his red turn-signal blink blink blinking surreally in the desert landscape. It made the terrain look like some bizarre darkroom image of the moon.

Brian had been coming to the state penitentiary for eight months now, ever since the dean of Brian's community college had made a deal with the warden to trade college credits for free grunt labor. It was a sweet deal for all involved. The dean got his campus cleaned and repaired for next to nothing; the warden got college-level classes taught on site, which kept the inmates occupied and therefore less likely to cause trouble. And Brian... Brian was guaranteed at least one night a week out of the house. A sort of work-release program from home.

A furlough from his wife.

"Evening, Professor," said the uniformed guard at the front gate. No one ever called Brian by name except the warden. They all seemed to like him fine, but he wasn't sure they even knew his name.

Brian nodded at the guard, watching the gate as it rose. He drove under it, then listened carefully as he headed for an open parking space. The heavy front gate always made a distinct *kthunk* when it closed. Not a loud noise, but one with finality that always gave him chills.

Hoisting his NexStar telescope case out of the back of the jeep, Brian staggered under its weight to the next guard post, this one just inside the door. Here he stopped to sign in. A new, young guard opened the case and began inspecting the telescope, making him quite anxious. Brian let the prisoners and guards look through his telescope, but only under very controlled conditions. He realized how obvious his concern must have been when the older guard, Lou, made the younger one stop.

"Don't mess with the perfessor's gear, kid."

"But we're supposed to—"

"I said don't mess with his stuff." Lou winked at Brian.

Brian's cell phone rang. He answered it, then stood listening. For a very long time. Periodically he nodded. It was the same speech Zelda always made. Home by 10:30; call when he left. Blah blah blah. With his free hand he stroked his pointer finger back and forth across his left eyebrow, feeling the hairs alternate between smooth and bristly, depending on which way he ran his finger. Smooth, bristly. Smooth, bristly.

Behind him, Brian overheard Lou saying to the younger guard, "His wife. Always checks up on him when he gets here. Gives 'im an earful."

On the phone Brian heard the last few words of what his wife was saying and realized he had been momentarily distracted by Lou's comment. And whatever Zelda had just said, it hadn't been the usual speech.

"I'm sorry, Zelda," Brian said. "Could you repeat that last part?"

"Excuse me?"

Zelda's tone was ice. When she was annoyed, she could single-handedly end global warming with her tongue.

"I'm sorry, honey. There was—"

"*Excuse me?*" Zelda repeated.

"I—"

Brian cut himself off.

Just shut up and take it, he thought. It will only get worse if you say anything but 'Yes, Dear.'

Zelda paused a moment, listening for silence. Making sure she had Brian's full attention. Then, in a voice that Brian imagined was what the serpent from the Garden of Eden sounded like, she said, "There will be consequences. Do I make myself clear?"

Brian remembered what happened the last time he had so much as hesitated when she was in a mood like this. Very quickly he said, "Yes, dear."

The phone line went dead.

Brian stared at his cell phone for a moment. Then he closed it, very slowly, trying to counteract his impulse to hurl it against the nearest wall. He wanted to see it shatter into a million glittering pieces, raining electronic shards onto the floor. Instead he stalked off.

"Carry your telescope for you?" Lou offered. He took hold of the telescope case's thick plastic handle.

"Don't touch it," Brian snapped.

He walked on. Lou walked next to him in silence.

"I'm sorry, Lou," Brian said after a minute.

" It's awright, perfesser. Don't you worry 'bout it."

Brian inhaled deeply, slowly. Gathering himself.

"Any chance I can see Warden Tomlinson tonight?" he asked. "I need to ask him—"

"You really don't want to talk to Tomlinson about nothing right now," Lou said. "Not tonight."

"Why's that?"

Lou whistled softly. "You haven't heard about Kit? Damn, I thought everybody knew. I forget sometimes that you're not in here every day like the rest of us."

"Knew what? What are you talking about?"

"I'm talkin' 'bout Kit Martens."

"I know who Kit *is*; he's a student in my class. But what happened to him?"

"His wife and baby girl got killed last week in a car wreck. On the way to talk to his lawyer about why Kit's appeal had been denied. So Kit applied for special leave to attend the funeral and the governor hisself turned him down. It's like it's personal or something. Like the governor's holding some kind of grudge. I never seen nothing like it. The warden got into a big fight with the governor about it this afternoon, so he's still pretty touchy 'bout dern near everything."

Brian breathed deeply. As bad as his own situation was, he couldn't begin to imagine what must be going through Kit's head right now.

Out in the yard the usual suspects had been assembled for their weekly session with the professor. Brian began setting up his NexStar's tripod in the middle of the basketball court. It was the smoothest, firmest surface available to him at the prison—better, really, than even his deck back at home. And it was certainly a more relaxing place to be, at least as far as the company was concerned.

Brian's cell phone rang. He tried to ignore it. Snickering came from the men in bright orange overalls. One voice called out, "That'll be the missus."

Brian stalked off a distance and answered his phone. It was bad enough when the guards gave him grief, but when the inmates did it, too...

"Look," he barked into the phone, surprising even himself with his venom, "You call me one more time tonight and I swear, I'll have them throw me in a cell and lose the key."

Snapping the phone shut, he immediately hoped that it had actually been his wife and not someone else.

Brian rolled his eyes. Yeah, like I have any friends left who might call. His parents were dead and his old friends had all been alienated by his wife's snobbery. Who else would it be??

Brian opened his cell phone long enough to change it from 'ring' to 'vibrate.' He didn't want everyone knowing when she called back again, and she would before long. There was no doubt about that.

Brian went back to setting up his telescope, and as he worked, he began speaking about the one thing that mattered to him anymore. And as he spoke about astronomy, his voice grew softer and calmer, and the men in orange suits drew nearer.

"Within the constellation Ursa Major is a group of stars known as the Big Dipper. Two of the stars within the Dipper can be used to locate Polaris, also known as the North Star. Fourteen thousand years ago, the Earth's axis was aligned slightly differently and another star, Vega, was the North Star. On my way here tonight I noticed that Vega was missing, so tonight we're going to look where it's supposed to be—"

Murmurs of dissent rose, until one inmate said, "We want to look at Mars again."

This comment was followed by a chorus of 'Yeahs,' and Brian stopped what he was doing. "Look, nobody loves Mars more than I do. You all know that. But we looked at Mars last week. And the week before. Now one of the brightest stars in the sky has vanished and you want to look at Mars?"

"Damn straight," said a voice in the middle of the pack. More 'yeahs' followed.

Brian looked at the crowd of men in orange. He thought to himself, *You think I don't recognize your voice back there, Striker? I'm whipped, not stupid...*

"All right, Mr. Striker. I'll make you a deal: you show me where the North Star is, and I'll let you look at anything you want. Just show me the North Star."

Striker came forward from the pack, stopping halfway to where Brian stood. Hands jammed in his pockets, he looked back and forth between Brian and the group, back and forth, until finally, defiantly, he thrust one finger toward the sky and said, "There. It's right there."

Striker was pointing directly at the North Star.

Brian's eyes went as wide as Jupiter and he staggered back a step.

Hadn't expected that, he thought. He wondered what to do next. Unconsciously, one hand drifted to his face and his pointer finger ran over his left eyebrow. Smooth, bristly. Smooth, bristly.

In the background, Brian spotted Kit. Brian couldn't believe Kit was here, considering what he had just learned from Lou. Maybe the man just needs a diversion, Brian thought. Something to take his mind off of what had happened. He's a stronger, braver man than I'll ever be.

That's when he noticed what Kit was doing. Kit held out one hand and pantomimed like he was throwing dice, then very slowly shook his head 'no.'

No? No what?

Then it hit Brian. Kit was saying that Striker had thrown the dice and taken a chance—and gotten lucky. The odds of Striker getting that lucky were, well, there was no other word for it, they were astronomical. But Kit was right: Striker had no idea where the North Star was; he had guessed and gotten lucky.

Brian looked Striker in the eye. "Are you sure?" he asked in as casual a voice as he could muster. "Because I'm feeling charitable. If you want, I'll give you another guess."

Striker turned his hand into a fist and stood ramrod stiff, looking like he might explode at any second. Then he stuffed his fist into his pocket and slunk back to the group. Brian suppressed a smile and the inclination to sigh in relief, then launched back into his lecture.

"The brightest stars in most constellations," he began, "are assigned a letter from the Greek alphabet, Alpha for the brightest, Beta for the next brightest, and so on. But Ursa Major is one of the few exceptions to this rule. The seven brightest stars that make up the Big Dipper are ordered from end to end, starting with the closest one to Polaris. We'll use Polaris to find Vega—or at least the place it used to be."

"Hey, professor." It was Kit. "I've got a question for you."

"Shoot."

"You told us last week that some of these stars are millions of light years away. But if it takes millions of years for their light to reach us, how do we know they're still there? Couldn't Vega have blown up or something and we just don't know it yet?"

Brian was pleased. Most of Brian's students at the community college didn't put this much thought into the subject.

"Excellent questi—"

Lights flickered. On and off. Off and on.

Then a whisper sounded in Brian's ear, so far in his ear that it was almost inside his head —*Who is the one?* —and every light in the McFarland Correctional Institute blinked out.

Back-up generators tried to kick in and the lights flickered again, just for an instant. Then it was dark. Brian knew better than to think the warden had changed his mind about turning off lights for an astronomy lesson. Something was wrong.

Amid shouts from the guards and mutterings from the prisoners, Brian became aware that it was not just dark, it was pitch black. Unnaturally so. And deathly silent. Aside from a few human voices, there was not another sound. Not dogs or birds, planes or cars, crickets. Nothing.

Brian looked up toward the sky, searching for Mars, or the moon—for *any* source of light—but it was like someone had dragged a lid over a pot, and he was inside the pot. A great semi-circle of blackness, an inverted crescent of nothing, had eased its way over the prison, blotting out everything.

Brian knew this wasn't any kind of eclipse; he had memorized the schedule of eclipses for the next three years.

Was it a jailbreak? Brian could sense the prisoners all

around him. But they hadn't made a move—not one of them. They hadn't moved toward the walls, nor had they tried to return to the building. They just stood there. This was no jailbreak.

Then suddenly Brian could *feel* something in the darkness moving, draping itself over him until he was engulfed. It was as if someone had dropped a silk parachute over him and the parachute was now seeping into his skin.

Next came the voices. Inside his mind, small voices, chattering unintelligibly.

As Brian strove to focus on individual voices, he found he was able to identify them. He heard Striker and Kit. Preacher. Gamedog. Little George and Lou and Tommy. Even the warden. A host of voices in the darkness, inside his mind. He heard his own voice, too, repeating over and over, *Dear God, what is going on?*

To Brian's surprise, another voice inside his mind answered, clear and sure. A powerful voice that Brian knew everyone else could hear, too.

"Who is the one?"

The chatter in Brian's head instantly rose to a crescendo. One who? One what? All the small voices of the inmates, wanting to know.

"Enough!" The sure voice cut through their minds, silencing them. *"How you creatures do prattle when you gather in large numbers. It's insufferable."*

A flash of blackness exploded around Brian, a burst of black even darker than the night that surrounded them, and something stood among them. The booming voice softened, no longer so overwhelming.

"We heard a mind that was desperate to escape. It drew us to this place. Never before have we encountered such a will to escape."

"Escape?!" Over and over, that word rippled through the minds and across the lips of the incarcerated men. "Escape!"

"Where are you?"

The chatter of the prisoner's voices around Brian rose to a crescendo. He could feel the bodies of the prisoners pressing forward, moving toward the darkness that surrounded the voice.

"Me!" "Take me." "I'm the one you want."

The voice continued, still soft, but more insistent. *"Do not misunderstand. We seek one of your kind to travel with us throughout the myriad galaxies. We need your unique perspective as a race that has never experienced interplanetary travel. But the one who goes with us will never return. Never see this planet again.*

Who is this one? We know you are here."

And all the small voices fell silent. Bodies stopped their forward press. And the darkness turned cold from fear.

Someone near Brian muttered, "I only got six months left."

Another voice said, "Six months? Hell, I'm outta here in six weeks."

Suddenly Brian became aware of a strange sensation. A feeling, a...

A vibration.

It was the cell phone in his pocket. Zelda.

That's when Brian realized it. Realized the truth. *He* was the one, the one they had come for. The one whose misery had become a tangible thing. The one so desperate to escape that aliens had sensed it from millions of miles away.

He was the one.

Good God, Brian thought, *I'm finally going to escape. To get away from her.*

The mere thought sent an electric thrill racing up Brian's

spine. He pulled the cell phone out of his pocket and let it fall to the ground, taking his first step toward freedom.

Some*thing* brushed against his arm...

• • • • • • • • ● • • • • • • • • •

Mars was fading. You had to know exactly where to look to find it. For months it had dominated the night sky; now it was just another prick of light, adrift among so many others—including Vega, which was plainly visible again next to Polaris.

In the middle of the darkened prison yard, Warden Tomlinson approached a lone figure standing next to a large telescope.

"I'm sorry to have to tell you this," the warden began, "but she's won. They're giving her permission to come in here with a team of investigators."

"But you said that was impossible, that the state would never—"

Warden Tomlinson ran his fingers through his hair. "I know what I said. I was wrong. What can I say? I'm sorry. Her husband disappeared and this is the last place he was seen."

The other man spread his arms, palms to the sky. "As long as I'm here, you've got the right head count. If she finds me, you're going to have some fancy explaining to do. And I don't care how many witnesses you produce, no one will ever believe a UFO took him."

"So what do we do?"

The man at the telescope brought his right hand to his face and ran his pointer finger over his eyebrow. Smooth, bristly. Smooth, bristly.

He said, "There's only one thing to do. 'Kit' has to go

into solitary confinement. When they get here, you'll have to put me in the hole."

The warden shook his head. "You don't want to go down there."

'Kit' looked up at the night sky. No, I don't want to go down, he thought. I want to go up. And for just a minute there, I thought I was. For just a minute I thought they had come for *me*...

He thought wistfully about that, but only for a twinkling of an instant. Every time he allowed his mind to explore that possibility, his feelings immediately turned from longing to embarrassed guilt. How had he ever thought that his situation was the worst imaginable?

But the wistfulness crept back in anyway. For ten seconds on that singular and fateful night last summer he thought he had seen his freedom: it had looked to be as close as Mars and then turned out to be as far away.

Finally, firmly, he said to the warden, "Going in the hole isn't my idea of a good time, but it beats the hell out of letting Zelda get hold of me again..."

Afterword

Oh, goody: another painful confession. Is this a short story collection, a memoir, or the diary a twelve-year-old...?

Let's just let it all hang out, shall we? We've already had life imitating art; this time art imitates life, and my oldest daughter dislikes this story because she immediately saw it for what it was. I didn't recognize it as such until years after I'd written it, but she saw it right away. And it made her uncomfortable.

I was just happy to finally get the ending I wanted. Early drafts of this story had the main character being whisked away by the aliens to a happily-ever-after-among-the-stars. But that struck me as too easy. Too obvious. I prize above all else those endings which make perfect sense, are completely consistent with the information given to the reader, and still manage to stand expectations on their head. And I think this story does a nice job of that. Structurally I'm very happy with it.

However...

On a subconscious level, I was telling a whole other story. A very personal one. And I didn't even know it.

Before I go any further, allow me to offer you this *spoiler alert.* The story I'm about to tell you has a happily-ever-after ending. It took a while to get there, but it did, eventually.

You see, without knowing it, I was writing about myself, my life, my wife, and my own marriage. My unhappiness turned into fiction. Bled all over the page.

How could I not see that, when it was instantly, painfully clear to my teenage daughter? That's a whole other session on the therapist's couch. But I didn't.

However, not long before I wrote this story, I had closed down a reasonably successful business in Virginia and moved to North Carolina because of a job my wife had been offered. I decided it was the perfect opportunity to pursue my dream to be a writer, and my wife ended up stuck in a soul-sucking corner of corporate America as our family's primary breadwinner. Let's just say it wasn't a healthy situation for either of us.

To be fair, she was nothing like the pushy, controlling character in this story; nor was I an innocent. Any relationship that struggles is the responsibility of both parties, and my wife needed things from our relationship that had nothing to do with money. In fact, money was one of the few things we *didn't* argue about. But life did get pretty rocky for several years.

Thankfully, we got through it. It was an act of will, of sheer determination, but we got through it. When we stood before an altar, a priest, and our families, and said 'for better or for worse,' we meant it. We were not giving up.

Hurray for happy endings.

Didn't even need help from any aliens.

That one therapist *was* pretty weird though…

THE LAST HAMMERSONG

Through the window of her elevated seaside shack, Jafartha watched as a deep red moon climbed out of the ocean to join the two copper orbs that had risen several hours earlier. Though she knew there was still time until the three moons aligned, Jafartha was increasingly anxious. Tonight was too important: it was time for the Procession of Queens. It was time for her youngest daughter, Kitja, to become a woman.

Kitja had always been smart, the smartest in their family by far, and in the past year she'd gotten immensely strong working the family's fishing nets. But Kitja was squeamish—and that made her weak. She wouldn't try to catch that damn simka fish; she wouldn't go near a cayalla beetle; and worst of all, she didn't want to cut off her father's upper left arm.

Jafartha could no longer lie patiently in bed, watching and waiting while the Sky Queens decided precisely when and where to converge. She swung her legs over the side of the bed and sat up, propping herself with her lower arms on her knees and her upper arms against the windowsill.

She gazed down below, at the tide surging against the pylons that held her shack high above the ebb and flow of the sea.

A chill breeze blew through the night.

Jafartha closed the window against the cold, but it was no use; the wind blew right through the cracks in the walls of their meager shack sending goosebumps creeping over her hairless body, radiating down both of her two legs and out all four arms.

Jafartha hated being cold.

Her husband sat up in bed and slid behind her, rubbing her back feebly with his underdeveloped lower hands.

She snorted. Men. Their lower arms possessed less strength than a whimpering newborn.

But when he caressed her scalp with his stronger, upper left hand, Jafartha closed her pale-green eyes and sighed with a deep satisfaction. That felt wonderful.

It didn't do anything to change her decision, but it felt wonderful.

Jafartha noticed the warmth of Yonhe's breath in her ear as he whispered, "If you make Kitja amputate my last good arm, I'll never be able to do this again."

Jafartha's eyes closed with disappointment. Did he really think—?

She shook her head.

"No," she said. "We have to look at the big picture. Consider the stature this will bring to our family and the business opportunities it will create."

Yonhe glanced at her, then at his left arm as if it had already been cut off. "Losing… losing the right arm wasn't so bad. But this other one is all I really have. Isn't there some other way?"

Sixteen-year-old Kitja entered the room with a steaming cup filled to the brim with… something. She passed it to her father.

"He's going to look absurd with nothing but those spindly lower arms," Kitja said.

"He's going to look elegant," Jafartha said, caressing the scar at her husband's right shoulder where their elder daughter, Mafirtha had done her work. Then she gestured at the cup in Yonhe's hand. "What is that?"

Kitja replied, "Thyne bark tea. It will make him sleep. Best that he doesn't see what's about to happen."

Jafartha had never heard of such a thing. "Where did you learn this?"

"Grandmother Boonha taught me the basics of making herbal tea, but this particular recipe is my own."

Jafartha saw the kindness in rendering Yonhe unconscious for the amputation; the ritual was a bloody business. Nevertheless, that damned old grandmother had no right meddling with Jafartha's affairs. This was her family, not Boonha's.

Yonhe raised the cup of tea in his hand, drained it in a single swallow, and nodded toward Kitja. Jafartha didn't like the look that passed between father and daughter. It wasn't mere gratitude Yonhe expressed; there was something else, something Jafartha couldn't identify. But before she could say anything, her husband slumped in bed, passing into unconsciousness.

Kitja ritually kissed his cheeks and forehead, then placed one blue feather into one each of his undeveloped lower hands.

Jafartha wished the girl would hurry.

No, what Jafartha wished was that Kitja would be more like her older sister.

On the night of the Procession of Queens four years ago, Mafirtha had proudly taken part in each step of the ceremony as prescribed in the Eighth HammerSong, culminating with the amputation of her father's upper right arm. Mafirtha had not blinked her pale-green eyes, not once, throughout the ritual. Nor had she dawdled with tea or obscure feather rituals that had long since lost all meaning.

But Kitja was different.

Kitja was always holding back—watching and listening to Boonha's stupid stories, studying the intricate carvings on Jafartha's wharkbone knife, collecting herbs from the dunes behind their house—instead of diving in and doing what needed to be done.

Kitja was just like that simka fish that followed Jafartha when she paddled her canoe over to the neighboring island each morning, and then followed her home again each evening. On a world full of islands, this damn fish had to take up residence in *her* lagoon? Jafartha wished the simka fish would either do something or leave her alone. But it merely bobbed on the surface, watching, watching, with its unblinking, golden eyes, studying and questioning everything.

Just like Kitja.

Jafartha looked grimly at her daughter. "Only the finest, wealthiest families can afford to see the ritual all the way through. We are going to show the People—every man, woman, and child on every island within sailing distance—that we are still one of those families."

Kitja shook her bald head and grimaced. "Why do we have to cut off his good arm? Why not something symbolic like the useless little ones? He'll barely be able to feed himself with those puny things."

"As his youngest daughter, you become his good arm. It reinforces the bond that exists between you."

Kitja's lip curled, projecting a perfect blend of disbelief and disdain. "It reinforces the bond? If a bond already exists, why do I have to—"

"—because that's the tradition, and you can't be considered a real woman until you honor the traditions. Poor families can't afford to lose the man's productivity. We are not poor. Now get outside."

But Kitja didn't move. She simply watched with her brilliant, unblinking blue eyes. Studying and questioning everything. Jafartha hated Kitja's blue eyes. Yonhe had been so thrilled when those eyes turned from white to blue in the first month after she was born. Mafirtha's eyes had turned green, the same as Jafartha's. Kitja's eyes, however... they were the exact same shade of blue as Yonhe's damnable mother.

Kitja said, "There was a time when we *were* rich. Rich with wharkbone. But you frittered that away."

Jafartha looked at the lone knife on the trunk by the door. Wharkbone knives were harder and sharper than anything else known to the People, which was appropriate, since wharks were the craftiest, most pitiless monsters in the sea. Hauling one in—in a net, of all things—and walking away from the experience alive, much less with all four arms intact, was rare. Single-handedly killing the beast, eating its meat, and making tools from its bones had made Yonhe's great-grandmother a legend on every island the sun ever shone on. And rich, too.

But things had been hard lately. Jafartha had chased a few high-risk trade deals, instead of pursuing many small ones (as Boonha had advised), and when none of them went her way, Jafartha had been forced to trade away most of the wharkbone tools that Boonha had given as Yonhe's dowry. Jafartha's relationship with her mother-in-law had grown more and more strained with every piece she traded away.

Jafartha picked up her last wharkbone knife and slid it into the sheath hanging from her belt. She knew the moons were moving closer together. "Make me proud. Make your ancestors proud."

But Kitja still refused to move.

Gripped by a fury beyond words, Jafartha seized her daughter between the upper and lower arms and hefted her into the air, snarling, squeezing all four hands in on Kitja's ribcage.

Equally rapidly, Kitja whirled her arms inside her mother's grip and knocked all four hands aside, landing squarely on her feet. She grasped her mother with her upper arms and lifted her off the floor. "My arms are as powerful as yours—if not more. Don't treat me like a child."

Jafartha seethed to see Kitja behaving so disrespectfully, but was simultaneously stunned by the display. Kitja had always been smart and had recently grown strong, too, but where had she learned the moves necessary to turn the tables so quickly?

Kitja set Jafartha down.

Strong and smart were beside the point. Jafartha wouldn't tolerate such insolence.

"Only the heads of the finest families get to be on the ruling council. I won't let your squeamishness spoil this opportunity for me."

Kitja stared at her mother. "Is that what this is about? You're willing to sacrifice father's arm so you can sit on the *council*?"

Jafartha glared back. "Councilor's descendants get a portion of the taxes levied for four generations. Four generations! I'm doing this for you, and for your children, and their children, and for your children's children's children."

Kitja took a half-step forward and stood with her nose almost touching her mother's. "Only if the Councilor doesn't spend a single pound of it, and we both know you don't have that kind of self-discipline. If you did, you'd have made the dozen deals each month that Grandmother advised instead of trying to make it all in one fat deal each year. I won't let *you* sacrifice father's arm to cover up your laziness."

In one smooth motion Jafartha wrapped her hand around the back of Kitja's skull, stepped to her left and pulled her daughter forward, smashing her face into the wall. Kitja fell at her mother's feet like a bird hit with a stone. The girl's nose and forehead bled freely.

Jafartha smiled. "One of us is going to see this ritual through tonight. I don't care who, but I do know you'll be a lot more gentle with your father than I will. Now clean up and meet me outside. If you go out there smelling of fresh blood, a cayalla beetle will have your eyes for a snack."

Jafartha turned her back on her daughter and strode to the trapdoor in the floor of their kitchen. She opened it and slid through, wrapping her sinewy arms around the shack's center pylon and climbing to the boulder-strewn shore. The cold wind continued to blow.

Kitja appeared next to her faster than expected. The girl wore a shirt with long sleeves to protect against the wind, while Jafartha still wore only knee-length pants.

"Merus and Morlos are already in alignment," Jafartha said, trying to ignore the wind. "You must complete the rituals before Tynus joins them. The first sacrifice must be from—"

"—from the sea. I know, Mother. I know."

Jafartha thought: *Yes, I'm sure you do know what the sacrifices are. By now, you had better. The question is, are you prepared to* make *them?*

Ignoring her daughter's disdain, Jafartha asked, "Did you set your lines then? Bait any hooks? Set any traps?"

The girl gazed out toward the empty sea, upper arms crossed over her chest, lower hands clasped behind her back.

"Sort of."

Jafartha looked in the same direction as her daughter but didn't see anything. She had no idea what the girl was looking at or talking about, but she was going to wait, too—wait for her daughter to do something decisive.

Mother and daughter stood side by side, each staring silently, motionless, at the same red ocean. Jafartha breathed deeply, inhaling the spiced scent of the sea. There were no words for her disappointment as Kitja stood there, doing nothing.

Abruptly Kitja strode to her canoe, which had been resting well above the waterline at sundown, staked. Now the canoe pitched in four restless feet of water, an agitated beast eager to escape its bonds.

When Jafartha caught sight of what was in the reed cage bobbing next to the canoe, she broke into a run, splashing through the water.

"Kitja!" she cried out, seizing the cage with her lower set of hands. She transferred the cage to her upper hands and gazed into the golden eyes looking wonderingly back at her. "Kitja," she repeated. "You actually caught one!"

The girl studied the fish, nodding with sad satisfaction. "My theory was right: the best bait to catch a simka fish is no bait at all. Tempting-looking treats make it suspicious; the lack of bait makes it curious."

Jafartha was thrilled; she had wanted to kill this fish for years. "The first sacrifice must be from the sea…"

"Yes. But why a simka fish?" burst Kitja. "Why not a fish we eat every day? I can catch one right now."

Jafartha's face pinched fiercely. "You set the trap. Are you going to dishonor the Queens by refusing what they've offered?"

Jafartha saw horror in her daughter's eyes as the legendary wharkbone blade was slipped from the sheath and handed to her. Sloshing around in the seething surf, waves threatening to steal the knife from her hand, Kitja rocked back and forth with the water. Staring into the reed cage.

She wavered far too long for Jafartha, who smacked the back of Kitja's head, pointed at the cloudless sky, and growled. "*Before* Tynus joins them."

The third, smaller moon was nearing the face of Merus and moving fast.

Inching the tip of the knife closer to the wide-eyed fish, Kitja froze at the edge of the cage. She looked over her shoulder at her mother, but ceased all movement.

Running out of time and patience, Jafartha grabbed her daughter's wrist and thrust the blade between the reed slats, piercing the fish directly between its eyes. Golden ichor trickled down to the water, floating in a glowing mass until the next wave washed it away.

Suddenly Kitja grew animated. As the fish's breathing reduced to short, labored puffs, the girl, with near-surgical precision, removed both of its eyes and threw them as far out into the lagoon as she could.

"What was that?" demanded Jafartha.

"The eyes of a simka fish are the eggs for the next generation. But they must be released before it dies, or else the eggs die, too. Simka fish have few natural enemies and their eyes usually fall out on their own, once the fish gets past a certain age."

A lifetime spent living near the sea and Jafartha never knew that.

About to ask, "Where did you learn this?" she stopped herself. Jafartha knew precisely where Kitja had gotten her information.

Angrily, Jafartha said to her daughter, "Do you think you can make this next sacrifice in a more decisive fashion? A more womanly fashion?"

Kitja took a step closer to her mother. "I'll do whatever's necessary." Her words were delivered quietly, but so hard, so fierce, they gave Jafartha a chill.

What was the girl up to?

Ever more defiantly, Kitja added, "Back in the house, you called me 'squeamish.' I'm not squeamish. I just don't like this. I think Father deserves better."

For a moment Jafartha wasn't sure if her daughter was referring to the ceremony or to Jafartha herself.

Without waiting for a reply, Kitja walked off through the still rising surf and nimbly climbed up one of the shack's outer pylons and onto the flat-topped roof. Jafartha followed.

On the roof Kitja pointed at a second reed cage, identical to the one that had been tethered to the canoe. "I heard you up here after dinner, Mother. Setting this trap. I guess you didn't think I could set one properly."

That was her daughter: always watching, always analyzing.

On a more positive note, though, there was a cayalla larva in the cage. Perfect, Jafartha thought. Air and land — two sacrifices in one. Good fortune; it would save precious time.

Three hand-lengths long and angry, the creamy, wrinkled larva buzzed louder as mother and daughter approached the cage. Lacking the ability of the adult cayalla beetle to spit its toxic, dart-like teeth, the larva was still dangerous. Its teeth had plenty of venom; they were just temporarily stuck in its mouth.

Jafartha walked up to the cage and stuck both left hands

into the trapdoor as casually as if she were grabbing a loaf of bread from the kitchen counter. Gripping the creature behind its blind eyes, she drew it from its cage, saying, "You're not afraid of this little thing, are you?"

Kitja took a step forward. "Of course not."

"Good. You hold it while I get the knife ready for you."

Sidling closer to her mother, however, Kitja seemed unsure of which hand to put where.

"Come on, girl," Jafartha snapped. She reached a free hand and grabbed her daughter's wrist, pulling her closer. She placed one of Kitja's hands, "Here—" she placed the other, "—and here. My mother wasn't half so gentle when she showed me how to hold a cayalla larva."

As if sensing Kitja's agitation, the larva jerked and twisted, biting the air, snapping and writhing.

Kitja extended her arms away from her body, saying, "Don't force me to do this. Please. It doesn't have to be this way."

Jafartha shook her head. "Of course it does. When the Mythographers wrote the twelve HammerSongs, the first eight were about the Procession of Queens. They could have chosen anything to be first. The fact that they chose the Procession should tell you how important this ceremony is."

"But all you ever want to sing are the first eight HammerSongs. Grandmother Boonha says the rest of them are just as—"

"Enough questions, and enough of your grandmother's prattling. The first eight teach us everything we need to know. Everything!"

Kitja threw the larvae emphatically down on the rooftop. It made a *whump* when it hit like someone had beaten a drum with all four hands.

Immediately the larva began wriggling across the flat surface and toward the roof's edge. If it tumbled over the side and fell to the beach below, it would burrow into the wet sand, emerging seconds later as an enormous and deadly cayalla beetle, the only thing that would render losing the sacrifice insignificant by comparison.

Without hesitation, Jafartha threw herself forward, wharkbone knife in hand. She stabbed at the larva even as she crashed down onto the wooden rooftop.

Jafartha's first blow missed and the blade stuck in the roof.

The larva wriggled closer to the edge as Jafartha struggled to free the blade. Yanking, pulling, heaving, finally wrenching it up and out.

One last chance. She raised the blade again...

And pierced the creature's body dead center.

Blood ran down the side of their home.

It would make a permanent stain; there was no washing away cayalla blood.

Jafartha climbed to her feet. "The Mythographers say that it's a bad omen to spill cayalla blood on your house."

Kitja replied, "It's an omen of your own making. I wouldn't have dropped the creature if you had been the least bit patient with me."

Jafartha glanced to the sky, scanning, looking from Tynus to the other two queens, then at her daughter. The final moon had almost arrived at its place in the Procession.

"We'll discuss your cowardice later; right now we have precious little time to finish."

Wordlessly, the two of them climbed back around to the kitchen trapdoor, entering the shack from below. They found Yonhe where they had left him, still deep in the grip of Kitja's herbal tea.

For the final time, Jafartha offered the knife to Kitja. Just as the girl was about to take it, Jafartha snatched her arm back, holding the knife high in the air.

"Are you sure you have what it takes to do this?"

"Depends on what you're talking about."

"Excuse me?"

Kitja began counting off points on her fingers. "Water sacrifice. The blade was in my hand, but who *really* did the deed?"

Jafartha's eyes twitched; something about her daughter's tone was troubling. She said, "Mine."

"And the air and land sacrifice? Whose hand spilled cayalla blood on our house?"

"Mine…"

Kitja nodded slowly. "That's right. *Yours.*"

"Your point?"

"Grandmother Boonha taught me about another tradition—the Succession of Queens. It's the last HammerSong, one of the ones you never want to sing. Grandmother taught me that song—and that there's more than one way to become a woman. You were so eager to cut off father's arm that you never realized I was making you do all the work. The last HammerSong says that if I can get you to perform all of the sacrifices for me, as well as spilling cayalla blood on your own home, then I get to invoke The Succession of Queens."

Quickly extending her strong upper right arm and wrapping her fingers around the knife's handle, Kitja stripped the weapon from her mother with ease, leaving Jafartha too stunned to even put up a fight.

Kitja said with regret, "I *knew* you'd never be able to resist killing that simka fish…"

Realizing the ramifications of what Kitja had done—what she had made Jafartha do—Jafartha's pale-green eyes turned yellow with fear. The Succession.

Kitja was actually going to invoke—

No. No, it couldn't be. No one had invoked the Succession in a hundred generations. It was archaic. Barbaric. It was... pointless.

All Jafartha could think to say was: "Why?"

Kitja raised the wharkbone knife high in the air, replying, "Because right now... Father doesn't need me to be his good new arm... nearly so much as this family needs a new *head*."

Afterword

In light of the last story's afterword, it would not be unreasonable for you to think this one also has personal albeit subconscious overtones. You'd be wrong, but I couldn't fault you for thinking it. However, I'm pleased to say that my kids—my daughters—never got involved in the temporary insanity that touched my marriage, nor did I want them to, even subconsciously. And I can say that with certainty because this is the oldest story in this collection, written years before "Breakout," years before Insanity came to Schubert-town.

My objective with this story was to write about an alien race with an alien way of thinking about things. To contrast our ideas about what constitutes acceptable behavior (as reflected by the daughter character), with something completely different (as reflected by the mother character). This is a theme that has always intrigued me and I've revisited it several times.

"HammerSong" still strikes me, with that perfect clarity known as hindsight, as being a little on the simplistic side in that the mother character is portrayed as clearly being the 'bad' one, and the daughter clearly the 'good' one. If I were to write this over today, I'd try to shade both of them much more on the gray side.

What I did do, however— something I feel good about— is to rewrite this story several years after its initial publication in a way that is completely unrelated to 'good guys' and 'bad guys.' You see, originally "HammerSong" was about a father and son, not a mother and daughter. But somewhere along the line, it occurred to me that I was being too narrow in my focus. I was writing too many stories from the perspective of characters who were, in most ways, just like myself: straight white men. And even in a story that was supposed to be about looking at things from an 'alien' perspective, I was still writing about straight, relatively white, male characters. So I rewrote the whole thing to change father to mother, son to daughter, and patriarchal society to a matriarchal one. Not a huge change, but one that I thought mattered. It's not that I had never written from the point of view of female characters; I had. But I had never stopped and asked myself if a story *needed* to be written from a male point of view, or if it was just my default setting as a male writer.

Now I'll be surprised if some people don't find something (or things) to complain about in my handling of this version of the story. Probably there are several justifiable complaints to be levied. And though I won't claim to have come anywhere near having gotten this 'right,' I do feel good about attempting it, about taking the step. If I never tried, I would never come close, never progress. And as the father of two daughters, I'd like to try. I'd like for them to see me writing female characters. I'd like for them to see me making that effort and know that I care, and hope that over time I'll get it *right enough* to step into some very different ways of seeing the world, as well as helping to make it okay for people to spend a little time looking at it that way themselves.

And our world would be better if that were not an alien idea at all. Our world would be better if it were a downright common one.

A LITTLE TROUBLE DYING

Waiting for the last contaminants of the plague to pass, I had sat in my underground bunker, surrounded by 55-gallon plastic drums of distilled water and mountains of canned vegetables with peeling paper labels. I had scribbled the days and weeks and years onto the wall like a prisoner marking time in solitary.

And that's exactly what I was: a prisoner. Except I hadn't been forced into a cell for crimes against society; I had gone down there alone, voluntarily, to escape death.

If only I had known quite how thoroughly I would accomplish my goal...

You see, until yesterday I had been alone, waiting, lingering, without seeing another living being in exactly two-hundred-fourteen years, eight months, and three days. But I was still here, still young, still healthy. Still *exactly* the same.

I was having a little trouble dying.

Now, I know what you're thinking, and no, I'm not crazy. I may have become a little obsessive about counting things, but you try spending 3,264 days alone in an underground bunker—no matter how well-stocked it might be with books, games, digital music and movies—and another 75,146 days above-ground but still alone, foraging for anything that might help ease the boredom, and see if you don't come out obsessed with *something*.

And I think it's important that you know I never intended

to go into that bunker alone. Despite being told repeatedly what a paranoid fool I was for building the damn thing in the first place, I was a social person. I loved being around people. They say the difference between an introvert and an extrovert is that the former derives their energy from being alone; the latter derives their energy from being with people. I was no introvert.

But when I told my co-workers at the lab that I thought the N7HV3 virus was about to explode across the planet, none of them grasped the urgency of the situation. And when I told my family and friends the same thing, I got the same response. They called me a 'Doomsday Prepper' and told me I should go on one of those reality TV shows.

Reduced from logic to cajoling, then pleading, I finally had no choice but to go into the bunker alone.

Six weeks later they were all pounding on the double-paned, bullet proof window next to the entrance, their eyes bleeding and their flesh flaking from their bodies in great gray chunks.

But by then letting anyone else in, even my sister and her infant daughter, was no longer an option. All that was left to do was talk—and sometimes cry—along with them, through the intercom, until they died on my doorstep.

A lot of people died on my doorstep.

I hated each and every one of them for making me watch them die like that. Hated them with a passion.

That's when I started counting. I counted family and friends as they died a few hermetically-sealed inches away, and I could feel myself age with the passing of each one.

Several centuries later, I'm still in the habit of counting things—but I haven't aged since.

And I only hate them a little...

• • • • • • • • • ● • • • • • • • • •

Despite my scientific background and having little to do but ponder the situation, I had no idea why I stopped aging. At first I thought it might've been related to the N7HV3 virus, or some mutant strain of another virus I worked on in the lab. Both of those theories made as much sense as anything else I could come up with. Unfortunately, I lacked the equipment to test them, and by the time it was safe to come out of the bunker, the lab where I had worked — along with everything else mankind ever created — had been reduced to so much rusted, rotted, moldering junk.

But as with so many other things, after the first century I stopped questioning it. A man can only stew for so long on the same problem without finding answers before he moves on.

Then, yesterday, over two hundred and five years after I determined it was finally safe to live above-ground again, I was standing in front of the entrance to my bunker when Death came to visit me. Actually, he walked right up to me.

He was about six foot two, had blond hair and hot pink eyes, and wore black jeans and a black t-shirt with a pirate's skull and cross bones printed on it. It was overkill in the most absurd sort of way, but there could be no doubt who he was.

I had never been so happy to see anyone in my very long life.

You see, I had thought about killing myself plenty — I had planned it out 407 different times — but I had never had the nerve to do it. Now Death had finally come. He would do his job and I would be *free*.

He sauntered up to me like it was a birthday party. "Jared Matheson?"

"Yes," I said excitedly. I extended my hand to shake his. "Yes, I am."

I had spent years talking to myself for fear I might forget how to speak, but it still felt odd to have someone standing in front of me as words came out of my mouth. Death looked at my hand as if it were covered with cockroaches and immediately stepped back, raising both hands in a gesture that was familiar even after two centuries of solitude.

"What's wrong?"

"No, no," he said quickly, firmly. "No touching."

"Why not?" But even before I had finished asking the question, I knew the answer. "Because if I touch you, I die," I said. "That's how it works, isn't it?"

He nodded once, decisively. "Pretty much. It takes a full second of contact, but if you touch my skin, that's the end."

Suddenly the sun didn't feel quite so warm on my face anymore. What kind of cosmic injustice was this? Death had finally come—and he wouldn't take me?

"But it's time for me to die. It's *past* time."

Death stared softly at me, as if measuring which words he might use. It seemed like he was purposely dragging this out.

"Well..."

"What do you mean 'well'? Do you have any idea how tired I am of living alone?" I lunged at him—

...but before I had completed my first step, Death was gone. Vanished.

I staggered, I fell to the ground. It's not easy lunging at nothing.

Had I finally lost my mind?

But no, he was still nearby; he had merely moved, apparently too quickly for my eye to follow. Now he was perched, squatting, settled atop the raised concrete entrance to my bunker. The afternoon sun was directly behind him, making him look like an ominous, blond-headed crow as he hopped down.

"It's actually painful for me to move this slowly. It's like *choosing* to be the Tin Woodsman after he rusted by the side of the Yellow Brick Road. I'm only doing it for your benefit, so don't try anything like that again. Otherwise I will leave you here, alone."

"No!" My stomach cringed at the thought. "God, please, no."

Death spread his hands. "No more nonsense? No more 'sudden' moves?"

"No," I agreed quickly. "No. I promise."

Death sat down in the tall green grass, his legs crossed in such an unusual way that I'd swear he had just bent his knees in the opposite direction. He said, "Let's chat, you and I. You must have questions, and I haven't spoken with anyone in nearly a century. Let's spend a few moments together."

I grew increasingly convinced he was stalling when he gestured grandly to the Eden-like world around us. "Impressive, no?"

It was an undeniably gorgeous world. Every river ran as clean and clear as an infant's conscience, fish and birds and animals teemed like snowflakes at the North Pole, fruit and berries filled the bushes thicker than people had once filled New York City.

Frankly, I didn't care about any of it. I might have once, but that was so long ago I couldn't even remember any more. Now I only cared about one thing.

"Why won't you take me?"

I was still on my feet, standing before him, looking at him longingly. And all the while, I kept thinking that there was no way, absolutely no way, he could avoid me if I threw myself at him.

Problem was, I was terrified to try.

In all the years gone by, I had never been able to come up with a means of killing myself that didn't look like it would hurt like hell—or worse yet, leave me suffering if I failed. My greatest fear was that I was somehow immortal and would live on in agony if I cut my throat or threw myself off a cliff. And believe you me, I'd stood at the top of sixteen different cliffs since that first one 73,186 days ago.

But Death could end this. One touch and it would be over. It was his job. His duty.

I ran my fingers through my hair, despairing. If I tried to touch him and missed, if he left me here alone again...

I couldn't stand it if that happened. It would break me. Utterly.

"Why?" I repeated. "Why won't you just do it?"

Death grinned cheerfully. I may as well have asked a child why he wouldn't clean his room. Don't feel like it, Ma.

Asshole.

I lay down, flat on my back in the grass, watching the sky drift by. I didn't feel calm. I didn't feel relaxed. I just knew that if I didn't get off my feet I would do something stupid.

"Isn't there anything else you want to know?" he asked. "Like why you're still alive after all these years?"

I had been focusing on a high, thin, wispy cloud lazing across a lagoon-blue sky, but that question froze me. For too many decades, that had been *the* consuming question. The one I had given up on.

I propped myself up on my elbows, realizing even as I did it that I was nodding my head, and that I couldn't seem to stop.

Death approved. He shrugged and spoke so matter-of-factly that you'd have thought I had just asked him why the ocean was wet. He said, "I couldn't find you."

I blinked, twice, thrice, lingering with the idea for a

moment to be sure I had heard him correctly. I couldn't have. It was ridiculously insane. Insanely ridiculous. I think my mouth tried to spit out the word "What?" but I was so flabbergasted I'm not sure anything actually made it all the way past my lips.

I gathered myself, convinced myself that yes, I had really just heard what I thought I heard, and said, "What do you mean you couldn't *find* me? How could you not find me?"

Thoroughly irritated, I started to climb to my feet. But Death made little fluttering motions with his hands. I'm not sure if he was saying I should sit back down or if he was threatening to fly away, but the result was the same: I stayed where I was.

"What do you mean you couldn't find me?" I repeated. "That's the stupidest thing I've ever heard."

Death laughed. It was a deep, rich, resonant, horrifying sound. The sound of a gigantic wave rising from the depths of the ocean and rushing over beaches and towns and fields, crushing, crashing, and shattering everything in its path.

"I couldn't find you," he repeated. "It's pretty simple. I'm naturally drawn to the terminally ill, injured, and old, and you managed to avoid all three."

This was making less sense all the time.

"Okay, that's—" I cut myself off. At this point I had no idea what question I should even be asking. "How...?"

"How does someone avoid aging?" he said for me.

I nodded.

Death was amused, but mercifully he did not laugh again. He said, "Ironically, by being one of the last people on Earth. Back when the planet was swarming with people, the ones that were, if you'll pardon the pun, *deathly* sick or injured, called out to me. I answered them. And on my way,

I brushed past the living—and they aged. Only slightly, but age they did.

"The problem was, when I got down to the last handful of humans, you started getting hard to find. Damned hard. I wasn't brushing past people on my way to claim other lives, so people weren't aging. And the world has become such a *healthy* paradise—" He said the word "healthy" as if it had been marinated in vinegar before it passed through his mouth "—that unless someone became mortally wounded or—as a few lonely souls did—intentionally killed themselves, I simply couldn't find them.

"And to be honest, I've stopped trying quite so hard in this last century. Maybe I'm just bored, but there's certainly no need for all that rush, rush, rush. Not when there are only four people left on the entire planet." He paused, pulled a small notebook and pencil out of his back pocket, flipped the notebook open and thumbed to a particular page. He made a little check mark. Then he looked back at me, suddenly all business. "Well, it was five. It'll be four—in a moment."

He slipped the notebook back into his pocket.

"Wait a minute," I said. "There are others? Besides me?"

"Oh yes," he said, climbing to his feet. The grass where he had been sitting was dead. He took another step toward me and another patch of green grass withered and turned scorched brown.

I backed up. "After all this time, *now* you tell me there are still people out there? That I'm not alone. That's not fair. You have to let me find them. See them."

"But you said you wanted to die." His demeanor was markedly different. Hard.

"No! I said I was tired of being alone." I jerked my head around, panicked, desperate to find some avenue of escape.

"That's better," he said softly. He began circling me, gliding, muscles rippling. "It's no fun when they *want* to die..." Louder, he added, "Those people have been out there all along. One man and three women. One of them is even on this continent. You just didn't look hard enough."

His inward spiral was bringing him closer and closer to me. I pivoted as I retreated, trying to keep him in front of me. "It took you over two hundred years to find me... and I didn't look hard enough?"

But with each word I uttered, he drew closer still. One second, he had said. All it took was one full second of contact.

"I got bored," he said. "I could have found you sooner, but I've learned to savor the moment, to relish the hunt. There are so few of you left."

I had been about to make a break for it, to try to run. But I knew it wouldn't do any good. On the other hand, when a man is about to be pounced on by a lion, doesn't he at least *try* to get away?

That was the answer.

I immediately stopped backpedaling.

He stopped pursuing.

"What are *you* doing?" he demanded. His eyes turned a deep shade of red, cherry red, if cherries grew in Hell.

"What are you doing?" I said. I jabbed a finger in his direction; he flinched away from it. "You say you're bored. You say you've learned to savor the hunt—" I moved toward him. He retreated two steps backward for every one I took forward. "—yet you're on the verge of killing me, killing off one of the last of the humans. If you think you're bored now, what are you going to do when we're all gone?"

Death stopped retreating. He crossed his arms, folding them over the skull and cross bones on his t-shirt. His pupils dilated until they completely disappeared.

I had his attention.

"What do you have in mind?" he asked.

That stopped me cold. What *did* I have in mind? My mind had been racing, trying to find a way to get him to wait, to think, but I never thought he'd actually listen. Now that I had his attention, what did I do with it?

"I don't know," I said.

I counted the nine dead-grass footprints he had left as he backed up. Then I assessed the wide swath of green that surrounded us.

I said, "You could give me time. If I can find the others and bring them together, it's inevitable that babies will be born. Then you'll have more people to kill. More work to do." It sounded reasonable to me.

But not to Death. "No," he said, and his eyes flushed pink again. "I don't think so. I'm enjoying these hunts precisely because they'll be my last. After all this time, I'll finally be done. You think it's tough being alive for a few hundred years, try living a few hundred thousand."

I might have felt sorry for him if he weren't here to kill me.

"You don't want to kill us off," I said. "It would be the biggest mistake you ever made."

Death looked at me like I was insane—but he was listening.

"I don't know if you ever were human," I said. "Maybe it's just that you've lived among us for so long, I don't know. But look at yourself. Look at all the human traits you're exhibiting. First you didn't want to take me when I wanted to die. No, you wanted to do it on your own terms. That's incredibly human. Then you said you were bored. In fact, you've said it twice now. Trust me, I counted. Boredom is a quintessentially human emotion.

"Well, let me tell you something—something I just figured out about myself. Seeing how excited I got when I learned there were still people out there? It made me realize I wasn't miserable simply because I was lonely. Yeah, I was lonely; I won't deny that. But I was miserable because I had no *purpose*. Without purpose, people are nothing. And without a sense of purpose—without humans to hunt—you'll be more miserable than I ever was."

As I spoke, Death's eye-color swirled like a Halloween hurricane before they finally settled on black.

It was the first time I had been glad to see them that color. They were still unnerving, but at least they weren't in flux.

"I can't sit around and wait another century for you to find these people," he said. "Patience is one thing, but asking me to sit around is another thing all together. And I honestly don't know where the others are." He paused, then narrowed his eyes and added, "So why don't we just get this over with?"

Before I knew it, Death was inches from my face, his fist clutching a handful of my shirt. I leaned back as far as the shirt's fabric would allow—which gained me maybe three inches.

"Wait," I gasped, eyes wide. "Don't you understand? That's exactly why this is going to work."

He didn't let go, but his demeanor shifted oh-so-slightly.

"Why *what's* going to work?"

"You don't know where the other people are. I don't know where the other people are. So we'll have a race. Or a treasure hunt. Call it whatever you like. We'll both go looking for the last people. Anybody you find first is yours. But anybody I find first, you can't touch for three generations."

"During which time you'll breed like bunnies."

I nodded. "I'm assuming that growing up is not the same thing as growing old, so you won't need to brush past the children in order for them to develop."

He nodded.

"And none of that 'faster-than-a-speeding-bullet' stuff," I added. "You move at my speed — regular human."

I could tell by the look on his face that he was considering it.

"And every five years we'll meet back up," I said, trying to sweeten the pot. "We'll compare notes, see how it's going."

"Make it ten years," he said. "Right here. I have fond memories of this little bunker of yours. Collected a lot of people here on your doorstep."

He extended his hand to shake on the deal and laughed heartily when I almost fell for it. His laugh didn't sound any less horrible than it did the first time around.

When he walked off, he was still laughing. It was clear that this wasn't going to be a friendly competition; it was going to be the strangest deathmatch ever.

But he had gone for it. That was all that mattered.

· · · · · · · ● · · · · · · · · ·

Or at least I think he went for it. As he walked away, I couldn't help but wonder if I had talked him into this race, or if he had tricked me into thinking it was my idea. It's possible he knew all along that he needed something to do, something to keep life interesting. Whether that something lasts for the next few years, the next few hundred, or more, I can't say. And it wouldn't surprise me at all to learn that he's set all five of us in motion at the same time, just to double the fun.

Whatever it is he's up to, I don't care. There are others

out there. Four of them. And I'm going to find them. Before he does.

This time I'm not going to escape Death; I'm going to beat him.

Considering the way things had turned out last time, I wonder how thoroughly I might be able to meet *that* goal...

Afterword

That same daughter who struggles with "Breakout"? I'm happy to report that she loves "A Little Trouble Dying." And to be completely honest, I have no idea why, and I'm afraid to ask.

You see, sometimes understanding a thing makes it more difficult to appreciate. The more I studied writing, the harder it became for me to appreciate novels because I couldn't help but break them down and try to analyze them. Why does this section work? What about this character works and what doesn't? I know enough about the craft of writing to answer those questions (*usually*—for instance, I think I can explain the appeal of *The DaVinci Code*, but have absolutely no idea why millions of people actually paid money for *50 Shades of Grey*).

All that analysis makes it difficult for me to get lost in a story, though. I've said to several people over the years that I will never ever ever study music because I don't want to spoil the magic. I enjoy that magic too much.

So with "A Little Trouble Dying" I happily settle into the blissful zen of ignorance.

Why does my daughter love it?

Who cares. She does, and that makes me smile.

FOR THE BIBLE TELLS ME SO
or
ANGELS, RAPISTS, AND OTHER DRUNKEN HEROES

"Where did you find him?" asked a gravelly-voiced blond man in a lab coat as they wheeled me into the generation-ship *Voyager's* primitive-looking med center.

"Area 451," replied one of the three jumpsuit-clad men who'd been standing over me when I first regained consciousness. All three wore identical orange-sleeved and brown-bodied jumpsuits.

"451? I thought that space had been cleared out years ago."

"So did everyone else, brother. Guess they were gonged off," said jumpsuit guy number two, an albino. "We were scavenging spare parts. Found this guy in a cryo-pod shoved into one corner. He was surrounded by a few dozen non-functioning pods, but his was hardwired right into the bulkhead. Must have happened right after The Wrecking. Don't know how they did it without losing him, but there he was. It's some kind of miracle, praise God."

"Save the 'miracle' talk for someone who buys that bullshit," the lab coat blond said sharply.

The third guy in a jumpsuit turned out to be a woman. Her feminine voice contrasted starkly with her short black hair, her grime-covered face, and her unnaturally, almost inhumanly prominent chin and lower lip.

"Think I could get on the litht to breed with him, doc?" she said, her high-pitched lisp cutting through the fuzz wrapped around my brain. If I wasn't completely awake before she started, I was by time she finished. Her words—their meaning—ignited a flame of panic to go along with the nausea that swept through my body. Have sex with a woman? If there had been any food left in my stomach, it would have been strewn across the floor like a bowl of frog leg soup.

"I'll have to check the computer's gene-pool program," the doctor answered. "Maybe in a year. Consider yourself lucky you found a guy. If you'd found a woman, the boys would probably never've had a chance to spread their genetic material around."

"A year?" the woman cried, wiping her brow with a faded orange sleeve. "Come on, doc, can't you work me in any thooner? I'm the one who notithed hith cryo-pod wath thtill working, you know."

"No promises," the doc said. "I'll see what I can do." He transferred an IV bag from a metal rod overhanging my gurney to a higher one protruding from the wall. Then he shooed the three jumpsuits out the door.

"Scoot," he said, even as they tried to hover and gawk. "I've got tests to run. It's going to be a while before anyone gets to bed him down."

My mind reeled, trying to process what was going on around me. This gen-ship was a mess. The people were a mess. But worst of all, the things they were talking about were appalling. I was a decent, God-fearing man, yet the first thing they wanted to do after waking me was figure out how many women I could have sex with and who got to have me first.

I tried to think of a way to voice my indignation—not that anyone had asked my opinion, or that I'd even tried speaking yet—when the doctor jabbed a hypodermic into my thigh. "I know this is going to sound counterintuitive," he said. "But you need to go back to sleep. Those three were well-intentioned, but they didn't follow protocol when they pulled you out of that pod. If we don't wake you correctly, it's going to screw up your metabolism. We'll talk again in a few hours."

Before I could say a word, my eyelids became unbearably heavy. I think I was unconsciousness before they even finished closing...

• • • • • • • • ● • • • • • • • • •

When I woke again, I found myself surrounded by three new people and the doctor again. This batch was better dressed than the last, but seemed no less intent on hovering and gawking. Apparently I was quite the novelty.

One of them, an albino woman, stepped forward and began speaking. I'd never before seen an albino in person; now I'd seen two in the same day.

"Mr. Fallgood," she said. "I'm sure you—" She shot her unnaturally pale blue eyes down to the tablet in her hands, the standard five-by-seven sheet of clear, hard glastic. It struck me as somewhat odd that in the 250-year transit from Earth to Kepler 186f, the technology hadn't changed, but before I could ask about it, the albino woman started over. "You are Jeremy Fallgood, yes? That's what it says on the crystal the techs pulled from your cryo-pod, but given the unusual location where you were found, maybe we shouldn't make assumptions. Are you Mr. Jeremy Fallgood, born October 10, 2669, in New Detroit, Ontario, Canada?"

I nodded, still unsure of my voice. Hearing this woman

refer to me as Jeremy made me think of my husband, Michael. I coughed a little, then squeaked, "Please, call me Jerry." The effort of speaking scratched my throat.

"Excellent," she said. "I'd hate to start with bad information. As I was about to say, I'm sure you have a lot of questions. We do, too."

It made no sense. After not using my voice for God knows how long, why would such a tiny effort be painful? Regardless, I wasn't about to test it again. I nodded.

The albino woman smiled. "I'm sorry. I forgot how uncomfortable speaking can be after hibernation. Your body didn't produce any saliva during that time, but I promise, it will come. It's been such a long time since anyone found a survivor of The Wrecking that I'd all but forgotten some of the problems you have."

Found a survivor? The Wrecking? Clearly things were bad, but what kind of disaster had I woken to?

The concern on my face must have been evident because she handed me her tablet, saying, "Use this to write your questions. But first give me a moment to explain what's going on."

I punched PLEASE DO into the image of a keyboard that materialized when I thought about typing. The tablet responded to commands as they passed through my mind, just as always. The tech was identical. I don't know why, but that troubled me.

A second woman, broad-faced with a hint of Asian in her ancestry, stepped up next to the albino, inserting herself into the conversation. "My name is Mary Ellen Trumbul," she said impatiently. "My pale colleague here is Tina Gareth, and the two gentlemen over there are Roy Markham and Dr. Chip Jones. Collectively, we are the greeting committee for what is left of the crew of *Voyager*. In a nutshell, what was supposed to be a 250-year, multi-generation journey to a planet known as Kepler 186f has become a voyage of the damned, with no real end in sight, and not much hope of survival. Welcome to our party."

I looked at the tablet in my hands, wanting to ask so many questions. The display swirled randomly, mirroring the chaos of my thoughts. If this device sought something in my mind to work with, it would have to wait in line; I had no idea where to begin. Fortunately, the doc stepped in.

"Nothing quite like foreplay, is there?" he said, smiling. "Please forgive Mary Ellen's bluntness. Still, she has a point: there's no way to say it and have it sound good, so we may as well say it straight. Maybe they solved their problems back on Earth, maybe they didn't. We don't know because we lost contact with them a long time ago. *Voyager* was always intended to be a one-way ticket someplace else—Earth's insurance policy when it became obvious the planet was unable to support human life for much longer. Overpopulation, food shortages, water shortages, air and soil toxicity levels off the charts. We had to get a bunch of people off-planet, quickly. I suspect that's why you entered the lottery in the first place.

"What you probably don't know is this: On its way out of the solar system the *Voyager* was scheduled to stop in the Oort Cloud to collect ice for water and methane. We're not sure exactly what happened because the damage was so extensive, but it looks like multiple collisions occurred in the Cloud with some pretty massive ice comets. From there it was a deep-space reenactment of the *Titanic* that we called The Wrecking. Power failed throughout much of the ship. Few in hibernation survived. Going back to Earth was never an option, so we've limped along ever since, making do with what we have.

Things have gotten tight in every way imaginable over the last 800 years, including genetically."

I could barely contain my astonishment. *800 YEARS?????*

Doc nodded.

"That's where you come in," said the albino woman, Tina. She clasped her hands as if she were about to pray. I felt a little embarrassed that I hadn't thought to do so myself.

"Your contribution to *Voyager's* genetic diversity is vital to our survival," she said. "Your DNA is new and different, and we need you to spread it as widely and as quickly as possible. So for you, it literally will be a party."

"More like an orgy," said Roy Markham with feigned disapproval and a cheesy grin. He was an older gentleman with smoke-gray hair that contrasted attractively with his hot-cocoa skin. "Scientifically speaking, we could do it through artificial insemination, but long ago we realized there were a lot more benefits to personal interaction, and now it's ingrained in our culture. Who sleeps with whom has a lot of status associated with it."

"You're just jealous because he's going to sleep with *everybody* and be king of the ship," Doc Jones chided. He turned back to me and said with surprising earnestness, "Jokes aside, we really do need your help. The ship's overall F-values are routinely above .12, sometimes spiking as high as .17, and we're seeing more and more cases of hemophilia, deformities, and still-births. Your genes are going to help us forestall a genetic mutational meltdown."

I shook my head vigorously, not liking the direction this conversation was heading. I stabbed one finger at a time onto the onscreen keys: NOT THAT WAY.

I held the tablet up for all to see. Then I turned it back to me and typed one more word.

CHRISTIAN!

Doc Jones rolled his eyes and turned on his heel. The other three joined him in a conversation so animated it was impossible to follow. Raised voices spoke over each other and hands exploded repeatedly into the air like five-fingered fireworks. I caught words and phrases like 'One of those elated people…' and '…that idea was gonged off almost a thousand years ago…' One of the women said something like "Make him do it anyway…', but besides that last comment, none of it made any sense; I had no context.

While they talked, I typed on the tablet.

CAN'T YOU DO IT WITH CLONING, THE WAY GOD INTENDED?

I held the tablet aloft, but they were so engrossed in their conversation they didn't notice me. I banged my hand against the metal bars of the gurney. It hurt, but it got their attention.

Roy noticed first. He walked over, shaking his head as he read what I'd typed.

"You're one of those 'elateds', aren't you? Part of that cult that bought into the government's bizarre reinterpretation of scripture when Earth's population got out of control."

Cult? I wasn't in any cult. Where I came from, the fanatics who demanded the right to have intergender sex were the cult—a small but noisy minority who insisted they had the right to breed outside of society's accepted limits, regardless of the consequences. And I had no idea what he meant by 'elated.' That word must not have meant what it once did, because elated was the last word I'd use to describe my mood right now.

I started typing again, frustrated with the futility of conversing this way. I prayed for strength, even as I searched for my voice.

Surprisingly, my throat suddenly stopped hurting. It was as if God had said, *Speak, my child.*

For the first time since being reawakened, I felt His loving hand on me.

"The government had nothing to do with it," I said, feeling invigorated. "The priests finally understood what certain passages of scripture meant. John 13:34-35 says: 'A new commandment I give to you, that you love one another, even as I have loved you. By this all men will know that you are My disciples, if you have love for one another.'

"Jesus traveled with men; he spread his gospel with men. We're meant to be together, just like women are meant to be together." I felt foolish explaining something so obvious to them, but they seemed to have lost the truth. "Cloning made it feasible. We could finally procreate without intergender sex, enabling us to embrace Jesus' commandments. It's mankind's ultimate destiny, the perfect hybrid of science and religion."

The doctor stalked over, fiercely gripping the bars of my gurney. I don't know where the friendly doctor went, but he had vanished, replaced by an angry Mr. Hyde on the verge of losing control. Exasperation dripped from every gravel-covered word.

"It was the government's way of manipulating the world's population, you moron. During Old Testament-times they used the Bible to tell people not to eat pork and shellfish because pork and shellfish carried germs that made them sick. God had nothing to do with it; it was the best way to influence people. This 'Biblical cloning' business was the same thing. By finding choice verses of scripture they could twist to their purposes, they could control population growth and—"

His sacrilege offended me. What's worse, he was wrong.

"There aren't just one or two verses," I said. "The Bible is rife with scripture telling us how we are meant to live and to love." I grew increasingly animated. I couldn't help it; if you challenge my faith, you challenge who I am. "Romans 12:9-10. 'Let love be without hypocrisy. Abhor what is evil; cling to what is good. Be devoted to one another in brotherly love; give preference to one another in honor...' Don't you see? Preference to brotherly love. I could quote countless verses. I won't abandon my principles!"

Romans 12:9-10 was my husband, Michael's, favorite verse. *...cling to what is good. Be devoted to one another in brotherly love...* It was like he'd been preparing me for this moment from the very beginning. Michael stood with God now, one of His angels, and together they would guide me.

"Oh yes," the doctor barked. "Please, quote as much scripture as possible. That never fails to fix things. In fact, have you got any verses about stupidity? Because we could use some help in that department, too. The government used scripture because this wasn't something they could legislate. It had to go deeper than that. Well, apparently it went so deep in you that it skipped right past your *brain*."

"What the doctor means to say is that we don't have the ability to do cloning anymore," Roy said, taking the doctor by the arm and creating a safe space between us. "Any technology that would have allowed us to manipulate human genes has long since been lost. Good old-fashioned sex is all that remains. Men and women did that in the Bible, too, didn't they? I seem to recall a few verses that mention it."

Dr. Jones gestured to me, though I'm not sure who he intended his comments for. "Of all the people to survive," he barked, "we had to end up with a damned elated Bible-thumper."

The sort-of-Asian woman—Mary Helen, I think her

name was — brought some sanity back to the med center.

"I think we need to take a break," she said. "We're not going to solve anything with tensions running this high. Doctor Jones, go write yourself a prescription for a chill pill. Mr. Fallgood, you need to think about what we've told you. With all due respect to your religious principles and your interpretation of scripture, we need your help. Plain and simple: this may be the end of the human race we're talking about."

• • • • • • • • ● • • • • • • • • •

I dreamt of Earth, hanging in space. The orb, the marble, the planet that gave us life. In my dream we were in the process of leaving it; far out, far away, but not so far that I couldn't still see the distinctive white whirl of clouds draped over the planet's surface.

Except this wasn't possible. I'd been placed in cryo before *Voyager* lifted off. I should have no memories of leaving Earth. No memories of —

Something slammed into the ship. It shook, and shook again, and I looked up and to the left, saw an iceberg — a literal iceberg — at the edge of my view. It loomed, pointy and slim at the top, rounded and immense at the bottom, floating against a background of star-freckled space. The ship rumbled again from another impact and now there were dozens of icebergs, more than I could count, filling my field of view.

There came another impact, another rumble, another —

My eyes sprang open; my heart pounded inside my ribcage.

Above me a dark silhouette in human form.

"Michael?" I asked hopefully.

"Wake up, Mr. Fallgood," the silhouette said.

My head cleared. No, not Michael…

I recognized the med-center even as the memory of the dream melted away to be replaced with the reality of someone shaking me, waking me.

"Mr. Fallgood," the silhouette repeated. "You need to rise, brother. You need to follow me. Quickly."

Random specks of light emanated from medical apparatuses; otherwise it was dark.

"Why?" I said. "What's going on?"

I wasn't going anywhere with someone I didn't know, and this was clearly no official visit.

"I want to introduce you to some people, folks I think you'll like more than that science-worshipping doctor. He hated you from the moment he found out what you believed. I want you to meet some folks who'll treat you better."

"There are Christians on this ship?"

"We have to hide in order to worship. They won't let us do it openly."

That was always the church's finest hour: when it met and worshipped and grew in secret, persecuted yet persevering. From 2nd century Rome to 20th century China, the church always thrived when it was oppressed.

"Take me to them," I said.

My mysterious benefactor lowered the rail on one side of the gurney and I sat up, swinging my legs over the edge. I scooted my rear forward, placed my feet on the floor, and promptly collapsed in an ignominious heap.

"You're still weak from cryo," the silhouette said, bending to help me. It was then, with his face close, that I recognized him. The albino in the orange-sleeved jumpsuit, part of the crew who found me.

"The electronic stimulations they run through you when you're in hibernation are barely enough to prevent total muscular atrophy. It'll be a while yet before you're walking on your own."

He knelt beside me, pulling my arm around his neck and standing us both upright. "You think you can walk if you lean on me?" he asked.

I wondered for a moment why The Lord hadn't provided me with the strength to walk like He'd earlier given me the ability to speak. Then I realized He didn't need to; He'd provided me with the albino.

Treasure *all* the gifts He gives you. That's what Michael always said.

"Happily," I replied.

• • • • • • • • ● • • • • • • • • •

The church group met in a large, half-lit room, which seemed appropriate, considering the oppression and abuse that my albino friend told me about. I had assumed ill-treatment based on the doctor's reaction when he heard me claim my Christianity, but the tales albino Oliver told were heartrending: Christians treated as slaves, forced to do the most menial tasks while others lived in relative comfort; told when and who to breed with, and severely punished if they did otherwise.

I was trying my best to think about *anything* besides that last detail when Oliver had led me into a room full of men and women with smudge-covered faces, all wearing the same style jumpsuit: brown body and legs, faded orange sleeves, everything frayed and worn.

The entire room reeked to the point of being

overwhelming, a vivid contrast to the sterile med-center. Oliver helped me take a seat in a plastic folding chair facing the rest of the room, while everyone else faced me in rows, some in plastic chairs, everyone else cross-legged on the floor.

"Brothers and sisters in Christ," began Oliver. "Let us bow our heads together in prayer.

"Heavenly Father, we gather tonight in Your Son's holy name to thank You for the miracle of Jeremy Fallgood; for allowing him to survive The Wrecking so that he could bring everyone on the *Voyager* the truth of your Word, so that we may stand up to the Brahis and Satis above us, and aid the Chucks beneath us."

"Amen!" rang every voice in the room.

It was encouraging to see so many Christians united in prayer. Oliver had mentioned this was one congregation among several, but that they couldn't meet in larger groups for fear of being shut down. Yet right now everyone in the room exuded a palpable excitement. I looked around at a shadowy pool of smiling faces, about thirty of them, packed tightly. I even spotted a familiar face: the short-haired, long-chinned, lisping woman who'd found me. She smiled and nodded when she saw I'd recognized her—an awkward smile given the extreme pronouncement of her chin and lower lip.

She and my albino friend weren't the only ones in the room with physical abnormalities. Truth be told, the 'normal' looking ones were the exception.

Oliver made settling gestures with his hands. "Okay, I know you're eager to hear from the walking miracle himself, so let's get to it. Tonight I am pleased to introduce to you the man who survived 800 years of cryo-sleep under the most miraculous circumstances. The man who told those Brahis that he was a Christian and wasn't going to play their games.

The man who told that Sati doctor what he could do with his computerized gene-pool program. I give you... Jeremy Fallgood!"

The room burst into applause and shouts of 'Halleluiah.'

I, however, was at a complete loss. Oliver hadn't said anything about me speaking. He said he would introduce me to some folks, that's all. I was no public speaker. That was...

that...

That was Michael's forte.

No.

No, damn it. I rejected that. It had only been one day, but I was tired of feeling sorry for myself. Done with it. Michael was gone and I had to learn to live with it.

"Um... Thank you... Oliver. For that introduction." I leaned forward in my chair, determined to do this well. "And thanks to all of you... brothers and sisters. You're too kind." I paused, nodding to the crowd, still trying to think what to say. "I don't mind sharing my faith with you. In fact, I'm happy to, though I don't know how much encouragement I can offer."

Cries of 'No,' and 'Testify, brother,' arose. I tamped it down.

"Seriously. There's so much I don't understand. I didn't understand half of what Oliver said when he introduced me. Why are you oppressed? Who or what are Brahis and Satis? For that matter, how did I end up here? Does Dr. Jones have any idea where..."

A chorus of boos sprang up at the mention of the doctor's name. Clearly not a popular figure.

"The Brahith and Thatith are—" began the long-chinned woman. She cut herself short, then tried again, "You have to imagine thingth here ath a thort of cathte thythtem, like a—"

"I'm sorry," I said. "Can you...?" I felt guilty interrupting, but I literally couldn't understand her. "Imagine what like a *what*?"

A younger woman with short-cropped blonde hair—I realized everyone in the room, male and female, had short-cropped hair—rose from the floor.

"Melba said, you have to think of it like a caste system," she began. "It's gonged off to call it that publically, but that's what it is. The Brahis are the politicians; they make all the rules, all the decisions. The Satis are mainly scientists and engineers—the next step down—except that half the time they're the ones telling the Brahis what to tell *us* to do."

"Yeah," called out a voice from the floor, "like flush their shit out an airlock when the plumbing breaks down."

The young woman ignored the interruption. "We're Madris: the worker bees, the ones who get the nasty jobs the Brahis and Satis don't want to sully their hands with. And the Chucks—well, they're halfway to the other side. They don't do much of anything because they're such a sickly lot. The caste distinctions are set according to our personal F-value—" she paused, adding bitterly, "—as if our F-value correlated to our value as human beings."

I raised a hand, stopping her. "That's the second time I've heard that term. What's it mean?"

"It's an indicator of how much genetic overlap a person has," said Oliver. "If your parents were brother and sister, you'd have an F-value of .25, because exactly 25% of your genetic material is duplicated. The Chucks' F-values are even higher than that. They're a pretty diseased, malformed lot." He indicated the pointy-chinned woman, "Melba there—she's a .248. Barely qualifies as a Madri."

The young blonde woman broke back in. "And none of the other castes will even touch a Chuck. If they get cared for at all, it's by us. It's not one of our official duties, but if we don't do it, no one will."

"Because we're Christians!" called yet another voice from the back of the room. "We don't abandon people."

"Amen!" shouted the rest of the room.

"Amen," I repeated, my head bobbing with approval. Now I understood why the people in the med-center got so excited about bedding me with half the people on the ship. The undertone of desperation they showed in that first conversation. Yet I also found myself respecting these dirty, jumpsuit-wearing men and women so much more. They may have been persecuted—the absolute dregs of *Voyager's* society—but they were the ones who were true to Christ's message. They understood His purpose when He opposed the Pharisees and associated with lepers and prostitutes and tax collectors.

I rose unsteadily to my feet. It required every ounce of strength I had, but I felt inspired by these true Christians. By their commitment to caring for the downtrodden even when they were downtrodden themselves.

"Brothers and sisters," I said, raising both hands. "Blessings on you all. As it says in Romans 12:9-10: 'Let love be without hypocrisy. Abhor what is evil; cling to what is good. Be devoted to one another in brotherly love.' You have embodied the essence of that verse better than anyone I've ever met, demonstrating true Christian love. That Bible verse was my husband's favorite verse, and every time it came up he always said—"

"Wait a minute," said the young blonde woman. "Did you say 'husband'? But you're a man."

"Of course," I answered. "Married for eighteen years. We actually got the lottery results about *Voyager* on our eighteenth anniversary—"

I had to stop there; I suddenly couldn't speak or breathe.

I hadn't thought about it until that very second, but the moment those words slipped through my lips, they came boomeranging back, hitting me between the eyes like the rock David had slung at Goliath. And with that painful blow, memories flooded my mind, overwhelming me, shutting out the room, the group, and everything else. That day—our anniversary—it should have been the happiest of my life.

But on our eighteenth anniversary, on that very day, Michael had come into our bedroom and woken me. At first I thought he wanted anniversary sex, but he'd kissed me so gently, so tenderly, telling me I'd won the lottery for *Voyager*. He held my face between his hands, and smiled, and cried.

And somehow he convinced me to get on that ship without him.

Had he really been *that* convincing? Or had I merely allowed it? Because I wanted to live…

A tidal wave of tears welled behind my eyes.

No. I would never do that to Michael, would I? Abandon him like that?

Then why did I feel the weight of… of…? Guilt? Pressing on my chest like a tombstone?

Because I had been afraid. Because I had *let* him convince me.

I had held the guilt at bay as long as I possibly could, and I had found my limit. Right here. I blinked, trying to hold back the tears.

Yet even as I sought to get control of my eyes, my ears heard something they could barely comprehend, much less believe. A cacophony of voices, protesting, disparaging, reviling. It was the med-center all over again, except this time I had context. This time their outrage was Biblical.

"Abomination!" "Sinner!" "False prophet!"

The kick in the teeth was the repeated shouts of "Leviticus 18:22!" That verse was shouted loudly and often, spreading like a living organism through the room, an organism that seemed to grow darker and more dangerous by the moment. "Leviticus 18:22!"

Thou shalt not lie with mankind as with woman kind: it is an abomination.

I collapsed into my chair, my legs weakened by the verbal assault. Yet even then, I protested. "But that's the Old Testament," I cried. "It was replaced by His New Commandments. Men are supposed to love men, and women are supposed to love women. 1 John 4:21. 'For the one who does not love his brother, whom he *has* seen, cannot love God whom he *has not* seen.'"

Even as I spoke, I made eye contact with Oliver, whose ultra-pale-blue eyes flashed with recognition at the verse I quoted.

"Wait a minute!" he said, calling for quiet, for calm. "Everybody wait a damn minute!"

Order was restored, albeit marginally. He turned his attention to me. "Are you saying that verse *endorses* homosexuality?"

The room burst out again, but Oliver wouldn't let the voices run rampant.

"Everybody SHUT UP!" he bellowed, his eyes looking at me, demanding answers.

"I'm saying it reveals His ultimate plan for us. The marriage of science and religion—cloning. We could finally love each other the way God intended."

From the quasi-darkness someone shouted, "That's a filthy lie!"

The previously charming low lighting had morphed

into a convenient hiding place for anger and resentment, and I suddenly wished I could see better.

"Hold on," said Oliver, intrigued. But he was shouted down as the room scuffled to its feet. "Liar!" "Sinner!" "Scum!"

They morphed from congregation to mob in a nanosecond, pressing forward—a mass of brown and orange jumpsuits intent on mayhem, violence, or worse. Never in my life had I witnessed such hatred. Their eyes burned like volcanoes, and I was the city of Pompeii.

And just as the lava looked as if it were about to flow in my direction, in through the door burst a horde of uniformed men and women.

Their uniforms were navy blue, somewhat faded, but cleaner than the frayed brown and orange jumpsuits. And in the hands of each uniformed individual was a two-foot metal rod that sparked with orange and yellow charges of electricity—charges that looked like tropical butterflies but kicked like mules when the officers swung them against the scattering congregants. Bodies fell before they could reach the exits, and seemingly before it began, it was over.

People lay on the floor, moaning, writhing, or plain unconscious; navy blue uniforms loomed over them, on the lookout for trouble. One of the few congregants still conscious glared at me from her position on her stomach, a blue-uniformed knee crushing down in the middle of her back.

And into the middle of this artless scene strolled Dr. Chip Jones.

"Had enough Christianity for one night, Mr. Fallgood?"

I had never felt so relieved to hear a gravelly voice in all my life.

Somewhat smugly, the doctor added, "I waited in that hall forever, wondering when you'd finally get to the good stuff."

I gazed at him in uncomprehending silence, still on the verge of tears. Despite the chaos, the memory of Michael haunted me. My betrayal of him.

Dr. Jones gestured to the woman lying face-first on the floor, the one who'd glared at me so hatefully. "Tell him," he ordered. "Tell him what being a Christian means to you."

The woman's eyes locked onto the doctor with even more venom than she had for me, stubbornly silent.

The doctor raised an eyebrow. "Do you need convincing?" he said. One of the guards raised his electric bat above her. "Tell him what it means to you to be a Christian. Tell him what you believe."

"I believe in the Bible. The Word of God."

She knew the answer Dr. Jones wanted. She also despised him—more than she did me, and she wasn't interested in cooperating.

The doctor stepped toward her. Something about his manner was suddenly far more frightening than the electric weapon the guard wielded.

"Tell him!"

"The Bible talks about being brothers and sisters in Christ," snarled the woman. "It talks about brotherhood and sisterhood more than anything else in the New Testament. And every Madri on this ship is genetically closer than most biological brothers or sisters. Therefore, it stands to reason that *we* are the true siblings of Christ. We have the right to breed with anyone we want, any time we want. That includes our biological siblings. God spits on your computer's gene-pool program, Dr. Jones." She spat when she said those words. "We are the Chosen People, brothers and sisters in both flesh and in spirit. The Bible tells us so."

"Breed with your siblings?" I said, stunned. "What happened to helping people? What happened to taking care of those who can't care for themselves?"

She looked at me incredulously, as if the answer were so obvious it pained her to speak it out loud.

"We can't do both?"

• • • • • • • • ● • • • • • • • • •

I sat in my prison cell, leaning against the glastic wall.

"Alice got out of Wonderland," I said. "Dorothy met the Wizard of Oz and then returned to Kansas. Frodo Baggins defeated Sauron and returned to the Shire. Even Sheva Rath, who explored twelve parallel universes in the Cycle of Rath — even Sheva got to go home again." I gazed vacantly across the cell the guards had me thrown in. "But I'll never see Earth again. It's the 36th century, and I've lost my husband and the better part of a millennium. And I'm going to be stuck in this hell-hole for the rest of my life."

Oliver stood and walked to the edge of the adjacent cell, splaying the fingers of one hand against the glastic wall in a gesture of support.

"No worries," he said. "Your crystal-pure genetics will have you out in an hour or two, tops. They're just making a point."

Oliver didn't get it. "I'm not talking about this two-bit jail cell. I'm talking about *Voyager*. I've been out of cryo less than twelve hours, and I already know I'm going to die here. I'm never going to see my family or friends again. Never going to feel sunlight on my face."

"Most likely not," scratched the doctor's voice from a speaker up above.

I jumped in my skin, which hurt my already aching body.

Oliver flicked both ghost-hands dismissively. "Pay him no mind. That's just the doc's way of letting us know he's eavesdropping through the security feed while resting comfortably in his quarters."

Oliver paused. "Have you really felt the sun on your face?"

I looked at him: so pale, so wan. He was lucky to never have lived under the sun; the skin-cancer issues alone…

But to have lived your entire life and never once felt the warmth of the sun? Skin cancer or no, I couldn't conceive of such an existence.

"Forget that," he said. "What I really want to know, Jeremy, is this: Were you actually married to another man?"

I'd been on edge from the moment they put me in this cell, but I was overwhelmed, out of mental and emotional resources. "That's the second time you've called me that!" I shouted. "My name is Jerry. Only Michael calls me Jeremy, and you're not Michael!"

The door to my cell made a double-clicking noise and popped open.

"There you go," said Oliver. "Told you you'd be out in no time."

The moment Oliver spoke, the doctor was on the intercom to correct him.

"No," said Dr. Jones. "He's not going anywhere."

A group of guards came around the corner. They were wheeling several pieces of medical equipment.

The doctor continued. "We're converting your cell into a hospital suite, Mr. Fallgood. Can't afford to have you going on any more unauthorized adventures. These men will tend to you in my absence, and when you're feeling better, we'll resume that conversation we started in the med-center. Because one way or the other, you will be making a contribution to keep mankind—and womankind—alive and kicking for a few more generations. The only question is how willingly you'll do it."

How willingly. That was funny—as if I had a buffet of choices before me. The only thing on this ship that looked like a buffet was the electric-wire spaghetti hanging from every wall and juncture, and, sadly, right now my choices were even less appealing.

・・・・・・・●・・・・・・・・

Over the course of the next week, I grew stronger and more bored each day. The only thing that kept me sane through the physical therapy was the fact that they left Oliver in his cell, too. He'd grown a beard while we were there—twice as fast as Michael ever did, yet somehow just as thin and wispy. Despite it being white, it made him look more than a little like my dearly departed Michael.

I said, "We're limping through space in a broken-down bucket of bolts, in a situation that puts a whole new spin on the term 'generation ship.' We're cut off from the rest of humanity and the only thing I can say with certainty is I'm going to die here."

Lord, it sounded worse out loud than it did in my head. I needed a distraction.

"Don't you have something amusing or entertaining? A story about hostile aliens who tried to force their way onboard *Voyager*? Or a wormhole you thought you could fly through to shorten the trip, but ended up going back in time? I could use something like that right now. Some good old-fashioned escapism."

"I can do that," said Dr. Jones. But his voice didn't come from the speaker up above like it had all week. It came from down the hall. The man was never where you thought he was going to be.

"You can do what?" I asked.

"Tell you a different story."

"Come to gloat in person?" said Oliver.

"It's been thirty-seven years since we last found anyone alive in a cryo-pod," the doctor replied. "Next to the life-support system, his genetic material is the most important thing on the entire ship."

"Don't I feel special," I said. "Stop or I'll blush."

The doctor pulled a small device from his pocket and pushed a button. Our cell doors opened with a hollow-sounding *kthunk*.

"Walk with me, gentlemen," he said.

Surprised to be included, Oliver moved quickly lest the doctor change his mind. As we walked three abreast down the detention center's hall, Oliver waved to the guards. I couldn't tell if it was intended as a friendly gesture or a provocative one.

"So," began the doctor. "Your requested tale opens in a post-apocalyptic wasteland: a place scourged of whatever human life it once held. The entire region has been devastated by a series of blasts—firebombs, atomic, biological; whatever devastation you care to name."

"Where are we headed?" asked Oliver.

"You'll know once we get closer," the doctor replied, hands clasped behind his back.

The hallways all looked alike to me—panels hanging open everywhere, wiring splayed, half the overhead lights burned out.

"Through this blasted setting the last three survivors struggle onward, a father and his two daughters. They've worked their way through a city where an EMP bomb was detonated, which destroyed anything technological but left all the buildings and roads, all of the infrastructure, undamaged."

We rounded a corner and found ourselves in a hallway crammed with crates of electronic junk. The light at the end of the hall flickered erratically.

"We're headed for Area 451," Oliver realized aloud.

"The father wants to stay in the city," continued Dr. Jones, ignoring him. "But both daughters are creeped out by the ghost town, so they push on, heading into the surrounding mountains where they stumble across a rocket ship—a rocket that's stocked and ready to go. It's a God-damn miracle."

Oliver and I simultaneously said, "Don't blaspheme."

The doctor grinned. "Begging your pardon."

The story had a familiar ring, but I couldn't place it.

We halted outside one of the closed doors, and Oliver picked up a trio of headlamps, putting one on and distributing the other two.

We walked through a doorway—and into darkness. Oliver seemed to know where the doctor wanted to go and took point. Good thing, because the headlamps barely scratched the surface of the blackness that owned the room.

"There's a problem, though," Dr. Jones continued. "There's tension between the father and his daughters. You see, right before the apocalypse, two men had come into the town where they lived, important representatives from the government. And because the father knew the town to be a dangerous place, he went out to meet them and offered them a place to stay. But when they got home, behind them came an angry mob who wanted to rape the men."

"This is the story of Lot," Oliver said, even as I recognized it. "The story of Sodom and Gomorrah."

"No, it's not," said the doctor. "You think I've read your silly little book?"

"It certainly is," I replied.

"Then tell me the rest."

I looked up and around me. This was no ordinary storeroom; it was a warehouse-sized space, desolate in some areas, packed with random stuff in others. But you could only see one speck of it at a time—just what appeared in the muddy yellow grapefruit-colored dot produced by the headlamp. It was like walking around with a peephole strapped to your eye.

I had to hope Oliver and the doctor knew where they were going because I was lost. So I focused on Dr. Jones' story. "The father offered his virgin daughters to the mob in place of your so-called government men—who were angels, by the way. He was prepared to let them rape his daughters instead. But the angels saved them and warned them about the coming apocalypse. Told them to flee town at once. On their way, Lot's wife turned into a pillar of salt. That's the most famous part of the story."

"Yes," the doctor said. "I've always admired your God for punishing Lot's wife for the unforgivable sin of looking over her shoulder."

"It's not our place to question God's orders," I replied.

"How convenient. So what happened in the rocket ship?"

"It was a cave," said Oliver. "Not a rocket ship."

"Yes, well," the doctor chuckled. "I thought a modern-day parable would be appropriate."

"A parable?"

"Parables were Jesus' favorite teaching tool. If you tell

people things directly, their defenses go up. But if you come at them sideways..."

Oliver said sharply, "You claimed you hadn't read our 'silly little book'."

"No, I asked if you *thought* I had read it. Thirty percent of the population of this ship believes everything that damn book tells them. I'd be an idiot not to familiarize myself with it. You think I'm an idiot?"

"Yes," Oliver said. "But not because of that."

I realized we'd stopped walking. Had, in fact, some time ago. But I was so engrossed in the conversation that I'd lost track of everything else.

Dr. Jones prompted, "So what happened? On the rocket ship?"

Oliver said, "It's one of the core teachings of Christianity." He glanced at me, adding, "Well, Christianity as I know it."

"So...?"

"So in this *cave* they find some wine. The daughters decide that since everyone else is dead, the pragmatic thing to do is get their father drunk and use him to get themselves pregnant. The story makes it clear that sex with your relatives isn't a sin. The incestuous bloodline that came from that coupling is a key part of the genealogy of Jesus Christ, so how can it be seen as anything but sacred?"

The doctor looked at me and gestured to Oliver. "You should know that not all Madris share his views. Many aren't even Christians. The guards I brought with me that night I saved you, for instance."

"Most of them *are* Christian," Oliver said, not bothering to hide his satisfaction. "They just know how to hide it from you."

"Yes, well..."

"In fact, some of your high and mighty Satis are

Christians, too."

"Let me guess: Tina Gareth?"

"That albino freak? Heaven forbid."

Oliver and Dr. Jones laughed. It was a strange sight, as much as they disliked each other.

"You're wrong, you know," the doctor said. "That story is a warning about the perils of disobeying God. The cities of Sodom and Gomorrah, Lot's wife—they disobeyed God and felt his wrath. He's not a nice God."

"I always appreciated the story of Sodom and Gomorrah for its poetic justice," I said. "A father offers up his own daughters for rape and ends up getting raped *by* them. It's about justice. It's also about doing whatever is necessary to survive."

Oliver and the doctor stared at me, mute.

"So what are we here for," I asked, afraid that waiting another minute would bring another interpretation.

"We're here so I can see this miraculous cryo-pod of yours," the doctor replied, content to change the subject. "I don't believe in divine intervention, but I do think there's a chance we might learn something that'll help us find other survivors."

Oliver held up one finger. "Give me a moment and I'll show you exactly where we found him."

Oliver scurried back to where we had entered, disappearing into the engulfing darkness until the only thing that remained was a dancing grapefruit. Some banging and clanging ensued and then a moment later he reappeared with a three-foot section of metal pipe.

"One of the pods shifted as we pulled him out, and I suspect it wedged in pretty tightly. I'm assuming you'll want to see the inside as well as the outside."

I know I did. I had never been part of a miracle before.

We climbed over and ducked under piles of gear, finally arriving at a group of cryo-pods, some of which stood upright and open, some leaned cockeyed, closed. Oliver pointed to a pair jammed into the corner, one leaning against the other, both standing silent and dark. Neither showed any sign of having functioned for a long time. In fact, each had a noticeable layer of dust. And if I saw it, so did they. What kind of game was this?

"Help me shove this aside," Oliver said, pointing to the cockeyed pod.

Doctor Jones and I positioned ourselves on one side of the pod and Oliver went to the other. I bent to get a good hand-hold, but even as I did, I kept one eye on Oliver and one on the doctor—who had both eyes on Oliver.

None of it mattered, because all of the open eyes in the world don't make a lick of difference when you've got two hands full of cryo-pod—which is precisely the moment Oliver struck. He lifted the length of pipe in the air and brought it crashing down on the back of the doctor's head.

For a moment I was too stunned to speak.

I heard a voice murmuring weakly, "What the hell?!?"

Except it wasn't me speaking. It was the doctor. He staggered, bloodied. But he hadn't been knocked out. Blood flowed down the right side of his face and neck.

Oliver raised the pipe again, and this time I found my voice. "No!" I grabbed his arm.

Doctor Jones struggled to stay on his feet, staggered, fell to his knees. Tried to rise, fell again. Oliver broke free of my grasp and swung again, but I threw myself at him, spoiling his aim. The pipe hit the doctor's shoulder instead of his head, but it was a solid blow. Screaming, the doctor collapsed to the floor.

Over top of the doctor's cries, I shouted, "Is this what you call Christian behavior? Is there something in your Bible that makes this okay?"

I expected argument. Struggles. But Oliver froze.

"Fine," he said, backing up a step. "You don't want me to hit him again, help me stuff him into the pod."

"They're not air-tight, are they?" I asked, keenly aware that he still held his makeshift weapon.

"Only when they're working properly, and none of these are." He waggled the pipe. "Make up your mind quickly. Club him, stuff him; it makes no difference to me."

"Okay, okay," I said. "Into the pod." Oliver put his hands under the doctor's armpits, I grabbed him behind the knees, and we hefted him into a cryo-pod. Oliver swung the glastic cover in place and wedged the length of pipe under the door handle so it was impossible to open it from the inside. It would be easy enough from the outside, but Oliver wasn't going to let me do that.

Inside the pod, the doctor groaned, bleeding but recovering from the initial blows, getting more clear-headed and irritated with each passing second.

Oliver leaned against the glastic door and grinned. "I knew sooner or later you'd *have* to see the place where we found him. It's nowhere near here, by the way. Area 451 is just the most out-of-the-way place I could think to bring you."

"You think I didn't expect treachery?" the doctor snarled. "You think I didn't expect this? The guards are two minutes behind us."

"Well then I guess I best not waste time telling you the details of my evil plan," Oliver said with child-like glee. He paused, bringing his hand to his white-whiskered chin, then added, "Oh wait, I have *loads* of time. I sealed the door. No one is getting in here until they backtrack and get tools to cut their way in, and I locked the tool room, too." He was immensely pleased with himself. "For years I've let you pull the same stupid trick over and over, letting you 'surprise' me with your stormtroopers. All so that one day, the day I needed it most, I could be one step ahead of you. Well, today is that day, Dr. Jones. Today the cavalry will not be riding in to save you."

Dr. Jones lost it. He screamed. He pounded on the glastic door. Curses flew from his mouth like hornets.

But the only thing his outburst succeeded in doing was amusing Oliver, who said to me, "I know we have our own ideas of what it means to be Christian, but I think ultimately we're more alike than different. If you'll help us, pretend to be our hostage, I think we can force the Brahis and Satis to make real concessions. They'll do anything to get you and your genetic material back. Even treat us like human beings."

He took a step forward, closing the gap between us. "And in the meantime…"

He ran the back of his fingers against my cheek, leaned in, and kissed me, his beard brushing my cheeks exactly the way Michael's used to. The hairs tickled, soft and feathery, just as his lips fluttered soft against my lips. For a second, for just one second, it was as if Michael were back from the dead. I closed my eyes and leaned into the kiss.

"I want to be a good Christian," Oliver said, suddenly breaking off. "But at the same time I need to be able to express who I am. I've always felt repulsed by the women they make me breed with—every one of them. Your reading of the Bible allows for something different."

I opened my eyes and before me stood Michael but not Michael. My Michael, who I had betrayed and left to die. And one week later—at least in terms of my being awake and alert — here I was, betraying him again by kissing another man.

I was a horrible human being.

"No," I said, backing away, unsure who I was more upset with, myself or Oliver. "I'm pleased to know you find my 'version' of Christianity convenient for expressing your sexuality, but convenience is a lousy reason to embrace something so important. I won't do this."

"Won't do what?" Oliver grabbed my arm, yanking me toward him hard enough to wrench my shoulder. "Help stop the abuse? Help us get access to food and medicine? Do you know they won't treat half the diseases we suffer from? They say there's no hope for us, so why waste resources?"

I gazed at Oliver in disbelief. I sympathized with his plight, but it didn't justify his actions.

I moved away and he yanked my arm again, harder.

But this time I was prepared. I spun toward him, using his own momentum, transferring it into a shove that sent him stumbling backwards — right into an open cryo-pod. I slammed the door and threw my weight against it, looking for something to wedge it. But I couldn't find anything — nothing that I could reach without releasing the door.

Oliver raged, but within the confines of the pod he had no leverage. The doctor laughed.

"What are you doing?!" Oliver shouted. "Let me out of here!"

But the look in his eyes… Even through the rage, he seemed genuinely wounded. He stared, still struggling, but it was half-hearted. "I thought we were kindred spirits."

"Just because what they're doing is wrong doesn't make you right."

Michael stopped struggling.

I mean Oliver. Oliver stopped.

"You have to pick a side," he said.

I shook my head. "No."

"Set me free, Jerry," the doctor said. "I'll make sure they know you had nothing to do with this. But if you go with him—if you let him out—I don't care how much we need your genetic material, I will make your life hell."

"Yes," I said, "That's the way to win me over. Nothing says 'Do the right thing' like threats."

I had a flash of insight and took off one of my shoes and wedged it under the door handle. It worked. Not as rigid as a pipe, but it didn't need to be. Now I could step back from Oliver's pod. Now I could think.

But what to do?

Oliver had a point. I'd only been awake for eight days, but it was clear that he and his people were being treated unfairly. They had some pretty strange ideas, but to call them second-class citizens would have belittled the extent to which they were mistreated. Using me as a hostage, though, that was no way to go about changing things.

On the other hand, though Dr. Jones and his people were rigid and controlling, I could see the sense in their gene-pool program. If things were this bad—and again, eight days was plenty of time to see that they were—then extreme measures were justifiable. If Earth had already died, we might be humanity's last chance for survival. Didn't that trump everything else?

Now that I thought about it, I realized Oliver had been correct about one thing: I had to pick a side. Eventually I was going to get used by someone. That much was clear. Inevitable even. The most I could hope for now was to decide by whom. And maybe use my fifteen minutes of power and influence to make some small, good thing come out of it.

But what? How?

I had no idea. None at all.

But I knew who did.

I knelt. And I prayed for guidance.

In the background two competing voices clamored for my attention, appealing to my sense of justice, pleading with me to see their point of view. They shouted and cajoled. They cursed and offered bribes. And they wouldn't shut up.

How was I supposed to hear God's voice over all that noise?

That's when I heard Michael, whispering in my ear…

• • • • • • • ● • • • • • • • •

I staggered drunkenly toward Dr. Jones, my robe flapping open and flashing my otherwise naked body. I was not ashamed. Alcohol was still available in the 36th century and it still did its job. Praise God.

"You have to admit, it's pretty amazing," I said. Or slurred. Did I slur? With Dr. Jones' homemade hootch flooding my system, I couldn't tell.

"What is?"

"How one book can do all that," I said. "How the Bible can remain relevant for over three thousand years."

The doctor shook his bandaged head. "What I find amazing is how people manage to find ways to make that book say exactly what they want it to, no matter what the facts might be."

"No," I corrected him emphatically. Possibly over-emphatically. I jabbed my right forefinger into my left palm, saying, "I'll tell you what's amazing. What's amazing is that for thousands of years that book has been able to say exactly what people need to hear in order to make society work."

Dr. Jones shrugged. "You say tomato, I say tomahawk. I don't mind disagreeing, as long as we can do it civilly."

"Says the man who lost his mind when I confessed I was a Christian."

"Admittedly not my finest hour."

"Tell me something," I said, hopeful, yet afraid of the answer. "Is there anyone left who believes what I believe? Anyone at all?"

The doctor shrugged. "Honestly? There may have been a few, for a while, but I'm certain that life after the Wrecking required a radical rethinking of many things. And that was a very, very long time ago."

I lumbered toward the doctor. I *needed* to hug him. I appreciated his honesty so much. And he was so cute, even with half his head wrapped in gauze.

He dodged me easily. "Did you really have to consume quite so much alcohol?"

Given what I had agreed to do, yes, I needed to be very drunk. Often and a lot. But at least I got to establish the ground rules. And being plastered was just the first of them.

"Getting wasted worked for Lot's daughters," I said. "Can't imagine that either of them were terribly excited about having sex with their father. But without that, there's no Lord and Savior. No one to save mankind."

"Did you actually go back in the Bible and follow all of those 'begats' or are you just taking Oliver's word for it?" The doctor immediately waved off his own question. "Never mind, I really don't care. I'm much more concerned that you're so drunk it'll keep you from performing sexually. Alcohol impairs people, you know."

The door opened, and in walked Melba, she of the pointy chin and loopy lower lip.

Dr. Jones said, "On the other hand, in order to have sex with that, I'd have to be so drunk I was blind, so…"

"I don't know 'bout that," I said, squinting. "If you look at her right, she kind of looks like a man."

"I'm thtanding right here," Melba said.

"Whatever gets you in the mood," the doc said to me, looking at her and grimacing.

Alcohol plus Melba looking like a man was exactly what would be required to get me in the mood, at least this first time. After that I had to hope I could find my way with only booze, because I had seen some of the Brahis and Satis, and they didn't look nearly as manly as sweet Melba.

Doc Jones insisted that the status of sleeping with me was as important to people socially as the genetic material I'd be sharing. So as much as it disgusted me, this was what the situation required. I flopped back onto the bed and patted the space on the mattress next to me. My robe fell open. "C'mere, Melba," I said. She looked aside modestly. It was a horribly feminine gesture.

The doctor headed out the doorway Melba had just entered, saying as he passed, "Be careful with him. He's had a hard day." He turned back to me and said, "I'm going to visit Oliver in his cell again, see if he's ready to tell us where he really found you. I still think there's valuable information to be gleaned. And before you ask again, yes, I will make sure he honors his part of your agreement and shaves that stupid beard."

"Tha's right," I said. This time I know I slurred. "He don't get out of jail until that awful thing is gone."

"Right," Dr. Jones said. "As we agreed. Might be a few

other things I require before he gets out, but that's definitely on the list. When you're done here with Melba, you should sleep it off. You're too drunk to go again anytime soon."

"Really?" That was wonderful news, because I was truly freaked out by the whole thing. Starting with Melba was the right place to begin—and it had the added benefit of meeting one of my other requirements: equal time for the Madris. But it was still going to be difficult. And unpleasant.

I realized my robe was open and pulled it closed.

"And for pity's sake, try to relax," said the doctor. "Even spacing things out so we don't have too many babies born at the same time, you're going to have to impregnate an average of eight women a month for a long time to come."

"As long as we do one Madri for each Brahi and Sati," I said. "I'll do 'em when and where you tell me." So many women, such stomach turning results. But it was the one thing I could think of that would bring balance to this system. The genetics were too far out of whack for the Madris to be viable as a breeding group, but if the status conferred by sleeping with me would change the way people treated them… well, it wasn't much, but it was a start.

Let love be without hypocrisy, right Michael? That's what he always said. That was my new prayer, every day.

"As we agreed," the doctor said. "Everybody gets a turn."

I looked at him longingly. Teasingly. Flirtatiously. I didn't mean it, but if he was going to put me in this awkward position with all these women, making him a little uncomfortable was the least I could do to pay him back. I waggled my eyebrows. "That's right: Everybody gets a turn. *Every*body."

He started to laugh, stopped, then started again, unsure if I were serious. Good.

He said, "God damn, you're drunk. No, not *every*

everybody. Not for all the cloning machines in the universe. That is never happening."

"Don't blaspheme," I said, even though I laughed when he said it.

But as I closed my eyes so as to avoid watching Melba get undressed, I couldn't help adding, "And don't say 'never' too quickly, my dear doctor. Stranger things have happened in this universe…"

Afterword

I'm a Christian who constantly feels the need to explain himself. Let me explain. No, there is too much, let me sum up. (I'll sneak a *Princess Bride* reference in any where, any time. I have no self-control…)

So anyway…

Far Right evangelicals and others of their ilk have hijacked the term 'Christian' in a way that I believe flies in the face of what Jesus Christ was all about. Christ hung out with tax collectors and lepers and *gasp* women. The outcasts and the unwelcome. He advocated for non-violent resistance. He praised love and acceptance. That's what I believe in. That, to me, is what Christianity is *supposed* to be about.

How the Evangelicals got from there, to what look (to me) like hatred and intolerance, I'll never know. But it often makes me hesitate to say I'm a Christian because I REALLY don't want to be lumped in with that lot.

The ironic thing here is that most of the point of "For the Bible Tells Me So" is to remind people that the Bible has evolved over the years. Not so much that the book itself has changed — the Bible's core message has remained unchanged for thousands of years — but the way we view it has changed as our cultures and societies have changed.

If you ask the average person today what the story of the Good Samaritan is about, they'll tell you it's about being nice to people, even strangers, and helping them when they need it most.

And while that's true, people have lost the original context of the story and have, therefore, lost an important piece of it. Back in the day, Samaritans were some of the most hated people in the region, and if that story were being told today in proper context, it would be titled the Good Taliban or even the Good ISIS Soldier. All those people who walked past the injured man and didn't lift a finger? They were supposed to be 'good guys.' The only one who stopped to help was a *serious* 'bad guy.' So the central message people back then would have taken (along with 'helping the helpless') is to judge people by their actions, not by their labels. But that's lost because most people don't know the context anymore.

Sadly, the Bible has also been used — and I say the word 'used' in the *worst* possible way — by people with their own agendas and their own purposes. And anyone who won't acknowledge that is a fool, a liar, or both. "For the Bible Tells Me So" is my attempt to address these issues.

This story was also the next step in my own evolution regarding something I mentioned in my afterword for "The Last HammerSong," namely looking at things in ways that are 'alien' to our normal thinking, and contrasting them with more traditional ideas. I'd been noodling around in my mind for a long time with a character who emerged after an extended time in suspended animation, only to find that the sexual landscape of the new world was very different from that which he or she came from. But it didn't go anywhere until I paired it with the idea of looking at Christianity down a long tunnel of time and seeing how it had changed and how it was used and abused by the powers that be.

In her book, *One Writer's Beginnings*, Eudora Welty said, "There is no story until there are two stories." There are multiple ways that this concept can be applied to fiction, but in every instance, I find it results in a better, more compelling story. And "For the Bible Tells Me So" was that way for me.

One story; one idea? Not so much. But when I mashed the two together? It all came alive.

I also feel like I managed to allow these characters also operate in more of that 'gray' territory I mentioned earlier; they're not as black-and-white 'good' or 'bad' as previous characters. Each simply has their own agenda, and when those agendas come into conflict with each other, well, that's when things get interesting.

LAIR OF THE ICE RAT

In April of 1935, Nikolai and four of his fellow *zeks* fled across the frozen swamps surrounding their Gulag, heading south between the Kolyma River and the adjacent mountain range. Nikolai knew that any escape attempt was doomed to failure, but when he accidentally killed a guard while stopping him from beating a prisoner to death, he didn't think he had much choice.

Four other men saw him run and seized the opportunity to follow him across the tundra. Nikolai's tendency toward action—even action that was less than logical—often resulted in men following him, though in this case he dearly wished that they hadn't. If these *zeks* thought he had a plan, they were mistaken. And he did not want to be responsible for their deaths.

Several hours of running later, as the group of escapees got closer to the rolling gray mountains, Nikolai headed for the area where a network of caves had been discovered and a crew of inmates briefly worked at establishing a mine. After a full day on the run, his fellow *zeks* were excited for the opportunity to take shelter—all but one. The oldest, a wrinkled bag of bones named Vasily who had lost his nose to frostbite the year before, trembled like a prisoner about to be interrogated for the first time.

"The ice beasts," he moaned. "The ice beasts will surely get us if we go in there."

"Calm yourself, old timer," Nikolai said, watching his breath drift through the air. "There's nothing to fear."

"Nothing to fear?" Vasily said. "The swamps of the Kolyma are the place where God forgot to separate the earth from the waters so he froze it all—and keeps it frozen for nearly the whole year so no one will notice. Then He left and never returned, leaving it to the ice beasts."

Nikolai scratched his head through his knitted cap. "What do frozen swamps have to do with going into the mountain?"

"That's where the ice beasts have taken refuge," Vasily said, as if it were the most obvious thing in the world.

Nikolai rolled his eyes. He had no trouble believing God had forsaken this place—one glance at any part of Siberia in winter made that obvious. And he did feel for the old man, who was clearly frightened out of his mind. But enough was enough. They didn't need peasant legends; what they needed was to find a hiding place before the guards caught up to them.

Frankly, at this point all Nikolai wanted was to get out of the wind and the ankle-deep snow. April may have meant spring in some places, but in Siberia it meant another month of winter.

The old man saw things differently. He became more agitated with each step the group took closer the cave. Finally, he stopped, refusing to go another step farther.

"Don't you understand?" he shouted. "There are great beasts that tunnel under the frozen earth. Some are so big their digging causes earthquakes. When I was a boy, I saw a dead one on the banks of the Berelkh River. Its fangs were three metres long!"

"Stop it, Vasily," Nikolai barked. Vapor billowed from

his mouth with each aggravated word. "There's nothing in there but supplies. I was part of the last digging crew here, and we left in a hurry because a blizzard was coming. There are tools and firewood. But there are no monst—"

Suddenly Vasily's forehead exploded, spraying blood and brains everywhere. One second later, the sound of a single shot reverberated in the distance.

Nikolai dove face first into the snow. A second later so did the others.

Nikolai had a flash of insight, suddenly realizing he wasn't going to see the shooter. If regular guards were near, he would already know about it. No, there was only one explanation for *that* precise a shot: the Gulag's commander has sent out Vlad with his sniper rifle.

Most men weren't foolish enough to run from the Gulag where Nikolai had been imprisoned; there was no place to go, no towns for hundreds of kilometres. More likely a man would stumble into another Gulag where he would be spotted as an escaped *zek* and tortured as an example.

But when someone was foolish enough to try running, the Gulag's commander sent out Vlad. Vlad the Hunter, they called him. Vlad didn't collect trophies. In fact, he never returned from his hunts with proof of any kind. He didn't need them. You could tell just from the way he walked that he had found and killed his prey.

Now he was on Nikolai's trail.

Nikolai glanced at Vasily's body, crumpled in the snow with a pool of blood congealing around his head. All Nikolai could think was how much the color reminded him of wild cherries.

"We've got to get into that cave," Nikolai whispered. There was no need for him to keep his voice low, but he couldn't help himself.

"Think for a minute," one of the other *zeks* shouted. "If we go in there, we'll be trapped."

"So stay here," Nikolai said. "Maybe you'll freeze to death before Vlad shoots you."

Without waiting, Nikolai was up and running, bent at the waist, snow flying in the air as he zigged and zagged. He got to the cave in less than half a minute, breathless, his heart pounding. Within another minute all of the others had joined him there as well. Not a single shot was fired. Nikolai wondered if Vlad never had a good line of sight or if the hunter was just toying with them. No one knew much about Vlad. There were never any survivors to tell stories.

Inside the low, deep cave, the four remaining zeks—Nikolai, Aleksandr, Sergei, and Pietr—clustered behind a rocky outcropping. A half-dozen pick-axes leaned up against one wall, neatly arranged right before the mining crew had fled from an approaching blizzard. A different kind of storm approached them now, and it wasn't one they could run from.

"So what now?" asked Pietr, the youngest of the bunch. Naïve Pietr had arrived at camp a few months earlier, and Nikolai had taken pity on him, teaching him survival tricks: the best way to wrap his hands and feet with rags to avoid frostbite, that sort of thing. Nikolai suspected it was why Pietr followed him across the tundra. But then, Nikolai suspected Pietr would have followed him anywhere; he was as impetuous as he was innocent.

"Yes, Nikolai. What now?" echoed Sergei.

If there was one man in the entire Gulag Nikolai did not want to be on the run with, it was angry, entitled Sergei. Sergei acted as if everyone he ever met owed him a lot of money.

"We wait here," Nikolai said, "until someone brings us

vodka. Then we invite Vlad to sit down and have a drink."

"I don't suppose I could get a cup of hot tea, could I?" asked Aleksandr. Aleksandr was a ridiculously short man with the most powerful arms Nikolai had ever seen. He had also spent four years studying at university in Great Britain and acquired a taste for tea.

"Anything hot sounds good to me," Nikolai agreed, rubbing his shoulders and realizing he was hungry. "Look, I didn't plan this escape any more than I planned on killing that guard. If I had planned this, I would have scheduled it for *after* a meal break, not before."

"Then why the devil did you lead us out here to die?" snapped Sergei.

"I didn't lead you anywhere," Nikolai snapped back. "You came on your own."

Without warning Sergei lunged at Nikolai, grabbing him by the collar. Nikolai slipped his arms inside Sergei's, knocking his clumsy hands away. Sergei staggered back. He was about to come at Nikolai again when Aleksandr wrapped his arms around Sergei's waist.

Nikolai growled. "I don't need your help dealing with the likes of him."

"And I don't need you two killing each other," Aleksandr said, his face pressed into Sergei's back. "If you'll recall, there's someone outside who'd very much like to do that for us."

Nikolai exhaled heavily and his shoulders drooped. He knew better than to get into such a stupid squabble.

"You're right, *tovarisch*," he said. "As always."

Aleksandr released Sergei. "You'll behave?"

Sergei glowered and stalked away.

"And you, my friend," Aleksandr said to Pietr. "You'll behave, too?"

Pietr's blue eyes widened beneath the edge of his knitted hat, and he held his hands up innocently. "What did I do?"

"Nothing," Aleksandr said. He winked. "Yet."

Nikolai followed Sergei into the depths of the cave. He found him sitting on a rock, his back to the rest of the group.

"Look," Nikolai said. "Whatever bad blood exists between us, we've got to put it aside. It's the only way we're going to survive."

"We're going to die no matter what," replied Sergei. "Vlad's going to come in here and shoot us all."

"No, he's too smart to risk coming in here. In close quarters we outnumber him. He'll wait outside and try to pick us off from there. If we can outwait him, the cold might drive him off."

"Fine," Sergei replied, turning and staring at Nikolai. "But at least build a fire. It's freezing in here. If I'm going to sit around waiting to die, at least let me be warm."

Nikolai couldn't argue that. He had hoped this cave would be more comfortable since it was out of the wind, but if anything it was worse. Nikolai couldn't remember ever feeling so cold, and in Siberia that was really saying something.

"We've got firewood," Nikolai said, pointing to a large bundle stacked neatly against one wall. He patted his pockets and said sarcastically, "But I seem to have forgotten my matches."

Without taking his eyes off of Nikolai, Sergei reached into his coat, pulled out a pack of paper matches, and opened it. There were a dozen matches inside. Sergei lit one and held it, staring at Nikolai. He let it burn down to his glove-covered finger tips, and before it went out, it left a small singe mark on the tip of his glove.

Matches! Nikolai couldn't believe their good fortune. He

wondered where Sergei had gotten them. Stolen, most likely. Not that it mattered. What mattered was that Sergei had just wasted one.

About to voice his displeasure, Nikolai noticed the thin wisp of smoke the match left behind was drifting toward the mouth of the cave. He watched it closely to be sure his eyes weren't playing tricks on him. If the wind were blowing into the cave, then the smoke would move away from the cave's entrance, not toward it.

"Wait a moment." He held very still, senses alert. Now that he was looking for it, he thought he felt it. Yes, there it was. A faint breeze coming from the back of the cave. It was too dark to see, but there had to be a tunnel back there — a tunnel with an exit. It was the only place air could be coming from.

"Come on," he called to the others. "We may have just gotten lucky."

Pietr eyed the darkness warily. He said, "That depends on whether or not you believe in ice creatures."

There was no time for nonsense. Nikolai said, "What happened to the last man who hesitated because of so-called ice creatures?"

Wordlessly, Pietr looked back toward the tundra. Nikolai was astounded. The boy was actually hesitating.

"I think old Vasily was talking about ice rats," Aleksandr ventured. "And there are no ice rats."

"There," Nikolai said, pointing at his muscular friend. "And he went to university. He should know."

"What are they?" Pietr asked, unconvinced.

"Actually, they're wooly mammoths," Aleksandr said. "And they've been dead for many thousands of years."

"What are you talking about?" asked Nikolai.

Aleksandr said, "I've heard people refer to wooly

mammoths as 'ice rats' before. Sometimes they're found half-buried in the ground, which is why people assumed they were subterranean. They looked like gigantic elephants with reddish-brown hair and tusks that grew three or four metres long. And because they're frozen, it's almost impossible to tell they've been dead for so long. But the last of them actually died four or five thousand years ago."

Nikolai pointed. "See? No ice rats. Now, there's nothing to fear but Vlad and his rifle. Maybe if we go this way, we can find something better."

Aleksandr moved up beside him. "Like tea?" he asked.

Nikolai grinned and patted the little man on top of his head.

• • • • • • • • ● • • • • • • • • •

They moved in total darkness.

Because he had the matches and would not relinquish them, Sergei led the way, and the group moved through a series of lefts and rights until the tunnel narrowed so much they had to turn sideways to pass. Sergei nearly got stuck. At that point he lit another one of his precious matches just to make sure they hadn't gone down a dead end. Nikolai didn't think it was a dead end because he could still feel the air moving against his skin, but it was better to be sure.

The matched flared, blinding them after such complete darkness, and it cast an eerie yellow light on the black rocks of the passageway. Above, the ceiling was barely higher than their heads; on the side, the walls were slick and reflective with ice. But ahead the way was clear.

Tight, but clear.

When the match burned out, nobody moved. It was as if

the brief moment of light made the darkness worse. They stood still for a long time, listening for the sound of a man following behind, or for the sound of something else, ahead. Nikolai's speech about having nothing to fear had been comforting — in the light. In the pitch dark even Nikolai wasn't so sure. There was something primal about this place. It was easy to believe God had abandoned it, and Nikolai found it hard to find comfort in a place that God turned his back on.

Eventually the sound of shuffling feet let Nikolai know Sergei was moving again. He followed, and after a moment, the tunnel widened again. As it expanded, it curved sharply to the left, where it was not quite so dark. The world was gray instead of black, and Nikolai thought he could see the silhouette of Sergei in front of him. One more curve and the tunnel blossomed into a full-fledged cavern.

There Nikolai saw where the light and breeze were coming from: an opening in the roof of the cavern four metres above. The opening was roughly the size of a train engine, with a mound of snow-covered ice beneath it. It looked to Nikolai as if part of the swamp had crashed through the roof of the cavern.

Nikolai immediately began climbing the pile of ice, intending to peer out the opening in the roof. It was treacherous going, but eventually Nikolai poked his head through the opening, surprised to find himself in the flatlands. Apparently the tunnel had wound away from the mountains and gone deep underground.

"What is it, Nikolai?" said a voice from below. "What do you see?"

"Nothing," he replied. "We're not inside the mountains anymore."

"Not inside the mountains?" Pietr repeated.

"We're in the flatlands, just below the surface."

Suddenly animated, Pietr ran to the base of the ice mound. "That means we can escape!"

"Yes," Nikolai said, turning, "we—"

About to climb down the ice again, Nikolai looked at his feet and froze. There was something there. Something beneath him. Beneath the very ice where he stood. It was massive, and hairy, and one eye was staring at him.

"Pietr!" he shouted. "Aleksandr! Get out! Get out!"

In his panic, Nikolai's feet shot out from under him. His head smacked against the ice, spears of pain jabbing through his head and neck and back. He tumbled down the ice, jangling every bone in his body.

Somewhere between the top and the bottom, he lost consciousness.

• • • • • • • • ● • • • • • • • • •

Nikolai woke up with a tremendous headache. He bolted upright, memories of the *thing* he had seen under the ice flooding his brain.

But there was no monster here, no sign of anything amiss.

Nikolai had no idea how long he'd been unconscious, but from the looks of things, the sun was just beginning to rise. Had been unconscious all night?

Apparently, because during that time, though, his comrades had built a good-sized fire. They now lay in a ring around the fire, sleeping.

But what immediately captured Nikolai's attention, even more than the warmth of the fire, was the rich scent that hung in the air. Meat. Fresh-cooked meat.

The odor was everywhere, permeating even his clothing, and it made Nikolai's stomach come alive with growling, grumbling its resentment of his neglect. Nikolai hadn't had meat since he caught that bat in the barracks on Christmas Day. *What a Christmas present that had been…*

In the back of his mind, some small part of Nikolai's brain grew concerned that the fire and smoke and, most of all, the pervasive, pungent scent of meat would bring Vlad down on them. That it would carry out the hole in the roof and lead Vlad to their hiding place.

But his stomach overrode his brain; it was as hungry as a wild animal and it didn't care about anything besides getting fed.

But there was no food to be seen. Nikolai spotted the wood pile, which his comrades had probably carried from the main cave, and three pick axes, also from the cave.

Nikolai's eyes drifted past the dancing flames, scanning the rest of the cavern, and it was there that he found something interesting: the side of the ice mound, chiseled away. His three comrades must have worked for hours with the pick axes to carve out such an opening, and their labor revealed the strangest sight Nikolai had ever beheld. He walked toward it, threading his way between Aleksandr's diminutive, slumbering form, and Sergei's, which lay with his arms and legs splayed, snoring like a bear.

At first the hole in the ice looked like a small cave with teeth. But as Nikolai drew nearer, he realized what he was seeing were ribs—gigantic bones, curving upward. Each rib bone was as tall as he was. This had been one gigantic creature. When he was close enough, Nikolai pulled off one glove and extended his hand to run his fingers over the rough and ancient bone.

It was not quite cream-colored, not quite brown, more

the color of the sand. Where the bone met the ice, bits of flesh and a reddish-brown hair could also be seen, and within the colossal, curving ribs was flesh. Frozen solid. And it looked for all the world as if—

"Looks like something had been eating it before it froze, doesn't it?" said a voice from behind him.

Nikolai jumped, unprepared for company. But when he turned, it was only Aleksandr.

"Unbelievable, eh?" Aleksandr said, yawning and stretching, rubbing the sleep from his eyes. "We actually found one of Vasily's 'ice rats.' It's amazingly well-preserved, too."

Aleksandr went back to the fire, grabbed a pick axe, and chipped away at the frozen *thing*. The sound stabbed inside Nikolai's still aching head.

"A wooly mammoth?" Nikolai asked, grimacing.

"Oh, yes," Aleksandr said, swinging the pick axe. "And a tasty one at that." He swung again and the pick stuck.

Prying on the handle until a piece of meat wrenched free, Aleksandr spun the handle around so the narrow end of the pick was pointing down. Then he impaled the piece of meat on the end of the pick.

"Instant cooking utensil," he said.

Nikolai and Aleksandr sat side-by-side while Aleksandr held the pick over the fire, slowly thawing and roasting the hunk of mammoth flesh. As the meat cooked, the strong, enticing aroma became even more pronounced. Sergei and Pietr stirred. They sat up, half asleep but sniffing the air.

Finally, Nikolai could stand it no longer; the scent was too much for him and he grabbed the meat off the pick axe, taking a desperate bite. It was hot, scalding hot, and it burned his mouth. It was tough, chewy, and hard, and so hot he couldn't even taste it, but he wolfed it down with relief and joy. It was the finest meal he'd ever eaten.

His stomach growled for more.

Then there was another, different growl. It didn't come from anyone's stomach.

This was a deep, guttural, primitive growl that made the hairs on the back of Nikolai's neck stand on end. In the confines of the cave it was impossible to tell where it came from, but whatever it was, wherever it was, it was coming toward them.

The flickering light of the fire did not extend all the way to the edges of the cavern, and the pre-dawn glow was only just beginning to fill the sky, so there were more shadows than anything else—shadows that all seemed to be moving. Creeping. Stalking.

Nikolai grabbed the end of a log from the fire and lifted it high in the air. No sooner had he done so than something suddenly burst into their midst.

Nikolai caught a glimpse of something immense and feline before being thrown to the floor by the impact of it hitting him. He rolled once, miraculously hanging on to the burning log.

Looking up, he saw bodies, people moving, vanishing into the shadows. The fire, scattered by the creature's attack, lay in orange glowing pieces.

But the patchy light of the glowing logs revealed a cat. Three metres long and a metre and half high at the shoulder, it loomed over Aleksandr, who was either too hurt or too frightened to move. Its hide was mottled, the color difficult to determine in this light, but there was no mistaking the long fangs that curved down out of its gaping mouth. No creature but one had ever walked the Earth with fangs like that—a sabretooth cat.

The sabretooth roared again and Aleksandr shook free of his stupor. He had just enough time to begin a scream — but not enough time to finish it. The cat swung its head down at him, knifing his body repeatedly with its fangs. Aleksandr raised his hands defensively, futilely, as his body tried to curl itself into a ball. The sabretooth hacked at him until he went limp.

"Nooo!" screamed Nikolai, climbing to his feet and advancing. He wildly swung his burning log, and the big cat surprised him by backing off a few paces.

Nikolai advanced, swinging the log until he was standing next to Aleksandr, who was bleeding from more places than Nikolai could count. The blood was on his face and hands; it flowed out of places in his pants and his jacket. But Aleksandr was not dead. He reached out, grabbing Nikolai's leg, saying, "Don't be in a hurry to die. It's not all it's cracked up to be..."

His eyes closed, and Nikolai knew Aleksandr was dead.

Nikolai looked down for only the briefest of seconds and then the sabretooth was on him again, charging, snarling, black claws extended. Nikolai was stunned by the attack. Weren't animals supposed to be afraid of fire? Was this creature afraid of anything?

At that moment Nikolai saw that he was alone with the sabretooth. He swung his log one more time, then threw it at the cat before running toward the tunnel that linked the main cave to this cavern of death. Running for all that he was worth. If he could only get through the narrow section of the tunnel, the cat would not be able to follow. If only.

He ran and did not look back. He did not want to know if the cat were right behind him, about to strike him down...

• • • • • • • • ● • • • • • • • • •

Nikolai made it. The tunnel where he stood was too narrow for the big cat, so he was safe. It did not sound like the cat had even tried to pursue him into the tunnel.

After he regained his breath, Nikolai cautiously edged his way back down the tunnel toward the cavern—listening for any sound of the cat, ready to break and run again in the opposite direction. But he heard nothing.

Nikolai came to the sharp curve in the ice tunnel and peered past the frozen stones of the wall. Inside the cavern, Sergei had climbed the ice mound, ready to pop out into the snow-covered tundra and run.

Aleksandr—what was left of him anyway—lay at the base of the mound. The sabretooth stood over his corpse, gnawing at it, crunching the occasional bone. The giant cat's oversized, curved fangs may have been ideal for bringing down big game, but they were far less efficient for eating. Still, the sabretooth seemed to enjoy the fresh meat of Aleksandr's steaming corpse.

But what about Pietr? Where was he? In the chaotic scramble to escape the sabretooth, Nikolai never saw where he went.

"Pietr?" The sabretooth's head jerked toward Nikolai.

"Pietr! Answer me!"

Almost immediately the answer came, Pietr's voice high-pitched with terror.

"I'm here, Nikolai. Trapped."

Up on the ice mound Sergei snickered.

"What do you mean 'trapped'," Nikolai said.

"I ran the wrong way," came the reply. Nikolai still couldn't see him. Pietr continued, "I thought the tunnel was this way, but it's a dead end."

Nikolai thought a moment. This wasn't good news, but it could be worse. He said, "If I can attract the sabretooth's attention, do you think you could make it to the ice mound?"

Silence.

"Pietr?"

"I, uh... I got my foot wedged in a crevice or something. I got it out again—" there was a pause "—but I'm pretty sure it's broken."

Nikolai closed his eyes in despair.

"Nikolai?" Pietr called from the darkness, sounding more terrified by the moment.

"Hold on a minute. I'm thinking."

"No wonder it's taking so long," said Sergei from his ice perch.

Nikolai looked around, assessing possibilities. He could go out the tunnel and back into the first cave. Sergei could go through the hole in the roof. Neither option did Pietr much good.

Nikolai snorted. Neither option did Nikolai or Sergei much good either, not with Vlad waiting out there. Damn Vlad. This would have been hard enough without him, but with him here, too...

...with him here too...

Nikolai took a step back, as if the idea that just hit him were a solid, physical thing. That was it. Vlad. Vlad *the Hunter*.

"Everybody hold tight," Nikolai shouted into the cave. "I'll be right back."

"Where are you going?" Pietr asked.

"To invite Vlad to join us."

"What, you have a death wish?" Sergei shouted. "He'll shoot you on sight."

"We'll find out in a minute, won't we?"

• • • • • • • ● • • • • • • • •

Nikolai began waving his arms the minute he walked out the cave and into the morning light. The rising sun behind the mountains cast long shadows in front of him as he walked into the open, entirely exposed.

"VLAD!" he shouted at the top of his lungs. He waved his arms vigorously. "Vlad!"

About two hundred metres away, a white-clad figure rose up out of nowhere. It waved one hand back at Nikolai.

"Don't shoot," Nikolai yelled as he walked toward the figure. "Don't shoot."

Nikolai sprinted half the distance before slowing to a jog, his lungs burning from the freezing-cold air. Vlad stood there, watching. When Nikolai was only twenty metres away, Vlad abruptly raised his rifle, set the stock against his shoulder and his eye to the scope, and squeezed off a shot.

Nikolai threw himself to the ground, scrambling, trying to keep low and get away.

"What are you doing?" he heard himself screaming. "What are you doing?"

As he dragged himself through a snowdrift, however, he realized there were no more shots, and that he wasn't wounded. He rose to his knees and felt his torso with his hands. No, he hadn't been shot.

He looked up and saw Vlad walking toward him, his rifle slung over his shoulder again.

"That was either an ill-conceived plan," Vlad said, "or your friend is quite impatient."

Nikolai stared, trying to figure out what had just happened. "You didn't shoot me."

Vlad shook his head. "I'm a hunter. I don't shoot defenseless prey. Of course, if you surrender and I take you back, they'll torture you to death. It would be better for you if you ran and let me shoot you. One clean shot. I promise you'll never feel a thing."

"Do you make that offer to a lot of prisoners?" Nikolai asked.

Vlad smiled. "You're the first. No one's ever been crazy enough to come to me like that."

"Wait a minute," Nikolai said. "Friend? Ill-conceived plan? Who did you just shoot?"

Vlad offered him a hand and helped him to his feet. Then he pointed to the left of the cave, where the hole in the roof of the cavern was. "Somebody popped out of the ground and tried to make a run for it. I guess he thought I'd be distracted by your presence."

Nikolai looked, but couldn't see anything. It had to have been Sergei though. He was the only one in a position to run. Nikolai didn't think he would have minded Sergei getting shot, but he was wrong.

"You're sure he's dead?" Nikolai asked.

Vlad's eyes made it abundantly clear why he never needed to bring his commander proof of the success of his hunts.

"So what's going to be," Vlad asked amicably. "Surrender or run?" He sounded like a man chatting with friends over a game of cards. Nikolai looked at him and wondered how anyone could sound so casual sixty seconds after killing another human being.

"I've come to offer you a trade," Nikolai said.

Vlad laughed like he had never heard anything so funny in his life. "I give you credit, *tovarisch*, you have courage. What could you possibly offer me?"

Nikolai simply said, "The greatest kill of your life. No," he corrected himself, "the greatest kill in thousands of years.

In exchange for—" he was about to say 'three lives,' but now Sergei was dead "—in exchange for two men's lives."

Vlad stopped laughing. He eyed Nikolai with critical interest.

"And that's not exaggeration," Nikolai said. "I mean *thousands* of years."

"You have my interest," Vlad said. He unslung his rifle and pointed it at Nikolai. "But not my trust. Show me."

Nikolai marched back to the opening in the roof of the cavern with his hands held high. He wasn't going to do anything that might provoke Vlad, no matter what the hunter said about shooting defenseless prey.

When he got near the hole, Nikolai could see that it was indeed Sergei that Vlad had shot. He lay on the ground not ten metres from the hole.

"So tell me," Vlad said, "were you intended to be a diversion, or did your friend here just get impatient?"

Nikolai looked at Sergei's corpse. "I had as much to do with him running now as I had to do with him running from the Gulag—nothing at all."

"What do you have to show me?"

Nikolai pointed down the hole. As if on cue, the sabretooth cat let out a ferocious roar.

Nikolai thought Vlad's eyes were going to start dancing in their sockets.

"It can't be," Vlad said excitedly. He walked up to Nikolai and grabbed him by the collar. "It's impossible. My God, do you know how impossible this is? A sabretooth?"

Nikolai hadn't had time to consider it before; he had been too busy trying not to be killed. But as improbable as it may have been, it was stalking and growling four metres beneath him.

"Nikolai?" called a voice from below.

"Yes, Pietr, I'm here. I brought help."

He turned to Vlad and said, "So what do you say? Is an opportunity to hunt a sabretooth cat worth two *zeks'* freedom?"

Vlad held out his arms as if to say, *You even have to ask?* Then he wrapped both arms around Nikolai in a great bear hug, kissed him on both cheeks, and said two words.

"Thank you."

Looking into the hole, Vlad got back to business. "So where did it come from?"

"I have no idea, it just appeared. What difference does it make? Shoot the beast and get it over with."

"Is there any other way out?" Vlad asked, ignoring Nikolai.

Nikolai wasn't interested in playing games, he wanted the thing killed so he could help Pietr.

But Vlad had the rifle, so Vlad was in charge.

Nikolai said, "There's a tunnel, but it's too narrow for the beast; it would never fit. Now will you please kill that thing?"

"Now?" Vlad said. "I'm not going to waste an opportunity like this by just shooting the thing while it's trapped down there. We've got to find a way to set it free so I can hunt it."

"Hunt it??" Nikolai said, taken aback. "Are you mad? How are we supposed to get it out of there? Push it up the ice?"

Vlad scanned the cavern. "That does seem to be the only way. The ice mound, I mean."

The sabretooth was pacing at the base of the mound. It had finished off Aleksandr and was looking interested in the men above. Nikolai was glad. It meant that the cat hadn't figured out where Pietr was. At least Pietr had the brains to keep quiet—he hoped. It seemed every time Nikolai thought that was exactly when the boy was most likely to say or do something foolish.

But no, Pietr remained quiet. Nikolai's relief quickly turned to concern, though, as he realized how out of character that was. Had the boy gone into shock? Depending on how badly his ankle was broken, it was a possibility. And even if it wasn't, the fact that he had been wedged in there, pressed up against the freezing cold rock for so long, meant he might be going into hypothermia.

"Pietr?" Nikolai called.

The sabretooth stopped pacing and put its two front paws on the base of the ice. Black claws came out for extra grip on the ice.

"Pietr?" Nikolai called again.

"Yes?" the answer came, faint and fading.

"Hold on, Pietr. Don't fall asleep. Do you hear me? Don't fall asleep."

"Okay," Pietr replied. He sounded like he was drunk.

Nikolai turned to Vlad. "All right. You want the sabretooth out. I want it away from Pietr. It seems we're after the same thing."

"Indeed it does," said Vlad, scanning the surrounding area. He walked through the low brush to where Sergei's corpse lay, one neat bullet hole in his head.

Nikolai thought, *the man has an affinity for headshots.*

"I think that sabretooth wants out of there, too," Vlad said. "I think he just needs a little motivation. Strip your friend naked," Vlad said as he started jogging away. "I'll be back in a few moments."

• • • • • • • ● • • • • • • • •

Vlad returned just as Nikolai finished the unsavory and difficult task of stripping Sergei. As dead weight, he was exceedingly difficult to maneuver. Vlad tossed a short line of rope to Nikolai and said, "You're going fishing. Tie this around his waist and push him down the hole. But make sure he doesn't go all the way to the bottom. Just far enough to tempt our prize."

Nikolai assessed the rope. "Where did you get this?"

Vlad chuckled incredulously. "You think I go hunting empty-handed? I've got a kit made up that's ready anytime a *zek* tries to run. Bedroll, one-man tent, all sorts of lightweight supplies."

Nikolai felt foolish. Of course the hunter would be prepared. He looked at Vlad and said, "Just promise me one thing. If that sabretooth comes up the ice too fast for me to get out of the way, put a bullet in its brain."

Vlad shook his head. "When that cat gets to the top, I intend to shoot at its feet to scare it off. Nothing more. I've never seen a creature yet, four-legged or two-legged, that didn't run when bullets were flying. If that's enough to save you, fine. But I won't deprive myself of this hunt. Not for the likes of you."

Nikolai wrapped the rope around Sergei's legs, tying it so tight he was sure Sergei would have complained if he were still alive. Then he walked back to the opening above the cavern, measuring out rope as he went.

Standing at the top of the hole, Nikolai pulled on the rope. Before committing himself to dropping Sergei down the hole and then hauling his weight back up, he wanted to make sure he could at least pull it across the snow-covered ground. But it was no use. Nikolai couldn't get good footing, and Sergei weighed too much.

Seeing his struggles, Vlad walked over to Sergei's body and began shoving it with his foot. It still didn't move. Nikolai wondered if it might not be freezing to the ground. He'd seen it happen before.

Nikolai turned and put the rope over his shoulder, leaning forward and putting his full weight into it, when the sabretooth roared. Something about the sound was wrong. It was too close. Nikolai looked over his shoulder just in time to see the cat come bounding up the ice in short, powerful bursts.

Nikolai threw himself out of the way just as the cat came flying past him. It landed on the ground halfway between him and Vlad, who immediately lifted his rifle and chambered a round. The cat hesitated, looking back and forth between Vlad and Nikolai as if trying to decide who looked tastier. It roared again and moved toward Nikolai, who was still on the ground.

Nikolai saw the muscles in its powerful hind legs coil, preparing to spring. He imagined monstrous fangs tearing and slashing him, ripping open his belly and then crunching down on his skull.

Suddenly small bits of ice began flying near the big cat's feet.

Nikolai looked past the beast. Vlad was trying to scare off the sabretooth — just as he said he would.

Only instead of causing the sabretooth cat to run, the sound only seemed to catch its interest. It turned to Vlad, not appearing to be the least bit frightened. Nikolai frowned. Not frightened of the gun? The sabretooth cat feared neither Vlad *nor* his gun.

Vlad didn't seem to notice. He kept firing at the cat's feet, firing and trying to scare it off — right up to the moment the cat launched itself at him and knocked him on top of Sergei's corpse. With one swipe of its primeval nightmare fangs, it tore out the man's throat. Vlad the Hunter died making the most horrible gurgling sounds.

The cat turned back to Nikolai. Nikolai knew he had seconds to do something, but he had no idea what.

In an instant his eye went from the sabretooth cat, to Sergei's corpse, to the rope tied around him. The other end of the rope lay on the ground between himself and the opening in the cavern roof.

Nikolai looked at the rope. He thought, this is the dumbest idea ever…

…and dove for the rope, praying that Sergei's body was as stuck as it seemed, and that the rope was not too long. He grabbed the end of it and pitched himself into the hole just as the sabretooth sprang.

Man and cat went into the opening at nearly the same time. Nikolai coiled the rope around his wrist as he fell and then hung on with both hands, falling for what felt like an eternity until—snap, yank, wrench—the rope went tight and he jerked to a stop. Even with his gloves on, the rope cut into his hands. His shoulder took an incredible strain, but he ignored the pain.

Beneath Nikolai's feet, the sabretooth cat lay dead. The momentum from its leap had carried it through the hole and beyond the ice mound, and its awkwardly twisted body told Nikolai that its neck broke when it hit the rocky floor.

"That was amazing, Nikolai," came Pietr's voice from the darkness. "Do it again."

Relief washed over Nikolai. The boy was still awake and alert—and channeling Aleksandr's sense of humor.

"You've spent too much time with Aleksandr," Nikolai said. "Next you'll be asking for tea."

Pietr crawled on his hands and knees out from his hiding place, and Nikolai dropped the last two metres from the end of his rope.

Pietr was pale but smiling. He began taking his coat off.

"It's getting warm in here," he said.

"No, Pietr," Nikolai said as he went to him. "That's hypothermia. Leave your coat on. Advanced stages of hypothermia make you feel warm."

Pietr's face went somber. "I'm going to die, aren't I." It wasn't a question; it was a statement of the inevitable.

"Not at all," Nikolai replied. "I've got Sergei's matches right here. I took them when Vlad made me take off his clothes. I'll rebuild the fire."

"But I still can't walk," Pietr said. He sounded tired. He sounded ready to give up.

"Look," Nikolai said, "we're in better shape than you think."

"How so?"

Nikolai began pulling the scattered pieces of the fire together. "Well," he said, "we've got Sergei and Vlad's clothing. We've got Vlad's rifle and we'll find his stockpile of supplies. And—" he pointed at the sabretooth carcass "—I think we have enough meat to last us quite a while. Though we might want to eat it raw."

"Raw?" Pietr said with a sick look on his face.

Nikolai gestured to the sabretooth with his eyes. "Maybe we thawed that thing with our bonfire, or maybe crazy old Vasily and his talk about God abandoning this place to the beasts wasn't so crazy after all. I don't know and I don't care. All I can say for sure is that that cat showed up after we started cooking the meat, and for a creature that was supposed to have been dead for thousands of years, it sure did a lot of damage. I'm not in a hurry to see if there's another one out there somewhere, so if I build a fire at all, this time it's going to be pretty small."

Afterword

I have long been fascinated by paleontology and cryptozoology, so to be able to write a story that essentially features both is more fun than one man ought to have. It's also a tale that my youngest daughter likes because she is, if anything, a bigger paleontology nut than I am.

I enjoy paleo, but I'm an armchair paleo guy at best. She is actually looking at colleges right now and planning to study paleontology and make a career of it. I envy her. Not as much as I envy the characters in this story who got to see first-hand a wooly mammoth and sabretooth cat (it's a sabretooth CAT, not a sabretooth TIGER), but still, I envy her. A lot. Digging around in the desert. Finding new species. Sweeping dust and debris with those little tiny whisk brooms.

God, I'm a nerd.

So what does this have to do with writing in general or this story in particular? How am I going to bring these ideas together to make a larger, nobler point?

I'm not. I'm a nerd, not a magician. I just like old dead animals — particularly ones that spring to life when they have no business doing so.

BATTING OUT OF ORDER

Fifteen-year-old Jerome Howard leaned against the small wooden desk in the bedroom of his family's Brooklyn apartment. The lamp to his right pushed back the darkness and illuminated the lone, baffling baseball card that lay before him—at least visually. In all other ways the card remained a dark mystery.

At the base of the lamp sat the rest of the cards, the full set from 2049, stacked tall and neat. Instead of arranging the cards in numerical order, Jerome had grouped the players into their respective teams: the New York Mets on top, then the Baltimore Orioles, then the New Orleans Dodgers, starting with his favorite teams and descending to those he had no interest in.

To the left of the stack, directly in front of him, rested the baseball card that had foretold his doom: card #874, Frank Ryan; pitcher; New York Mets. The card's voice-over had said that in ten years Jerome would suffer permanent brain damage at Ryan's hands.

There had to be some way to find out if that card was... was... what? Defective? A joke?

An impossible, unwelcome messenger from the future?

Jerome weighed the idea of sneaking back into his father's room and using his 3-D nano-printer to create another set of cards, wishing there were a way to print singles. Maybe another Ryan card might tell him something more helpful, more hopeful. But the program he'd downloaded didn't allow for that. It was the full set or nothing.

Earlier that day he'd watched his father install a fresh cartridge of nanites into the family's 3-D nano-printer and then print a replacement for his broken geniusphone, so Jerome knew there were nanites to spare. The question was, could he get away with printing a whole new 1,048-card set without his father catching him? It had been risky enough to do once. Nanite cartridges were expensive, and his ex-Navy father was notoriously tight-fisted — a dangerous combination.

On the one hand, the idea of brain damage was terrifying — especially if it was going to happen by the time he'd celebrated his 25th birthday. Jerome was as good a student as he was an athlete, and he'd quickly calculated that was barely one-quarter of his expected lifespan.

On the other hand, even news of his semi-impending doom wasn't enough to squash the excitement of the fact that the card had said he was going to be a Major League baseball player. *A Major Leaguer!* He'd dreamt of playing professional ball ever since his mother put a first-baseman's mitt on his tiny hand on his second birthday. He'd immediately grabbed a huge hunk of cake with the glove, and his mother crowed hysterically at the sight of icing all over the webbing, even as his father barked in his most commanding, military voice about damaging the leather. It was the beginning of the baseball dream.

Of course, Jerome had no actual memory of the event, but his grandfather had taken a holo-vid of the party and Jerome watched it so often that it felt like one.

His mother was gone now, his parents long ago separated for reasons he didn't know. That's why he watched those holo-vids as often as he did. He hadn't seen his mother in a decade.

So he'd make it to the bigs. An All-Star, no less. At least, that's what the card had said, right before adding that his promising career would be cut short by a fastball to the temple.

But how could the card know what would happen? Was he even the Jerome 'Cal' Howard the card referred to?

That last question was the easiest to guess at. Jerome's all-time favorite player was Cal Ripken, the Iron Man, whose record of 2,632 consecutive-games-played was over fifty years old and still standing. Jerome had always planned on calling himself 'Cal' in honor of his hero if he ever broke into the Majors — and how many "Jerome 'Cal' Howards" could there be?

So the card was talking about him. It had to be.

And the rest? The bigger questions? *Death* by fastball would have been better; at least that would be quick and clean and truly over with. But brain-damaged? How badly? How long did he have to live with it? Jerome could imagine more options that were horrifying than ones that weren't.

Jerome snuck down the hall and peered into the living room where his father was watching baseball on the wall. The Dodgers were playing the Astros, the biggest rivalry in the Gulf of Mexico Division. His dad became a big Dodgers fan while stationed outside of New Orleans for three years.

Just above his dad's new geniusphone, a holographic image of a cartoon balding man in a toga said, "Pizza pizza, delivery in twelve point five minutes." His father disconnected the call by swatting away the image with an openhanded swipe like he was snatching a fly out of midair.

No, Jerome thought. He'd better not try printing out another set of cards right now. His father would be too alert listening for the approaching pizza-oven truck. Those trucks didn't ever want to stop rolling, so if you met them by the curb, delivery was free; if they had to wait for you for more than thirty seconds, it was a huge extra charge. The Howard family wasn't poor, but they also didn't pay extra charges. Jerome's father saw to that.

Jerome returned to his room. To the card.

It lay there, inert, looking like an ordinary piece of plasticardboard with an old-fashioned color photograph printed on the front. Jerome picked it up and studied it.

It weighed next to nothing, was slick on both sides, and was artificially impregnated with the scent of bubblegum for a retro smell to match the 2-D retro look. The stats listed on the back were pretty standard.

- 2046: Games, 23; Innings, 132; Wins, 6; Losses 9, Strikeouts, 144, ERA 3.55

- 2047: Games, 26; Innings, 147; Wins, 9; Losses 14, Strikeouts, 171, ERA 5.42

- 2048: Games, 29; Innings, 208; Wins, 10; Losses 11, Strikeouts, 195, ERA 4.33

And that was that. It was this year's set, 2049, and Ryan had been pitching for three full seasons. He'd come up rapidly through the Mets farm system because of his 100-mph fastball, but he lost more games than he won because that fastball was his only pitch. If he couldn't effectively move it around the strike zone, a lot of hitters would launch it out of the stadium. The announcers had even taken to calling them 'Home Ryans' because of their frequency. He could ring up the strike-outs, but strike-outs alone didn't win games.

Jerome gripped card #874 between his thumb and

forefinger and accidentally slapped it down on the desk harder than necessary. The embedded nanites required only the slightest impact to activate, but Jerome knew what was coming and was anxious about it.

As the nanites worked their digital voodoo, a full-color 3-D hologram of Frank Ryan sprang to life above the card.

Holographic Ryan nodded to an invisible catcher and went into his wind-up while a voice-over announcer called the play—just as it had the first time Jerome activated the card. And just as had happened the first time—and the second, and the third—as Ryan reached full extension, the card glitched, white static and digital square blue sparks flying above his desk like a miniature fireworks display. Jerome didn't flinch this time; he knew the square sparks were coming. This time he studied them, trying to figure out what was happening.

But he didn't understand what occurred this time any more than previously. The square blue sparks were too bright to look at for long, and when they subsided, a haggard and clearly older Ryan stood on the mound, halfheartedly doffing his cap to an invisible but adoring crowd. Through the cheers, Jerome heard the announcer:

"After several years of mediocrity as a starter, Frank Ryan was converted into one of the most dominant relievers in baseball history. But early in 2059, his seventh year as a reliever, Ryan put a fastball into the temple of 2058's Rookie of the Year and one-time All-Star, Jerome 'Cal' Howard. Unable to shake off the effects of causing permanent brain damage and ending the promising young slugger's career, Ryan once again became ineffective and announced his retirement before the end of the 2059 season. Who knows what records the fireballer might have broken if not for that one ill-fated pitch."

The voice stopped, the hologram collapsed, and the card sat in plasticardboard silence. Jerome stared at it, Ryan's flat, unblinking eyes returning his gaze.

Impulsively Jerome grabbed a fistful of other cards—Mets players all—and slapped down one after another after another onto the desk, watching as they sprang to life. All projected as they normally did; all delivered last season's information: 2048. Most modern holocards gave stats for the current year, updated daily through the nanites' online link as the season progressed. Not using this year's data was intended to be part of the set's retro feel, but the idea hadn't been well-received by fans—they were too accustomed to immediate updates—which is why Jerome had been able to download the program so cheaply.

More than anything else, right now he regretted buying the stupid program, because the more he watched this one particular card, the more convinced he became that the story it told was real. But what was he supposed to do? How was he supposed to react? Could he change it, stop it? What if he simply chose not to play baseball?

Jerome tried to slow this tornado of thoughts; he was getting swept away by their negativity.

Consider the possibilities, he told himself. Even if he played only one season, it would be worth millions of dollars. That would set his father and sister up for life. His father could finally stop worrying about money, and his sister could go to any college she wanted, instead of the community college their dad always talked about.

And his mother…

He hadn't seen her since she left ten years ago, but she'd been an even bigger baseball fan than his father. That's where his parents had met, the baseball stadium; she was sitting near third base, his father was making extra cash by working the radar gun behind home plate. He'd abandoned his position and talked to her for two full innings before realizing how much time had passed and how much trouble he was going to be in.

His father had lost the job, but he'd always said it was worth it.

Maybe if Jerome played professionally, she might come to see him. Maybe he could arrange for his dad and sister to be there that day, too. Just, you know... coincidentally.

Yeah, right. And all he had to do was find a way to live through the next ten years, every day knowing that a fastball was going to turn him into a vegetable. Jerome wished he could be that noble, but he was too human to embrace such a fate. He was a fifteen-year-old kid, for cripes sake, not Captain America. He could imagine himself too vividly as a drooling, vacant-eyed *thing*, shuffling down the hall of some white-painted, semi-sterile institution, surrounded by other patients who were as likely to walk face-first into a wall as they were to find and operate a doorknob.

God, what an image. And now that he'd thought it, he couldn't get it out of his mind.

No! This wasn't fair! And he wouldn't believe it! He couldn't. It was a defective card made with defective nanites spewed out by a defective printer, telling him about a defective pitcher for a defective team that hadn't won a World Series since 1986. Nineteen freakin' eighty-six! Even the Cubs had finally won a World Series. But the Mets? The Amazingly Futile Mets? Two-thirds of a century of nothing.

No, Jerome would not accept this.

He walked out of his room and was partway down the worn linoleum-lined hallway when his father came in the front door with their pizza. "Kids! Dinner."

With that pronouncement, his eleven-year-old sister, Eliza, exploded from her room. She ran past him, rounding the corner and flying into the living room just ahead of their pizza-bearing father. She launched herself into his decrepit recliner with glee, shouting, "Mine!"

It was their weekly Saturday-night ritual, the one thing they still did from before mom had left them. The rest of the year they ate hot dogs and spaghetti and frozen lasagnas, but during baseball season, Saturday night meant pizza and baseball. Eliza in Dad's chair. Dad cross-legged, leaning against the couch, slice in hand, grousing about losing his chair in a voice that no one could take seriously. For just a few hours, things almost felt normal again, even if mom wasn't pacing back and forth behind the chair, coaching the game in perpetual motion.

But Jerome couldn't embrace the moment. He couldn't get this beanball madness out of his head, and now that his wheels were turning, there were other things clamoring for attention as well.

"Dad?" Jerome said. "Why did Mom leave? Why don't we see her anymore?"

Dad paused, slice halfway to his mouth.

He lowered the slice.

Then he raised it again and took a large bite—like he did every time one of his children asked that question. He would chew that mouthful of pizza until it was cheese-flavored paste before he so much as acknowledged the issue. The look of sadness on his father's face was unmistakable, but it changed nothing. It never did.

"I'm not feeling so good," Jerome announced sharply. "I'm gonna go to my room and lay down."

Jerome stalked back down the hall, fuming, but not to his room. To his father's. Forget him. If he couldn't answer one simple question, Jerome wasn't going to worry about pinching pennies. He was going to print another set of baseball cards and find out what happened in the future. Jerome couldn't say why, but every instinct told him that was the key: finding another card that could tell him more about what had happened. Or was going to happen. Or... whatever.

Inside his father's room, he closed the door and went straight to the printer, hitting the power button. It hummed and whirred. He heard the familiar zzt-tik-zzt of the priming nanite-cartridge. He heard the nozzle emerge from its housing and center itself over top of the print zone.

He heard the doorknob of the bedroom door slowly turning.

Crap!

He dove for the power button, praying it would shut down quieter and faster than it powered up, knowing full well that wasn't how it worked.

The printer's digital voice spoke, even as his father entered the room.

"Cancelling print operation. Are you sure? Press enter to confirm."

"Yeah," said his father. "You sure?" His tone was calm, even, and measured—which meant he was *really* pissed. "I came to check on you, to see if you were alright. I guess I won't need to take your temperature."

"Dad," Jerome said. "Let me explain."

"Not interested."

"But Dad, this is really important."

"I'm sure it is. And you can tell me all about it next week, but until then you're going to be in your room. If you're not at school, you'll be sitting at your desk pondering the meaning of words like 'privacy' and 'respect'."

"But Dad—"

"Your room. Now. Not another word." He pointed down the hall. "Unless you want to make it two weeks."

"But Dad!"

His father stepped forward. "Two weeks it is, then." He never raised his voice; he just grabbed Jerome with one hand by the collar and with the other by the back of the belt. Jerome stood nearly six feet tall and weighed 175 pounds. His ex-Navy father hoisted him like an inflatable doll and dragged him bodily down the hall, his stockinged feet scraping the floor all the way.

Standing him up in the bedroom's doorway, his father patted him on the head. "See you in two weeks, kiddo."

Jerome bit his tongue and stepped across the threshold, closing the door behind him. He couldn't remember the last time he'd felt so disrespected, so like a child. But he wasn't a child; he was fifteen, nearly a man. A man who was going to play professional baseball—if only for one season.

He leaned against the door, listening as his father walked away. He wanted to rage, to tantrum, to scream at the injustice. But if his father heard so much as a peep, he'd be stuck in this room for the rest of his life.

Not fair!

He strode across the room, a hurricane building inside of him. *Two weeks!*

As he neared his desk, his first impulse was to grab the chair and throw it against the wall.

Too noisy. He'd get into even more trouble.

He prowled to one side of the room, then the other, then back to the desk again.

He looked at the lamp, immediately rejecting the idea

of hitting it. That's when his eye fell on the tall, neat stack of cards under the lamp. The neatness offended him, and with a sidearm swing he launched them into the air. They fluttered up and out like a flock of pigeons.

It wasn't as satisfying as smashing the chair, but it was something.

But the relative silence lasted only a second or two. As the cards hit the wall, then the floor, the nanites activated, and one by one, baseball cards flared to life, holograms popping up, baseball players swinging at pitches and throwing them, fielding grounders and diving into the stands after pop-ups.

And one card, somewhere amongst them all — one card in an army of holographic baseball players — glitched, sending up a miniature fireworks display of square blue sparks and white static.

But before Jerome could identify which one, the fireworks ended.

His eyes flashed instantly to his desk, but the Ryan card sat precisely where he'd left it. Unmoved. Unglitched. Unsparked.

On the floor, hundreds of voice-over announcers yammered over each other, demanding his attention, describing deeds heroic and mundane. Then just as quickly as it began, the cards fell silent again.

The room lingered in suspended tension.

Something in the back of Jerome's mind told him he should be worried about his father hearing the racket the cards had made, but a larger piece of him focused on the place where the cards had fallen. He had no way of knowing which one had sparked, but his eyes locked onto the general area where the lightshow had come from. It might take a few minutes to find the right card, but it was only a matter of time.

He went to the spot, to the pile, to the cards scattered at the base of the wall. Picked a fistful of them up and threw one down.

Normal.

He threw another.

Not yet. Jerome remained calm and focused.

Finally, the thirteenth card—that was the one. Lucky thirteen.

He hadn't bothered to look at what was pictured on the front; he'd just flung it. Of all things, it turned out to be a team card. The Baltimore Orioles. Under normal circumstances Jerome skipped the team cards; they were useless and uninteresting.

When this card hit the floor, a hologram of Orioles Park at New Camden Yards came to life before his eyes—literally; it was a time-lapse holo-vid of the construction of the team's new stadium. But before it was half-completed, the now familiar display of glitch-static-squarespark occurred. It ended with a transition to an interior shot of the stadium, focused at home plate.

The faces of the trio holding court there were instantly recognizable, but they weren't baseball players. It was his family.

His sister Eliza, grown and beautiful. She was standing on the left. His father, as imposing as ever, stood on the right. And in the center was a figure he knew instantly from grandfather's holo-vids: his mother.

She sat in a wheel chair, her torso entombed in some kind of awkward looking metal and plastic brace.

Dad and Eliza flanked her, each with one hand on her shoulder, and there was a baseball nestled in her lap. The three of them had the oddest expression on their faces, as if they'd been simultaneously laughing and crying from their very core.

The voice-announcer began: "After the tragic loss of the popular young first baseman Jerome 'Cal' Howard in a freak accident on Opening Day, the Orioles dedicated the remainder of the 2059 season to his memory, winning the World Series in his honor. The notoriously divided, argumentative team came together in swift and unexpected fashion, and, defying all pre-season predictions, ended up winning 120 games against only 64 losses and sweeping all four rounds of the playoffs. In a moving, impromptu ceremony, Howard's family was brought onto the field immediately following the game's final out, with the game ball passed around among teammates who took turns inscribing it to the family."

Jerome... was stunned.

He didn't know what to think.

He picked up the team card and studied it. It looked and felt exactly like the rest of the cards, including the Frank Ryan card that had set this whole nightmare in motion.

He considered throwing it down again, watching it again, but he didn't need to. The whole thing was emblazoned in his memory as thoroughly as if he'd watched it a thousand times, as thoroughly as the holo-vid his grandfather had taken of his second birthday party.

Jerome went to the door of his bedroom and opened it. He walked down the hall to where his father and Eliza were still watching the game.

The minute his father saw him, irritation flooded the man's face like Noah's worst nightmare. He popped to his feet, pizza falling upside-down onto the carpet, words ready to fly from his mouth like hornets. But Jerome spoke first, softly, just barely audible over the game on the wall.

"How bad is it?" he said. "Is it just her legs or is it full paralysis?"

The flames dimmed in his father's eyes for the briefest of seconds, and Jerome knew the answer.

"Was she in a wheelchair when she left?" Jerome continued. "Or did that come later? I bet it was later. I think I would've remembered."

And like a Frank Ryan fastball down the middle of the plate, the pieces grooved into place for Jerome. His mother's absence. His father's tight-fistedness with money. His father simultaneously clinging to their Saturday night pizza-and-baseball ritual, yet steadfastly refusing to talk about their mother.

Suddenly it all made sense.

"She's in a home someplace, isn't she? She's embarrassed to see us, and you're letting her hide."

"She's not hiding!" his father snapped, finally breaking his silence. "She's... she's..."

"Are you secretly visiting her?" Jerome took a sudden, angry step into the living room, closing the distance and jabbing a finger into his father's immense chest. "Are you seeing her without us?"

His father exploded, backhanding Jerome across his face, shouting, "*She won't let me!*"

As if in slow motion, Jerome felt his body lift up, off the floor and drift backward. And as he fell, the oddest thought crossed his mind. *I wonder if this is what it will feel like when that baseball gets me...*

He hit the ground, but it wasn't so bad. It hurt—but he could handle it.

Eliza sprang from the recliner. "Daddy, no!" She threw herself over top of Jerome, shielding his body with her own.

Their father stepped back, horrified at what he'd done,

yet barely able to contain the torrent of emotions that coursed through him. He put his hand over his mouth, unblinking, lost in thought. "It's what she wants," he said. "She wants to be left alone."

Jerome rolled onto his back. Blood ran down his nose as Eliza climbed off him.

"Does she always get what she wants?" Jerome asked. He put a tentative finger to his bloody nose, then blotted it with his sleeve.

"Yes. Yes, she does."

"Well, at least someone does."

Jerome bolted down the hall to his room, but before he could get through the doorway Eliza materialized right behind him.

"It's not Dad's fault," she said gently.

Jerome stepped back, startled. "What?"

Eliza pushed him into his room, looking over her shoulder for their father. "You're supposed to be in your room," she said. "Two weeks. Remember?" Jerome always grew uncomfortable with how quickly she became protective over him. He was supposed to be the big brother, not the other way around. Yet here she was, looking out for him. Again.

Eliza said, "It's not Dad's fault that Mom's gone."

"Who said anything about fault? I just want to know what happened."

His sister shook her head. "If you're going to be mad at anybody, be mad at me. It's probably my fault."

"What are you talking about?"

"Think about it; she left right after I was born. Something must have gone wrong with the pregnancy. A complication or something."

Jerome was taken aback. "How long have you been

thinking this? I can't believe you're blaming yourself…"

Eliza rolled her eyes. "Doofus. I only found out five minutes ago that she's in a wheelchair. How did you figure that out, anyway?"

Jerome didn't know what to say, but before he could even think, Eliza went surprisingly quickly to a dark, brooding place.

"Still, Mom did leave right after I was born."

"So you *have* been blaming yourself."

Eliza's gaze wandered the room, looking at everything except her brother. She shrugged a tiny shrug. "Who else could it be?"

Jerome didn't know. But that was kind of the point; they *couldn't* know.

Except in this case, he did. He knew. Not how it began, but how he could make it end well. End right for Eliza.

He embraced it. It was time for him to be the big brother that he should have been all along. He would do this for her. He owed it to her.

Jerome hugged his sister. "It's going to be okay," he said. "I promise."

Eliza squeezed him back. She didn't say a word, but somehow, the longer she squeezed, the more it felt as if her hug were saying, *If you say so.*

Jerome took a deep breath, let go of his sister, and went to his closet. He got out his two favorite bats, one wooden and one carbon-fiber composite; then he put on his Orioles cap, the one his father gave him for Christmas two years ago but he'd never worn.

And he walked out of his bedroom.

Down the hall.

Through the living room and up to the apartment's main door.

And as he put his left hand on the door knob, two bats propped on his right shoulder, his father barked, "Where the devil do you think you're going? You're so grounded that a dozen Harrier drones couldn't get you off the flight deck. Do not even think about opening that door."

Jerome stopped. After tonight he'd probably be grounded for more like two months than two weeks, but at this moment he had to act. If he didn't take this first step, right now, he might still chicken out.

He looked back.

"I need you to trust me, Dad," he said. "You can ground me for the rest of the year if you want, but for just this one night, you need to trust me. There's an indoor batting cage that's open late, and I have to practice. I've got a lot of work to do."

Jerome looked hopefully at his dad, feeling the tightness from the dried blood around his nostril and upper lip even as he tried to put on his bravest smile.

Dad studied him: his new O's cap, his resolute eyes, his bloodied nose. And he softened. "You've never defied me before. Not like this."

"Nothing has ever been this important."

"Nothing?"

Jerome shook his head.

"And someday you'll tell me what this is all about?"

Jerome shrugged, and the baseball bats rose and fell with his shoulders. He said, "I think someday, when the time is right, you'll know. You'll look back on tonight, and it'll be like a fastball down the center of the plate. When that happens, hit a home run for me, okay? One perfect shot that brings everybody home again. Will you do that for me? Bring 'em all home?"

Dad nodded like he understood what Jerome was asking him to do. Exactly how he'd pull all the pieces together wasn't something Jerome would ever know for sure—because it wouldn't happen until after he was gone.

But he could live with the uncertainty.

In fact, he kind of preferred it that way.

Afterword

I feel guilty about this, but just a little. I'm going to tell you a story about this story, but I'm going to leave out names because I don't want to make a certain someone feel bad. She might not (feel bad). She might even laugh. But just in case, I'm going to leave her name out.

Some stories take eons. Like "Hint of Fresh Peaches." Measure the production of that one in years. Many of them.

Not "Batting Out of Order." "Batting" took ten days from start to finish. I will admit that there was a little polishing done after it was accepted, but essentially it took as many days to write as I have fingers on my hands.

In mid-November of 2014, I got an email from a writer friend of mine (the one who's going to remain nameless) asking me to critique a draft of a story she'd written for an anthology called *Temporally Out of Order*. She asked me to look it over and let her know what I thought. We all do that for each other when we can, and I was happy to help out.

She also sent me a link to the anthology's guidelines so I could help make sure she was hitting the marks the editor was looking for: essentially, devices that were malfunctioning in a temporal sort of way. Cell phone receiving calls from Abraham Lincoln. TVs in 2015 showing the Super Bowl being played in 2218. That sort of thing. But bonus points were being awarded for creativity, so things like TVs and cell phones were easy examples but not the sort of devices the editor was really looking for.

My friend's story was okay. It was a unique take on the concept, but not one that excited me. For what it was, it was passable, but not one I'd have published if I were the editor. And I didn't see a way to put a fresh spin on it, nor did I think she had time for a major rewrite because the deadline was only ten days away.

So I sent her some notes, suggesting a few line edits and wording changes, and wished her the best of luck.

But the idea, the concept, the novelty of something being temporally out of order, had wormed its way into my brain. I couldn't stop thinking about.

I didn't have an idea; I just had to write something and get into this anthology.

To this day I have no idea where the baseball card thing came from. I have no idea where any of it came from. It just showed up on my doorstep, and I just grabbed the tiger by the tail and rode it for all it was worth.

Ten days later I had "Batting Out of Order." Submitted it about an hour before the deadline.

The guilty moment came when my story was accepted but my friend's was not.

But like I said, I only felt a *little* guilty. It was kind of hard to find the guilt in and among the giddy laughter.

Hey, I'm human, right?

FEELS LIKE JUSTICE TO ME

Jonah sat on a thigh-thick limb in the highest part of a pine tree, his hands sticky from the climb. He didn't mind the sap so much, except for on his trigger finger. That was a nuisance.

On the ground below him, a shirtless man with a pair of hatchets strolled unknowingly toward a zombie. Coming from the other direction, Ben-the-zombie stumbled up the creek bed with typical erraticness. Jonah popped his right index finger into his mouth, licking and sucking it, trying to remove the pine sap. For something that smelled as invigorating as a freshly cleaned toilet bowl, it tasted God-awful.

Hatchet-man and Ben-the-zombie drew closer still, unaware of each other because of the dense, green foliage. Only from his perch up above did Jonah have a clear view.

They'd meet in less than a minute. Jonah tried rubbing his finger against his teeth, brushing, except in reverse, trying to use his molars to clean his fingertip. He didn't have enough ammunition to waste on multiple shots; the first one had to be perfect. It wasn't that the sap would interfere with his shot—not physically, anyway—but it was terribly distracting when your finger felt like something from the underside of a bus-stop bench, and Jonah had a tendency to get obsessive about things.

Hatchet-man crested the ridge of a small hill at the same time that Zombie-Ben plowed through a copse of trees.

Twenty yards apart and they still hadn't spotted each other.

"Forget this," Jonah said, slinging his rifle into position and firing in one practiced, nearly mindless motion. *Practically zombie-like,* he mused, reflecting on his technique. The bullet went through the man's right shoulder. Blood sprayed and he fell to the ground, screaming.

The zombie was on him in an instant.

"Eat well, Ben," Jonah muttered. "You son of a garbage bag."

Unfortunately, hatchet-man wasn't ready to be eaten just yet. He swung the weapon in his left hand, slicing into what remained of Ben's neck. The zombie's head lolled at an unnatural angle and Jonah bellowed in dismay. "Noooooo!"

He snapped his rifle back into position and fired three more shots: left shoulder, center-mass, head-shot, all in rapid succession. Brains sprayed up into Ben's face, driving him into a feeding frenzy. The undead thing tried to jam its face into hatchet-man's shattered skull, the force of its lunge doing even more damage to its tenuously attached neck. Now the head was attached to the body only by the spinal cord and a few tendons on one side.

"No, no, no, no no no!" Jonah spit rapid-fire anguish, working his way down the tree. He looked repeatedly over his shoulder at the zombie's flobbing head. With its short-cropped black hair and dark-hued skin, Ben looked like a rotting Alex Rodriguez bobble-head doll. A-Rod had been Jonah's idol before the D Plague turned the world into a buffet for the undead, but seeing Ben's head like this was anything but inspiring. There had to be some way to secure the head; to sew it in place, to keep it from falling off; to keep him from —

When he was almost down from the pine tree, a crusty, gravel-filled voice shouted from the leafy green nothingness: "Is he your brother?"

Jonah froze in place, trying to determine where the voice was coming from. "Your son?"

He remained silent, his head swiveling. He needed one more...

"Your boyfriend?"

Behind him.

Jonah grabbed a tree branch and pivoted to the right, swinging his rifle up with one hand, tucking his elbow against his side for stability. He was sure the owner of the voice was somewhere in this direction, but whoever it was, he was well-hidden.

He also wasn't shooting. If their roles had been reversed, Jonah would have put a bullet in someone by now. He glanced down at Ben, who was no longer trying to eat hatchet-man. Damn it, these zombies lost interest in corpses faster than Jonah could squeeze a trigger. If the heart wasn't beatin', Ben wasn't eatin'.

Crusty-voice called out, "I don't mind that you killed him. Frank was a serious piece of shit. But if you're killing people to protect zombies, that must be one special zombie."

Jonah called out. "Show yourself. Who am I talking to? How many of you are there?"

Zombie-Ben shambled back toward the creek, oblivious.

Jonah jumped out of the tree, eyeing the ground as he dropped the final eight feet so he didn't land on a root or rock and turn his ankle. A turned ankle equaled death in this D Plague world.

His knees flexed as he hit the ground and he rolled to disperse his momentum, popping up on one knee fifteen feet from a massive oak tree. He still couldn't see anyone, but this tree was the only one with a trunk thick enough for a grown man to hide behind. He quickly put his hand behind his back to make sure his revolver hadn't fallen out of the holster, then snapped his rifle into position.

A bald old man who was somehow well-dressed yet simultaneously filthy stepped out from behind the lichen-covered trunk of the tree, hands held aloft as if someone were filming a post-apocalyptic episode of C.O.P.S. "Easy there, chief. Like I said, no love lost for Frankie-boy. Just want to know what your deal is."

"Who else is out here with you," Jonah demanded. He glanced at Ben so he didn't lose track of him.

"Just me, chief," the old man croaked. He appeared to be unarmed.

No one wandered into the woods unarmed unless he was surrounded by a troop of guardians, and one shirtless goober with a couple of hatchets didn't qualify.

"Who else?" Jonah repeated. "Where are the others?" But even as he asked, he knew it didn't matter. Ben hadn't eaten in three weeks. They hadn't seen another living human since Gettysburg.

He was going to have to risk it.

He rose and took three steps closer to the old man, lowering his rifle's barrel.

The old man smiled, sending creases rippling across his bald head like water. He put his hands down—

...and Jonah pulled his revolver from behind his back and shot him, right below the belly. Shattered his pelvis into God-knows-how-many-pieces.

Between the sound of the gunshot and the old man's screams, there was enough noise to wake the dead. Or at least get their attention. Ben reversed course and shuffled toward them. Jonah knew zombie speeds intimately; it would take Ben over a minute to arrive, so Jonah divided his attention between the old man, in case he had any hidden weapons, and the surrounding woods, in case the old man's friends were close by.

Neither seemed to be the case, which stunned Jonah.

How about that. An honest man still walked the Earth. Well, not so much walked as lay bleeding all over it, but the basic concept applied.

The old man's screaming abated quickly; he was now breathing shallowly and rapidly through the pain, clutching his belly as if giving birth.

An honest man. Maybe the last one left in this world. Jonah felt he owed this honest man something, some sort of recognition before Ben slurped his brains out through his hairy ear.

"Do you think there's anything left of the people that zombies used to be?" Jonah asked, kneeling next to the old man and speaking loudly enough to be heard over his Lamaze-like breathing exercises. "Do you think there's any piece of their mind — their pre-zombie mind — that still lives?"

"You. Can't. Believe. There's. Hope. For." The old man gasped his incredulity one word at a time. But his mind was going in the wrong direction.

"Good Lord, no." Jonah corrected him. "Hope? For what? A cure? I'm not hoping for a cure. I pray every night to God — a God who I know full-well doesn't give a rat's ass about us — that the man who used to be Ben Peterson is still awake in there, fully aware of what he's become. That he's aware and suffering and tormented, knowing *exactly* what he is and what he's doing. I want Ben Peterson trapped for all eternity in his own personal Hell, unable to stop himself from killing." He pushed the emotions away, but his voice still trembled. "If there's even the remotest chance that he's still in there somewhere, I want his misery to last as long as possible, and I will protect him with my last bullet, with my last breath, to see that his Hell does not end one second too soon."

The old man's breathing was slowing, more like fish-gasping now. "That's. Really. Twisted."

Jonah stepped back to make room for Ben, who was almost upon them. "Feels like justice to me," he replied flatly.

"Fucking. Twisted," the oldster said even as Ben descended noisily upon him.

Jonah shook his head, reclaiming his composure. Anger was not a luxury he could indulge in for long; it was too distracting. "You really ought not to cuss like that," he said, even as Ben bit into the old man's face. "There's no call for that kind of language."

Out of respect for the about-to-be dead, Jonah stepped around to the other side of the thick-trunked oak. He didn't feel good about shattering the old man's pelvis and turning him into Purina Brand Zombie Chow. He just didn't see as he had much choice. Zombies needed to eat, too.

• • • • • • • • ● • • • • • • • • •

Ten minutes later, Jonah studied Ben as the zombie shuffled off, sated for the moment. That zombie bobble-head business needed attending to.

Jonah had lived with the undead long enough to know that a decapitated zombie stayed awake and alert for quite a while, but eventually any zombie—headless or otherwise—that didn't eat some brains would go into a coma-like state, nearly impossible to re-awaken. And unless he wanted to be reduced to hand-feeding a zombie-head, Jonah had to find a way to keep Ben's noggin in place.

He looked at the old man's corpse. Where had he come from? It couldn't have been too far away; he obviously wasn't passing through. That meant a home base. It meant supplies.

The old man—

No.

No, the answer was not the honest old man. The answer was Frank, the shirtless, hatchet-wielding idiot.

Frank had been coming up over that small hill, moving in a straight line, very purposefully. He was either coming from or heading toward something. If it wasn't his home base, it would be something that might at least provide a clue.

Frank was the answer.

Jonah smiled as he walked toward the bullet-riddled corpse. He had only taken three steps when something smashed into the back of his head, smashed it so hard that he barely had time to register the pain before he blacked out and pitched face first…

· · · · · · · ● · · · · · · · ·

Jonah awoke tied to a wooden chair, head throbbing, sitting beneath a single, bare bulb in a supply closet that was stacked to the ceiling with cans of food. He hadn't seen this much food in one place since before the D Plague broke out, back when supermarkets were still an ongoing part of reality. Big cans, small cans, family-sized cans; peas, corn, carrots, baked-beans, tuna and chicken; with labels from every brand he had ever heard of. The wealth of food was almost inconceivable.

Even as his mouth watered, his mind raced, assessing the meaning of it all.

First, there had to be a lot of people here. There was no

way a small group could have collected this many cans.

Second, these people were highly organized and under the control of a particularly strong-willed and insightful individual. Without potent leadership, this kind of ready food-supply would have been consumed in no time by desperate, short-term thinking people.

And third—and most importantly—that 'honest old man' had lied to him.

Jonah strained and heaved, pulling against his bonds with all his strength.

Lied!

There was no greater sin. No greater offense imaginable.

Jonah tried to straighten his legs so he could drop down heavily, trying to smash his way free from the chair. If this rotten old chair crumbled as easily he thought it would, he could get himself free of the ropes. He'd... He'd...

In his Hulk-smash rage, Jonah doubled his efforts and then doubled them again. He had *opened up* to that old man. He had repaid honesty with honesty. He had confided in him, told him things he had only ever told two other people in the entire world, and it had been based on a lie!

Except Jonah couldn't straighten his legs far enough, couldn't get high enough to put any real oomph into his attempts to shatter the chair.

He strained and jumped, but bunny-hopping around the supply closet wasn't enough to break the rickety old thing. It was enough to get someone's attention, though, because thirty seconds after Jonah began his futile attempt to destroy the chair, the closet's metal door swung open. A guard leaned into the room holding a revolver—his revolver, Jonah realized.

Jonah instantly shifted his attention and his demeanor. He didn't like showing emotion to others. "Where is Ben?"

"Who?" the guard asked.

"The zombie I've been following around," Jonah explained. "He looks like Alex Rodriguez, though not quite as attractive. Have you seen him?"

"What are you, fucking queer?" The guard's disdain dripped from every word like drops of water from a tree after the rain.

Jonah took a deep breath, trying not to get drenched by the guard's foul demeanor. The guard immediately went on his short list of people to feed to Ben.

Composed, Jonah replied, "Neither cursing nor homophobic slurs are necessary."

The guard raised the butt of the revolver threateningly. "Well then how about if I just smash your head in again? How about I—"

"How about you get the fuck out of my interrogation room?" snapped a slender young man in a faded camouflage jacket, standing in the doorway, filling it with his presence in a way he couldn't possibly fill it with his slight frame. He was so slim he could have been sixteen or twenty-five or anything in between.

The guard raised the butt of the revolver even higher over Jonah's head, then spun and stomped away, wordlessly closing the metal door behind him with a sharp clang.

"Greetings," said the man-boy, extending his hand, as friendly as he had been harsh just seconds earlier. "I'm the voice of reason in this insane asylum. Name's Martin, but most folks around here call me Robin—as in 'Robin Hood'."

Jonah nodded. "Nice to find someone civilized enough to offer a proper greeting…" He paused a moment before adding, "As you can clearly see, I'm not in a position to shake your hand."

"Right, right," the man-boy said, putting his hand in his

pocket. "Force of habit. My apologies."

They stared at each other in silence.

Stared.

Silently.

Until finally Martin spoke. Martin—not Robin. Jonah refused to think of him as a medieval comic book character.

"So... you want to tell me why you murdered my grandfather?"

"I didn't," Jonah replied automatically.

Martin stared at him like a parent assessing a lying kindergartner. He raised one eyebrow.

"Wait a minute. Your grandfather?" Jonah said. "And the other guy—"

Martin shook his head dismissively. "A trouble-making buffoon. Grandpa hated him."

"Well they were both about to be eaten alive by a zombie. Shooting them seemed kinder than allowing them to be... you know. I hardly think that qualifies as murder. I did them a favor."

Martin shook his head, disappointed. "Too convenient by half. The world isn't that tidy. At least offer me something original; God knows how many times I've heard that lie before."

"Look," Jonah said. "I can't help it if the truth happens to be 'tidy'. Those two were about to be eaten. Period. I could have watched it happen. But I didn't. I took action."

Martin leaned against the closed door. "Oh, so you're one of those." He nodded. "Okay. We can play it that way. I'm curious to see how far you'll take it."

"I'm not playing," Jonah snapped. He was fed up with this kid, and it was becoming increasingly difficult to keep his frustration from bleeding out. "One of what? What are you talking about?"

"So they were about to die, were they?"

"Yes," Jonah replied, calming himself. He would remain in control.

"And there isn't anything else you want to add to that story? Or change? Or... whatever? Did they stumble over a root and find themselves face down in the dirt? Did that zombie just catch up to them because it was faster than they were? Give me details."

The boy was trying to trap him. Trying to trick him. Most likely looking for an excuse to execute him.

"I don't recall the details. I was fighting for my life, not keeping a diary."

Martin nodded again. "Okay, this is helpful. Very helpful indeed. A temper, but controlled. Sells his bullshit like it was Biblical Scripture, but smart enough to refrain from making stupid mistakes. I think I'm getting a picture of the kind of man you are."

Jonah fumed. All he wanted was get out of here so he could find Ben and fix him. What was this man-boy babbling about?

Martin leaned in close, putting his hands on top of Jonah's bound and still tacky forearms, his nose inches away. He was so close that Jonah had trouble focusing his eyes on the boy's features.

"I know everything," Martin breathed hotly on him. "I know how easily you climbed up and down that tree, even while holding your rifle. I know how quickly and precisely you shot Frank. I know all four places you shot him. I know which hand you used when you drew that pistol and shot my grandfather." He smiled. "I don't care, by the way. About Frank, I mean. Grandpa was right: Frank was a piece of shit."

He paused. "I do care that you killed my grandfather, though, but if it makes you feel any better, he has... excuse me, he *had*... brain cancer and volunteered for every suicide mission that came along. I was prepared for him to die a long time ago.

"You know," Martin continued, "in a funny way, you told the truth and didn't even know it." Tears appeared in his eyes and he apparently had no qualms about letting Jonah see them. "You *did* do him a favor when you let that zombie kill him. Of course, you also let your zombie BFF eat a brain that was riddled with cancer. I'll be very interested to see how that affects him."

Jonah's thoughts pinballed wildly. Brain-cancer? Four shots? Suicide mission? The relevant pieces clicked into place. "You were watching me the whole time."

Martin stood up straight and impossibly tall, let out a hearty laugh. "No, dumb-ass, I guessed. Made the whole thing up to see if you would confess." The man-boy laughed again, though there was little humor in it. "Of course I was watching you. No one comes into Sherwood Forest without my knowing about it. And before you ask a stupid question, yes I just called it Sherwood Forest. It goes with my nickname."

"What are you going to do with me?" Jonah demanded.

Martin stepped back and, without ever breaking eye contact, banged his fist against the metal door. The door rang out like it had been a gong in a previous life. It opened immediately and the guard with Jonah's revolver poked his head into the room.

"We're ready," Martin said.

"Okay, Robin." His head disappeared behind the door again, only to reappear seconds later when the door was pushed open by a tall, narrow cage sitting atop a dolly. The wheels squeaked noisily as the guard rolled it into the supply room.

It was Ben, his bobble-head still flobbing around like it was attached to his shoulders with a slinky.

These bastards had caught Ben. Caged him.

When Jonah got loose, Martin would die. Everyone in this compound would die. Every single one of them. Dead.

Martin snapped his fingers a few times. Jonah caught himself staring at Ben and turned to look at the boy.

"You really have an unhealthy obsession with that thing, don't you?"

Jonah looked at him silently, vowing not to speak another word. Everything he had said today had been turned against him.

"Not talking, eh?" Martin said. "That's okay. You've said plenty. It never fails to amaze me how much you can learn about a man when you *know* he's lying. What you need to do now is listen, because believe it or not, I'm going to offer you safe haven here. I think we could use you. No, I know we could use you. You're better with a gun than anyone I've ever seen."

Jonah listened to Martin, but he couldn't believe what he was hearing. He *wouldn't* believe what he was hearing. No one had reached out to him in years. No one had asked him to be a part of anything since… Ben. Ben Peterson had made an impassioned speech about the importance of family and the power of teamwork—and Jonah had bought into it wholeheartedly.

"You're screwing with me," Jonah said. "Don't do that."

"This is on the level," Martin replied. "I know you've done some awful things, but I've got sixty-three people here, including eight children. I need all the help I can get, and your skill with guns makes you worth ten of Frank."

"Stop," Jonah hissed. "Stop messing with my head.

You'd never trust me after what I did. Never."

"Well…" Martin began. Slowly, carefully. "I might. But you're not going to like what I ask in return."

Jonah's gaze flicked from Martin to Ben and back to Martin again. He knew instantly what the boy would require.

"No," Jonah answered. "I won't kill him."

Martin eyed him. "It's the only way to be sure you won't betray us."

As if he knew what was going on, inside his cage Ben began rocking and moaning. Ben hadn't made a sound since Gettysburg. Jonah had assumed he was too weak. Was he stronger now, now that he had fed? Or was he responding to what was happening around him?

If he was responding—whether to convey a desire for life or a desire for true death—either way, it would be the proof that Jonah had been seeking all along. Proof that somewhere, deep down in his zombified self, Ben was still aware. That he understood what was happening.

On the other hand, Ben had just eaten. Maybe he was simply more energized, in his own undead sort of way. Maybe it was nothing more than animalistic hunger.

Jonah had no idea—and he suspected he never would.

"Say it," Jonah said softly.

"What do you want to hear me say?"

"I want you to tell me exactly what you want me to do. I want to hear you say the words."

Martin nodded gently, thoughtfully. "Okay."

Ben moaned again, aggressively, a throaty, whispered roar. He thrust his arms out as if to grab someone, but the bars of the cage were too strong. No one in the room flinched. They had been around too many zombies for too many years to be startled by something like that.

Martin squatted down so he was eye to eye with Jonah.

"I want…" the boy began, then paused. Hesitated. Came to a conclusion, then restarted. "I want you to tell me what Ben did."

Jonah blinked. He blinked again.

What?

Martin continued, calmly, coolly, but with increasing ardor. "Tell me what this man did to you. To your family, to your friends, to whoever it was he hurt. Tell me what he did that messed you up so badly that you're willing to kill living people to protect an undead monster. Tell me what was so awful that you have to keep him undead. Tell me that and I'll turn you loose right now."

The old scene immediately replayed itself in Jonah's mind. It always came too quickly, too easily; at the slightest mention, the slightest memory, the slightest scent, it flooded through him, unbidden. He hated it. He hated Martin for making him think about it. He always strove, and failed, to hold that memory at bay.

It began with Jonah running from a zombie and tripping over a root. A *root*, of all the stupid, clichéd ways to die.

He was about to be eaten. About to be consumed. Turned into one of the undead himself.

Until Ben pushed Emily and Hannah into the creature's arms. Just shoved them, without a moment's thought or hesitation.

"You're worth more to me than the two of them put together," Ben had said afterward, as Jonah wept for the last time in his life. "I need you to help keep me alive."

That was the moment Jonah had vowed to do exactly that. No matter what.

Ben was disgusted by zombies more than he feared

them. Every time he so much as looked at one, you'd have thought he'd just been force-fed a rotted fish. So holding Ben down while a zombie chewed him into a state of undeath, and then focusing on keeping him that way no matter the cost— those had been all Jonah could think to do to bury the guilt he felt for living. For surviving instead of his wife and daughter.

He was alive because they had died. It was supposed to be the other way around. He was supposed to protect them, defend them with his life.

Just thinking about it hurt more than words could express. Saying it out loud...

Saying it...

Saying it wasn't going to happen. Not now, not ever.

Jonah said quietly, "I thought you were going to ask me to kill him. Put a bullet in his brain."

"Oh, I will. Eventually." Martin was still squatting in front of Jonah.

"What difference does it make what he did?"

"It makes all the difference in the world because it gets it out of your system. As long as this stays bottled up inside of you, it owns you. You'll never be free of it until *you* set it free. Set it free, Jonah."

Jonah stared dumbly at Martin. He had been right when he first woke up under this bare light bulb and deduced that there must be an exceptionally insightful leader in this camp. He just had no idea the extent to which it would prove to be true.

Jonah said, "Let me shoot him first. Then I'll tell you what you want to know."

Martin leaned back on his heels. "Why in the world would I put a gun in your hands?"

Jonah stared, looking beyond the walls and cans and the

bare bulb, just to the left of infinity. Then he did the hardest thing he had done in four years: he pictured Emily. He pictured Hannah. Not being torn apart by a zombie. No. He envisioned them smiling, their faces lit from above by golden beams of sunlight. It was beautiful.

He let a tear fall from his eye. Just one. He didn't want to overdo it.

Then he pushed the image away.

"Killing Ben is the only way I can talk about this. I won't do it in front of him." He gestured with his chin to Ben, who had gone quiet in his tiny cage. "Not in front of him."

Martin rose, looking down on Jonah for a moment. "Alright. We'll try it your way. If I've learned nothing else in the past few years, I've learned to be flexible." He fished in his jacket's outermost pocket and produced a Bowie knife, flicked it twice, and just like that Jonah's arms were free. Martin knelt down and repeated the process on the ropes around Jonah's legs.

Jonah waited patiently, moving slowly so as not to startle anyone, especially the guard, who was waiting a few paces away, revolver pointed at Jonah's chest. His arms and legs tingled as blood flowed back into them.

Martin stepped back and held his hand out to the guard. "Give me the gun," he ordered.

"I don't like this," the guard replied. "No sir."

Martin turned on him with the speed of a cobra, snapping venomously, "I don't give a shit what you like. Give me the gun!"

The guard eyed him severely but turned the butt of the revolver around and handed it over.

Martin grabbed it by the black barrel, pivoted, and handed it to Jonah. "One shot," he said. "No need to waste ammo." He gave a half smile and stepped back to the edge of the room, tuna fish peering over his shoulder from the cans stacked behind him.

Jonah nodded, taking the revolver. He laid his finger on the trigger and considered bringing another tear to his eye. He decided against it. He didn't want this to look contrived.

With the tip of the barrel between the bars, he raised the muzzle of the revolver until it was pointed straight at Ben's forehead. Ben was strangely silent.

Jonah stared into his eyes...

—and pulled the trigger.

Click.

He pulled the trigger again. Again it clicked.

Click, click, click.

Nothing. It was empty. *As he had known all along.*

Martin crossed the room, put his hand on the revolver and eased it down, away from the cage, away from Ben. He moved his hand to Jonah's shoulder. "It's empty. I couldn't take the chance. But now that I know you're really ready..."

He pulled a bullet out of his pocket and offered it to Jonah—

...which is when Jonah whipped the butt of the revolver around, smashing Martin across the bridge of his nose. The man-boy crumpled to the ground, and even as he fell, Jonah turned and stomped his foot on Martin's throat. Then he dropped smoothly to one knee, snatched up the boy's Bowie knife and threw it at the guard, who was lunging toward him. The knife went into one eye socket and the guard dropped like a leaf in autumn.

It was over in less than ten seconds.

Jonah bent over and picked up the bullet that the man-boy had just offered him, sliding it into the revolver. He put his boot on the boy's chest and aimed the gun at his head.

"Do you really think I don't know when my own

revolver is unloaded? Are you really stupid enough to bluff me with my own weapon? For a minute there I thought you were smart."

"I meant every word," the boy croaked, voice sounding just like his grandfather out in the woods. "I need your help. There's a lot of kids here."

Jonah was done talking with this buffoon. He was annoying. And to make matters worse, he realized he wasn't going to get the satisfaction of feeding the guard to Ben. The guard was already dead.

Damn it.

Jonah shot the boy in the pelvis. It was the best way to immobilize without killing. The small room immediately filled with the smell of blood, and from within his cage Ben growled hungrily.

Jonah closed the closet's metal door and locked it. Then he flicked open the latch that held Ben's cage shut. Ben could have pushed against it, but he just stood there, watching.

"Why?" came a weak voice from the floor.

Martin had never shouted or screamed when Jonah shot him. He just lay on the floor, legs akimbo, hands clutching the crimson wound.

"Why?" he croaked again, sounding so much like his grandfather. "Why do you hate him so much?"

Jonah eyed him. He cocked his head to one side. The kid's focus was amazing.

When Jonah didn't reply, Martin spoke again. "You know you're never getting out of here alive, don't you? They heard that shot; they're on their way."

Jonah shook his head, resigned. "I was *never* getting out of here alive."

Martin shook his head, rolling it around on the floor.

"But we would have accepted you, taken you in. We really do need someone with your skills. All you had to do was tell me what he did."

Jonah exhaled softly, heavily, longingly through his nose. "I believe you. I truly do. And I think I could have endured almost anything else. But not that. Not that..."

Jonah looked around at all the cans of food. Through the door came the slapping sounds of running feet. "You've got a nice set up here," Jonah observed.

Voices shouted from outside the door, demanding that it be opened, calling out, "Robin!"

"It's not too late for you," Martin said. "I'll tell them it was an accident. They'll believe me. Just tell me what Ben did. I won't tell another soul, I swear." He coughed, then repeated, "It's not too late."

The boy was bleeding out, getting desperate. But what was killing him wasn't blood loss; it was not knowing.

If it hadn't been so tragic, Jonah might have laughed. "Life's not that tidy. You said so yourself."

The pounding on the door surged in volume and urgency.

Jonah continued, "Remember earlier, when you told me that you see everything that happens in these woods? Do you hear everything, too? Did you hear me tell your grandfather that I would protect Ben with my last bullet and my last breath? That I would do everything in my power to make sure that Ben's personal Hell didn't end one second sooner than absolutely necessary?"

Shots were fired into the metal door. It rang out its old gong song, but it didn't break.

"It was too late then," Jonah said. "It was too late for me a long, long time ago."

The people on the other side of the door changed tactics

and began shooting into the wooden frame around the door. Splinters flew throughout the room. That metal door would yield any minute now.

Jonah reached out and swung open the door to Ben's cage.

"It's certainly too late now."

Martin's hands fell away from his wound, too weak to hold on anymore. There was almost as much blood on the floor as there was left in his body. He said thinly, "You already used your only bullet on me. You're good, but you won't last five minutes against them. There are too many."

Jonah nodded. "Probably. But it's five more minutes than Ben would have had otherwise. I'll take it."

Martin's fingers clawed at the air, searching for meaning. "I can't believe you'd rather… die… than…"

Jonah didn't reply. There was no reply possible.

He moved toward the door.

As he did so, Ben lurched out of the cage. They glanced at each other as they passed, moving in opposite directions, Zombie-Ben shambling toward Martin, Jonah striding toward the metal door.

Jonah would hold off the attacking masses as long as he could.

With his last bullet.

With his last breath.

Afterword

And so we have come to the end. I hope you enjoyed the ride. More than the narrator of the last story anyway.

I have to give a shout out of thanks to John Hartness and Emily Leverett for sending "Feels Like Justice to Me" in a far more interesting direction than the one I first intended. I was originally going to write it from the POV (point of view) of a character who was being hunted by someone who wanted to feed him to a zombie. But when Emily and John announced they were accepting submissions for *Big Bad 2*, featuring stories from the POV of the bad guy, I knew I had to flip the zombie story I was planning, and that if I did so, I'd have something workable. Turned out a whole lot better than workable, but I never would have even considered telling it from the POV of the Bad Guy it if it hadn't been for their anthology. It's dark, but I think it's impactful and affecting. That always makes me happy.

I also see now that it was also the natural next step in the evolution I've been talking about in several of these afterwords: the exploration of foreign, alien, *other* ways of looking at things. Giving a guided tour inside the mind of this character was genuinely fascinating, dominated above all by one question: how do I make this character's actions understandable and relatable? Not justifiable or likable. But something the reader might identify with.

There's a saying among writers: Everyone is the hero of their own story, including the antagonist. Especially the antagonist, if you're doing your job well.

And that *is* my job now. Not the one I get paid to do from

9 to 5; not the one with a 401k and medical benefits. But the one I've embraced, the one I've longed for. The one whose benefits can't be itemized on my income taxes because they are worth far too much to be quantified.

Editing was a fascinating, educational detour, but that journey has come to its end.

Writing?

This Giant Leap is merely the (next) beginning.